Forgiving Her First Love

Forgiving Her First Love

A Raven's Cove Romance

Dani Collins

Forgiving Her First Love
Copyright© 2024 Dani Collins
Tule Publishing First Printing, July 2024

The Tule Publishing, Inc.

ALL RIGHTS RESERVED

First Publication by Tule Publishing 2024

Cover design by Lee Hyat Designs

No part of this book may be used or reproduced in any manner whatsoever without written permission except in the case of brief quotations embodied in critical articles and reviews.

This is a work of fiction. Names, characters, places, and incidents are products of the author's imagination or are used fictitiously. Any resemblance to actual events, locales, organizations, or persons, living or dead, is entirely coincidental.

AI was not used to create any part of this book and no part of this book may be used for generative training.

ISBN: 978-1-962707-97-8

Dedication

To the amazing team at Tule Publishing for always making me feel like I've found the absolute best home for my stories.

Dear Reader

Thank you so much for the love you've been showing for the first book in my Raven's Cove trilogy, *Marrying the Nanny*. I'm thrilled that you connected so closely with Reid, Emma and Storm.

Forgiving Her First Love can be read as a standalone. While Reid and Emma are in this story, it focuses on Reid's brother, Logan as he mends fences with Sophie. She loved him her whole life—until he broke her heart. Their journey is funny and heartbreaking and healing, but there is also a loss. If you struggle with grief, you should be aware of that content before you continue.

Trystan's story, *Wanting a Family Man*, will be out a few short months after this one. I won't spoil the identity of his heroine, but some of you have already written to me with the correct guess. Want a sneak peek? Visit my website: danicollins.com/books/**wanting-a-family-man**

Also, if you haven't read the bonus epilogue to *Marrying the Nanny*, you can get it here: danicollins.com/marrying-the-nanny-epilogue

Enjoy your visit to Raven's Cove!

All my best,
Dani

Prologue

April 2nd

AS LOGAN FRASER stepped out into the overcast day, he wondered how he had thought getting pissed to the gills last night would help his situation. He was so hungover, he was liable to throw up in the weeds before he'd walked to the end of the driveway, let alone all the way to the marina.

Prior to crawling out of bed this morning, he had thought yesterday was the worst day of his life. The truth was, 'worst days' had been growing exponentially since he'd received the call three days ago that his father had been killed in a small plane crash.

Logan had immediately departed the sunny humidity of the Florida Keys to wake jet-lagged in the frigid damp of Victoria, BC. When he had arrived at the lawyer's office yesterday, and met up with his two half brothers, Reid and Trystan, he'd had to let go of his dim hope that Wilf Fraser's death was an April Fool's Day prank. Their father's death had become all too real, especially when they were introduced to their baby half sister.

Quarter sister? What did you call it when your father made a fourth child with yet another woman? No matter how they were related, Storm was literally a baby, one who had crapped all over a boardroom table and, metaphorically, all over their lives.

The reading of Wilf's will had forced Logan to accept that his father was genuinely dead, and that he would never get to tell him what he really thought of him.

Maybe that was for the best, since what Logan thought kept changing. As the gravity of Dad's finances had piled up, so had Logan's acrimony. It had reached critical mass when they'd been forced to fly up here to Raven's Cove, a tiny island among many in the middle of the BC coast.

Traipsing around the collection of buildings they had called home throughout their childhood, they had discovered things were far, far worse here than the lawyers and accountants in Victoria had warned. The house they'd grown up in was showing its age. Wilf's almost wife, Tiffany, had started making updates, but the renovation had been halted mid-construction due to nonpayment of invoices.

It was the same story at the lodge where sports fishermen had always filled the utilitarian rooms, topping up the company coffers while they caught their limit. Tiffany had talked Wilf into upgrading the whole resort, hoping to draw higher-end visitors and ecotourism.

She was trying to gentrify a truck stop roadhouse on the otherwise desolate West Coast. Raven's Cove was a place to gas up, restock the galley, or get an emergency repair. Plenty of summer traffic was leisure craft, sure, but they were headed to more populous places like Prince

Rupert, Haida Gwaii, and farther north to Alaska.

Raven's Cove's lifeblood was commercial fishing vessels or other working boats. No one flew this far for a family vacation that didn't offer roller coasters or white sand beaches. There were more accessible places to go whale watching.

Tiffany seemed to have taken an "if you build it" attitude, but who knew what she had been thinking? She had lost her life in the same plane crash.

Logan and his brothers had flown here to Raven's Cove expecting to use the days leading up to their father's service to prepare this place for sale and extract an inheritance—not for themselves, but for their sister.

Wilf had given each of his sons money for school when they had left for university. They'd all used it wisely. Logan had expected Wilf to use his own money wisely, not throw it away on costly upgrades that left the whole place under water.

Selling Raven's Cove it wouldn't cover it's debts. No, they had to bring this place back into the black so they could sell it at a profit or there would be nothing for Storm's upbringing and head start as an adult. There was no one to physically look after her, either. Aside from the three of them, she had a nanny who trembled more than a Chihuahua on a frosty morning, and an absent aunt who may or may not be in trouble with the law.

Logan didn't know how they would turn this place around and find her a guardian, only that it had to be done. That overwhelming reality was sitting like radioactive waste in his stomach.

Of course, that curdled sensation might also be the cheap scotch and IPA chasers he'd downed last night. Or the guilt baked into hating a man who was beloved by all the people who had stuck around and spent time with him.

Logan passed Moody, the short order cook, heading into the pub. He also looked worse for wear after last night, stubbled and heavy-lidded, but he smiled and waved. Last night, Moody had told Logan that Wilf had paid for him to go to Rupert for some much-needed dental work last year. Quinley, one of the servers, said Wilf had covered the consultation fee for a divorce lawyer, when her ex-husband had tried to move their kids to Nova Scotia.

Umi was coming out of the coffee shop as Logan passed it.

"Morning." She waved and turned into the first door on the marina building, heading up the stairs inside to the resort office where she ran accounting. She had told them that Wilf had paid her salary without interruption, even when her pregnancy complications had forced her onto bedrest.

Randy, the apprentice marine mechanic, was opening the hardware store that fronted the machine shop. He had screwed up his dates and missed an exam, nearly putting his certification back a semester. Wilf had paid the fee to write the makeup test and arranged for him to get back to Nanaimo to do it.

Everyone seemed to have a story like that, and they had all been eager to share them with Logan and his brothers.

Maybe they had thought it would help with the grief, but mostly they left Logan feeling more infuriated with his father than ever.

Wilf had always been a spendthrift. He had wanted to be loved, so he had purchased affection. How could they not see that? If he was so compassionate, how had he been so stupidly thoughtless so many times to the people he was supposed to love?

As he rounded the corner of the marina building and looked at the boatyard in the watery light of morning, all Logan saw was the giant mess that Wilf had left, one that he and his brothers would have to clean up.

Oh Christ. He wasn't going to make it upstairs to the marina office. He'd only had coffee, but it refused to stay down. Better to lose it out here, rather than inside.

He hurried behind the brick building and leaned a hand against a tree trunk while he retched out all sorts of poor life decisions.

Above him, where the road rose up the bank toward the one-room schoolhouse, a young voice asked, "Are you okay?"

This was why he loathed this town. It wasn't even a town. It was a hundred and fifty people living cheek by jowl in a cluster of houses around a marina. The military had built this place on First Nations land during World War II, to service the navy. It was still the only place to repair a boat within a day's sail from anywhere. Nobody *wanted* to be here. If your boat broke down, you were stuck here. It shouldn't be a sentence, but for most it was.

Not him, though. Nope. No way. He was giving it one week. *That's all.*

Please let it only be one week.

"I'm fine," he lied, spitting and straightening to look up at the boy of seven or eight. He wore a blue raincoat with dinosaur skeletons on it, rubber boots, and a red backpack.

"My mom gives me ginger ale when I'm sick. Do you want some?"

"You got some in your backpack?" Something in the kid's big, earnest eyes tickled a memory in Logan's chest.

"No." He chuckled. "I can go to the store for you."

"Thanks, but I'm not sick. I'm suffering the consequences of my actions." A cold ginger ale sounded amazing, though.

"I thought you were having a hangover."

"I do have a hangover. How do you know what a hangover is?"

"My grandpa has one. Mom is really mad."

Oh shit. Now he was going to retch for an entirely different reason.

Those eyes. He knew those eyes way too well. And that helpful personality, the one that wanted to take care of him. His entire youth and a very hot angry week in his early twenties had been cushioned by big brown eyes exactly like those ones.

A piledriver had arrived to pound the knowledge into the back of his screaming skull, reminding him that yesterday was not the worst day of his life. That would be today, but he still asked with faint hope, "Who's your grandpa, little man?"

"Arthur Marshall."

"Thought so. I was drinking his scotch last night." He regretted it even more now.

"Is that like butterscotch? Is it good?"

"Not really. Your mom is Sophie Hughes?"

"Mmm-hmm." He nodded his head inside the hood of his raincoat.

"How old are you?" Logan was doing math that he'd done several times. The first time had been eight years ago, when his mother had told him Sophie was pregnant. He'd run the same figures four years later, when he'd seen her at his mother's wedding. Sophie had been there with another man and a preschooler who had disappeared after an hour. She had ignored Logan the entire evening.

"I'm seven."

"And who's your dad?"

"Nolan Yantz. Do you want to know my name?"

"Brian?" Logan recollected vaguely.

"Everyone thinks that. No. It's Biyen. Bye-En," he pronounced slowly. "My dad picked it." In the distance, the school bell rang. He looked up the hill. "I should go or I'll be marked late."

"Okay. Seeya later." *I'm going to stand here and lose a little bit more of the guts your mother hates.*

Sophie wouldn't have lied to him about something as important as whether he was the father of her kid. He had to believe that. She wouldn't have lied to her mother or his.

Not to her grandfather, either. Or her own kid.

Which meant she really had leapt from his bed into another man's, despite a crush on him that had lasted a decade. A crush he had crushed beneath his Nike runners on his way to the ferry slip.

He had no right to be hurt or disgusted or even curious about her life or her son. *He* was the one who had left. He would do it again inside of a week.

Whatever had been between him and Sophie back in the day was very much over.

But his belly twisted with one more spasm. He had another spit before he rallied himself to walk inside and face her.

Chapter One

Two and a half months later…

LIKE EVERYTHING THESE days, Sophie was late putting in the potatoes. She should have been turning this soil three weeks ago, but the weather had been nothing but rain and work at the marina had been an equal deluge.

Today, however, she finally had dry weather and a full day off.

It wasn't the worst way to spend it. She liked physical work. It was satisfying and gave her time to think. Or not. As she jumped on the shovel and levered the clumps out, the noise in her head faded. She absorbed the smell of the earth while a breeze meandered off the water down at the eastern edge of Gramps's property, floating up the sun-warmed hill to caress her arms and legs. A raven squawked as it commuted overhead and bees buzzed into the nearby chives that came up all on their own.

"Hey, Soph."

"No," she said reflexively. Belligerently, because she didn't have to look to know who had spoken. Much to her chagrin, she had been reacting to Logan Fraser from the time he had picked up her sweater on the first day of school and brushed the grass from it before handing it back to her.

"It's my day off," she added, even though her irritation was more about the fact he'd caught her in cut-off bib overalls with only a faded tank top beneath. She was wearing gloves and heavy boots and hadn't made any effort to tame her hair before rolling it into a messy topknot.

Why did she care? She had never been a girly girl, didn't wear makeup, and he saw her in shapeless coveralls every day at work.

Also, *he* didn't care. He'd made that so clear, so many times.

"I promised Gramps I'd get the potatoes in." She jumped on the blade of her shovel again.

"It's not work. It's something else."

"Then definitely no. I only talk to you about work." At twenty-six, she was finally learning how to set clear boundaries.

"I need to stay here."

The dirt rolled off the blade of her shovel. She held the handle in her lax hand as she turned to look at him.

He was annoyingly sexy, of course, wearing a striped button-down shirt with his sleeves rolled up his forearms. His linen trousers had a knife-sharp crease pressed into them and were rolled up to reveal his naked ankles in deck shoes. Being summer, he only allowed his stubble to grow in for a few days before shaving it off. This morning it was a light coat of glinting bronze, tidily precise down the slope of his cheeks and clean on his neck and under his jaw. His blue eyes were not the least bit apologetic or even entreating as he met her affronted gaze.

"This isn't a B and B anymore." Her mother had run it as one on and off, but that had been years ago. Much as Sophie would greedily accept extra cash working overtime at the marina, she didn't have the bandwidth for cooking and cleaning up after strangers or making the necessary chitchat.

"There's nowhere else. Not at this time of year. The lodge is buried in renovations, the completed rooms are booked. Anything else has to be used for contractors so they can stay and finish the rest."

"Is this because Reid and Emma are married now? Are they asking for privacy or something?" She glanced up the hill toward the house on the bluff where the Fraser boys had grown up.

Logan's older brother had married Sophie's best friend, Emma, a month ago. Initially they'd been trying to turn Emma from Storm's nanny into her stepmother, but they'd fallen in love, and good for Emma. She deserved to be loved by someone great. Reid was uptight and wore a resting-glower face, but he seemed to think Em was the cat's pajamas so that's all that mattered to Sophie.

"I *wish* they'd start giving a shit about privacy," Logan muttered.

Sophie bit back a smirk. She had noticed the pair locked lips a lot, no longer caring if they had an audience. Reid couldn't seem to walk by his new wife without rubbing her ass like it was a magic lantern, and Emma had taken to wearing low-cut tops and lip gloss on her way to see him at the office.

"Emma's family is coming," Logan continued. "Her mom and niece and nephew. They need the beds at the house."

Oh. Right. Sophie had forgotten about that.

"Don't you have a fancy boat you can sleep on?"

"Much as I would love to go back to Florida and sleep in my own bed on my own yacht, I can't. I leased it to help pay for all of this shit." He waved to indicate the marina and resort, out of sight behind the hillock where the road at the end of her driveway meandered toward the village.

Sophie had meant the shiny new tour boats that also belonged to the resort, but the casual way he threw out "my own yacht" irritated her. She ought to be proud of him and his brothers. They were local boys who had done well. They'd grown up here with roughly the same start she'd had. Granted, Wilf had handed them a six-figure check to get them through school and on their way to building a life. She hadn't had that leg up, but she could have had a very different life right now if she had made some smarter choices along the way.

Don't, her inner mama bear warned. She would never regret Biyen and would never *ever* regret that her mother had lived long enough to hold her grandson. Still, Sophie had caught some really shitty breaks over the years while Logan had lived his best life after refusing to bring her into it.

Which was for the best, she insisted to herself. If a man wasn't prepared to build a life with you, then the best thing to do was walk away from him. She'd learned that with

Biyen's father.

"I'll still take my shifts with Storm," Logan said.

"You guys are still doing that?" Days after they had arrived, Logan's mother, Glenda, had come along with her nursing background and no-nonsense parenting. She had laid out a schedule for the men to look after their sister in twelve-hour rotations. As much as Emma wanted to be Storm's mother, she had been hired as a nanny, so they could only rely on her for a standard forty hours a week.

"As my mother has made very clear"—Logan looked for his patience in the fluffy clouds overhead—"Emma marrying Reid does not miraculously give her more time in her day for childcare. I don't mind," he conceded with a twist of his lips. "The little turnip is growing on me."

Storm was cute as a bow tie on a bunny, that was a true fact. Seeing one of these grown-ass men wandering around with her in a sling put a smile on faces all over the village, but Sophie was determined to remain impervious to whatever paternal instincts Logan was developing. They were transitory. He was transitory.

"Between Storm and work, I'll only be here to sleep," he pressed. "It's only for a few weeks."

"That's what you said when you showed up here ten weeks ago! 'It's only for a week.'" She stomped the shovel back into the dirt.

"You think I don't know that? Look." He pinched the bridge of his nose. "As much as I would love to fuck right off, I can't. There's a chance that Tiffany's sister will show up and try to take custody of Storm."

"What?" Sophie almost dropped the shovel altogether.

Logan gave a shrug-nod that said, *Yeah, can you believe that shit?*

"But Reid and Emma are adopting her."

"Not until Em's immigration papers are sorted. It's a whole thing." He sighed heavily. "Trys and I have agreed to stay the rest of the summer. We might need money for a court challenge so we *have* to get this place turning a profit, in case we need to sell it like that." He snapped his fingers.

Sophie reflexively shoved aside that disturbing possibility. Wilf had been a wildcard of a boss, but he'd been the devil she knew, and he had said many times that this was his home and he intended to die here. Which he kind of had.

The threat of selling had been hanging over her head since the Fraser brothers had returned, though. She had pushed it onto a back burner, unwilling to stress about it until it happened.

"When did you learn this?"

"A few days ago."

"How's Emma?" Sophie tightened her grip on the shovel as she looked to the house on the hill again. Em had fallen hard for the baby she had been hired to nanny six months ago, back in January, before Wilf and Tiffany had died on the way to their elopement. When that happened, Emma's first words to Sophie had been a fearful, *What will happen to Storm?* A custody challenge must be freaking her out.

"She's handling it, now that she knows we're all committed to keeping her and Storm, together. It'll take time for everything to iron out, though. Meanwhile, I need a room."

"Why *here?*" she demanded.

"For Christ's sake, Sophie. Why are you making this such a big deal? This house is close to the marina and the baby. It's convenient. You and I are adults and there are two other people here. Surely, we can get along for three weeks. I'll pay rent," Logan said with exasperation.

"*I* pay rent! I buy groceries and cook and clean for Gramps. *Him.* It's his house, in case you didn't know."

"I do know. He's the one who said I could stay. This is a courtesy call, not a request."

Seriously, Gramps? Seriously?

She stabbed the shovel into the dirt and stomped on it. "I guess I could quit and leave. There's a job in Comox I was thinking of applying for."

"You're not quitting," he said tiredly. "You won't leave Art. He won't leave the island. You're stuck here, same as me. Let's both accept that and move on."

"Oh, you're very good at that, aren't you?" she muttered.

"What?"

"Moving on."

"Are *you* really saying that to *me?*"

They held a glower a little too long. Something squirmed in her stomach that was both culpable and defiant, burning hot and uncomfortably cold. There was a sting of shame, yet a dark pride in having provoked that small show of resentment from him.

But aside from antagonistic bickering, they didn't talk about the past.

Boundaries. Good fences and all that.

He was supposed to stay on his side, though, in that house up on the hill, not in her freaking attic bedroom.

"How long is Emma's family staying?" she asked begrudgingly.

"Three weeks," he repeated.

"Is Reid likely to survive that?"

"It'll be fun to watch and see."

"Where is Trystan staying while they're here?"

"On the *Storm Ridge*." It was one of the pair of tour boats that had been part of Tiffany's Great Revitalization Plan. Poor Trys, who was a loner at heart, was now hosting tourists on five-day cruises.

"It's booked to the gunwales and gone half the week so I can't stay there with him," Logan reminded her. "But Reid and Emma are taking her family on one of the tours so I'll stay at the house with Storm while they're gone. See? Once the math shakes out, I'll be here for ten sleeps. Max."

"Are they leaving Storm with *you*?" She pulled her bottom lip in a wide, *Yikes*.

"I thought we agreed to keep things civil."

She rolled her eyes.

"I'm not cooking for you," she stated. "I'm not picking up your socks and washing your underwear."

She was accepting her fate was what she was doing. *Damn it, Gramps.*

"Buy your own groceries," she added. "Don't swear in front of Biyen. Don't even think of getting between the two of us. *Ever*," she warned in a dangerous voice. "And don't get Gramps drunk. A beer at the end of the day is fine, but—"

"That was one time. I've barely had anything to drink myself since then."

"That is not the story those flats of beer cans told when Biyen did his bottle drive for school last Saturday."

"Those were Emma's," he lied shamelessly. Sophie knew Emma drank wine because they often polished a bottle between them. There wasn't a lot to do here. Drinking was a popular hobby.

"I'm saying if you want to have a piss-up, do it elsewhere," she warned. "This isn't a party house."

"Aye-aye, Cap'n. Anything else?"

"No shop talk. If you want my professional opinion, call me in and pay me for it. But not today. It's my day off. And who is minding the hardware store if you're here?"

"Trys. I'm going to give that kid a try, by the way. The one you said was looking for a summer job. But Trystan has Storm so I should get back. I'll bring my stuff over Sunday."

"Can't wait," she muttered, and stomped the shovel into the earth once more.

IF THERE WAS one thing that revved Logan's engine, it was

a scantily clad woman wielding tools. Heavy gloves and a low-neck top; naked arms operating a hammer drill; safety goggles and a ponytail... They all did it for him. When a tanned, flexed calf muscle wore a smudge of dirt above a steel-toed boot, he was pretty much done. Cooked like Sunday dinner.

When it was Sophie? That got complicated real fast. She worked for him, among other reasons.

But she was objectively hot with a figure toned by physical labor. She twisted wrenches and carried propellers and machined drive shafts all day. She had the confidence to stare him down and she had so many *freckles*. When he looked at her kinky red hair, he always remembered the way it had caught in his combing fingers back when—

Don't, he warned himself for the millionth time.

In fact, her grandfather had made it clear there would be no funny business on his watch.

You need a bed, you always have one under my roof, Art had said. *But you aren't sharing Sophie's. Not unless she invites you, and you damned well better be fixing to stay there if that happens. I won't have a repeat of eight years ago.*

Had he meant Sophie getting pregnant? Logan didn't intend to make any kids, ever. He wasn't his father, willy-nilly with his willy. His resolve had been strengthened by these last weeks of caring for his little sister. Babies were a complete pain in the ass.

He pulled the door open on the hardware store and heard Storm let out a cry of genuine pain.

A jolt of alarm went through him because babies were

also helpless and fragile and wormed their way into the rotten-cored apple of your heart even when you wished they wouldn't.

"What happened?" Logan hurried to the counter where Trystan stood with their seven-month-old sister strapped in the sling against his chest. She faced out and her face was crumpled up while her staccato cries pierced the air.

Tall, dark, and unflappable Trystan was holding her hand, examining her tiny, wet finger while a customer stood before the counter wearing a look of tested patience. The customer glanced hopefully at Logan, but Logan was more concerned about Storm.

"You have more teeth now," Trystan chided the baby. "It's going to hurt if you chew whatever you put in your mouth."

Storm sniffled down to a whimper as she noticed Logan. She gave him a very pitiful look as she held out her hand to him, entreating him to fix it since Trystan had failed her.

She was their father's daughter, very quick to switch affections, always willing to love the one she was with, especially if they loved her back.

Logan was starting to think he might, damn it.

The customer held up a valve, asking Trystan, "So, this one?"

"That should do it." Trystan nodded. "If you need to come back and exchange it, that's no problem." Trystan rang it through, then gave Storm's tummy a comforting pat as the man left. "Okay now, Jaws? If you'd quit dropping your teething ring in the dirt, we wouldn't have this problem."

"Want me to take her?" Logan held out his hands.

Storm smiled and kicked with excitement, exactly as he had known she would.

Trystan grunted and caught her feet.

"I don't think that game is as funny as you do." He clasped her in one firm arm while he released the buckles on the sling. "I need to adjust these straps again. Either she's growing or your balls are a lot droopier than mine. How come you never get sacked when you wear this thing?"

"I wear a cup." He didn't. And he got sacked on the regular when he carried her.

Logan took Storm while Trystan fiddled with the straps and buckles.

They'd been here ten weeks, Sophie had said. In some ways it sounded like forever, but he couldn't believe how much this mix of sunshine and vinegar had changed in that time. She moved nonstop and was grabbing at everything. When she was on the floor, she scooted around, trying to crawl. She knew their names because when he said, "Where's Trystan?" she turned her head to look for him.

She was strong enough to hold herself in a plank like a figure skater when Logan held her over his head—careful to watch for sudden spills out of those grinning lips.

"How'd it go?" Trystan asked.

Logan had asked him to cover for him while he went to "see a man about a room." He had known Sophie would rather dig him a grave to sleep in. That's why he'd walked over to tell her himself, away from work while her kid was at school. It had gone exactly as well as he'd expected.

"Art's letting me stay with them," he said very casually.

Trystan dropped the carrier back onto the counter. "*No.*"

"Tell me about my options." Logan refused to sound defensive. "I could couch-surf, but we're trying to make people believe we have our shit together. The lodge is overbooked. We need every contractor and laborer housed here so they can solve that problem for us. I looked into sleeping in one of the salvage boats in the boneyard. They all smell like rotten kelp and lung disease. Art was here yesterday, I asked him if he knew of anyone renting a room and he said I could stay in Biyen's playroom. It has a bed. Mom slept there when she was here for Dad's service."

"What about Sophie?"

"What about her? Why are you so possessive of her?" He scowled at Trystan as Trys took Storm. "Maybe you're the one we should be worried about where she's concerned."

"So we agree she ought to be worried about? I'm not possessive, I'm *protective*. She's my friend."

"She's my friend, too."

"She has never been your friend." Trystan was pulling the sling back into place with one arm, firmly holding Storm against his chest with the other. "She had a hard case of hero worship that you encouraged because it fed your ego. Then you screwed her and left. That's not how *I* treat *my* friends."

"Is that what she said happened?"

"She didn't have to."

"Well, you have your facts wrong." Not that wrong. He'd been immature and selfish. He knew that. But, "I'm not talking about her with you. Especially when you left this place on your own high horse, same as Reid and I did. Quit acting like your loyalty runs any deeper than our shallow ponds. Sophie and I are fine. That's all you need to know."

They were not fine. They got on with it, as Emma would say. They behaved like grown-ups when talking about work, bickered when it wasn't, and spent a lot of time ignoring the elephant that took up all the air in any room they occupied together.

It was kind of exhausting to keep everything so filtered and corralled, to be honest. Hopefully, they could alleviate some of that while he was staying with her.

"I also told her we're staying longer," he admitted.

That decision had only happened a couple of days ago, on the heels of the news about Tiffany's family. Or rather, the sister who seemed to comprise all that remained of Tiffany's family.

"I thought Emma would have told her by now."

"Sophie's been busy at work." The marina was nonstop this time of year. "Randy went back to Nanaimo for his final semester and exams." When Logan had realized Sophie hadn't had a proper day off in more than two weeks, he had insisted she take today.

Had he hoped that would put her in a slightly more receptive mood to his moving in? Sure. But he was also trying to at least glance at the labor standard laws.

Trystan did a safety check, running his hands across all the catches on the sling, ensuring Storm was firmly secured to his front before he released her and gathered her diaper bag onto his shoulder.

"I wish I wasn't going to be away half the summer, but I guess we're doing what we can, right?"

"Get those tours turning a profit. Or at least breaking even." It would take years for the boats to be paid for, but they were already taking bookings for next season, which was promising.

Logan gave a quick wipe of his fingertip across Storm's drooling chin, no longer squeamish about all the goop that came out of this kid.

No, he was far more apprehensive of what might happen with her aunt. And disturbed by how relieved he'd been when he and Trystan had agreed to stay.

He didn't like it here. He *wanted* to go back to Florida. Didn't he?

Storm, the little piranha, grabbed his finger and bit it.

Chapter Two

SOPHIE HURRIED TO finish planting the potatoes, not even showering before she hiked up the trail to the Fraser house.

This house had seemed like a castle the first time she'd seen it, when her mother had brought her here twenty years ago. Gramps's house was a modest homestead on the flats above the high-water mark, accessed by a lane that wound behind the bluff from the village. This one was perched to overlook the cove and marina.

After losing her husband to a logging accident, Janine Hughes had brought her young daughter to Raven's Cove, where her father, Art, had been running the marina. Janine had taken a job at the general store, and Sophie had started kindergarten at the one-room schoolhouse up the hill.

Sophie could still remember how awed she had been when she had learned *that boy* lived in this house. Heading into her very first day of school, she had been intimidated by the rambunctious kids who were big and loud and all knew each other's names. She had accidentally dropped her sweater and *that boy* had picked it up to give it back to her.

When school let out that day, on the teacher's instruction, he had escorted her to the general store. The only other child her age, Trystan, had come with them.

"We live up there," Trystan had said, pointing to where Reid was striding up the driveway ahead of them, moving with purpose and ignoring his younger brothers.

Reid had never been mean, but he'd never been warm or friendly, mostly keeping to himself. Trystan had become her playmate, disappearing regularly to spend time with his mother's family, but always paired up with her for lessons, becoming a reliable companion and confidante.

Logan had been godlike, outgoing, and full of jokes. He'd been allowed to say, "Let's go look at the boats," and run down to the wharf with his little brother.

Sophie had had to sit at a table by the window in the general store, practicing her printing while her mother finished her shift.

Those early memories of watching Logan disappear down the ramp had ignited her interest in boats and their engines. Her grandfather had nurtured it, eventually taking her down to the wharf himself, then bringing her into the repair shop. Had he ever guessed the real source of her passion for marine mechanics?

Working alongside her grandfather meant seeing Logan. *His* passion for watercraft—how they were shaped and crafted and propelled—was in his DNA.

She had fallen in love with Logan the way a puppy imprinted on an alpha dog. She cringed thinking of how obvious she'd been with her terminal case of adoration. It had lasted all through their school years and might have been killed by teasing from her schoolmates if Reid and

Trystan hadn't stepped in at different times, telling other kids to, "Shut up. She can like who she wants."

The fact her mother had been best friends with Glenda, Logan's mother, had made it worse. So had her close friendship with Trystan. Sophie's life had been so intertwined with Logan's, it had made a romantic connection with him seem sensible and feasible. Inevitable. As though they were meant to be together.

She had completely taken for granted that they would marry and live happily ever after.

Meanwhile, he had left the minute he could, same as Reid had done before him. Same as Trystan did after him. All without any intention of coming back.

Glenda had put it nicely, saying the Fraser boys were "restless spirits." A more accurate statement was that they had had a very complicated relationship with their father and each other. That was no surprise, given they had all been born from different mothers and crammed into the same house where Logan's mother, Glenda, insisted they all get along. They had done their best for her sake, then got the hell out the minute they could.

Sophie had been convinced, deep in her heart, that Logan would come back for her, though.

Sure enough, as he was heading into his final year at university, he had returned. Glenda had finally had enough of Wilf's cheating. Logan came back to help her move to Port Hardy.

Sophie had just graduated high school. She had been accepted at a trade school in Nanaimo, planning to become a marine mechanic. In some ways, it was a formality. Like Logan, she'd been learning at Art's knee, sent into diesel-infused engine rooms from the time she could hold a wrench. Maybe she didn't love boats the way Logan did, but she liked the work. She was good at it. It was a solid living, especially for a woman, and she found the work satisfying.

Three long, yearning years had slipped by at that point. Her feelings toward Logan hadn't shifted one iota. If anything, they'd been fed and watered by fantasies of their making a future together.

The day he returned, he saw her. Really saw her. She had reveled in his surprise and sudden interest. They talked like equals. He asked her about her plans, and she told him she was leaving Raven's Cove. He had congratulated her as though it was a huge accomplishment to move south seven hundred kilometers despite the fact he had chosen a school back east.

Their long catch-up that day had turned into a good night kiss. Several. They were as potent a match as Sophie had always believed they would be. She had always wanted him to be her first and, during a walk on the beach the next day, she asked him if he would be.

Logan had seemed startled but touched.

"Are you sure?" he had asked her a thousand times.

She had been more than certain. They were meant to be, weren't they?

He had initiated her in a way that had seemed utterly perfect. Sexy and playful, tender and passionate. Maybe it hadn't been exactly the way all those romance novels of her mother's played out, but afterward, she'd been more in love than ever.

Then, two days later, when Glenda had flown to her new home in Port Hardy, and the trailer Logan was driving onto the ferry was loaded and locked, he had said goodbye.

Good luck at school. Make yourself a good life.

Sophie had packed a bag and caught up to him at the ferry slip. She would live with Logan while he finished university and go with him if he got into that program in Italy he was applying for. Trade school? Who needed it! She wanted their future together to start now.

Oh, to be that young and naïve. She had been so excited to surprise him with her decision. It was romantic, wasn't it?

No, it definitely was not.

He had been floored that she thought he wanted her to come with him. Uncomfortable.

"You asked me to be your first, Sophie. Not your last."

She shuddered, shaking off the ice water of that memory as she knocked on the door of the Fraser house.

She cracked the door seconds later, calling out, "Emma? You here? It's me."

"I'm downstairs," Emma called.

The split level made the most of its position overlooking the cove and marina. It had plenty of windows and jutting decks, but stairs. Man, did it have stairs.

Sophie left her dirty boots on the stoop and slipped

from the foyer through the living room to the kitchen, then down the stairs to the basement where Emma was folding laundry that she piled onto a bench press with a barbell across it.

"Who let you off your overtime chain?" Emma teased.

"I know. Logan's covering the office, the store, and all the callouts today. Good luck with that," she said with an eye-roll. "I live in terror that Randy will fail his exam and have to stay for another rewrite. Or won't come back at all. That would actually kill me."

"You really think he wouldn't come back?"

"Forty-sixty?" She wavered her hand to indicate she didn't like the odds. "He would have to pay the company for his tuition and everything, since we sponsored him, but he has a girlfriend in Nanaimo. *And* he has a wedding to go to. This is probably my only day off until he gets back in July."

"And you used it to come see me?" Emma clutched a sleeper to her chest. "I'm touched."

"Logan told me Storm's aunt might make a play for custody? What's going on with that?" Sophie shifted a box of framed photos off a paint-spattered kitchen chair and sat on it.

"I'm trying not to think about it." Emma grimaced and shook out a receiving blanket covered in yellow ducks, halved it, then halved it again, before she ironed it down her front. She rolled it to the size of a burrito, then added it to the ones already in the basket. "I thought you and Logan only talk about work?"

"That's the deal, but he told me they're all staying longer. Gramps told Logan he can stay *in our house*," she added with outrage.

"Because my family's coming?" Guilt flashed across Emma's oval face. "I'm sorry, mate. Does Art not realize you two lock horns?"

"Gramps has a soft spot for him." For all the Fraser boys, really, but especially Logan. Logan had been more than a willing pupil. He'd extracted every scrap of knowledge he could from Gramps, but she suspected he'd confided in him, too. "Gramps probably feels he owes something to Wilf. They were friends all those years. And Glenda, for that matter. She used to come up to cook for Gramps when Mom was sick."

Glenda had been a godsend throughout Sophie's life, but especially while Janine had been in treatment. Sophie had been stretched thin between her new baby and her terminal mother, unable to travel up here to look after Gramps as well.

Neighbors help neighbors, was Gramps's view. Especially in a small community like this one. If Logan needed a bed, then Gramps would give him one.

Sophie was less inclined to be neighborly, especially to him.

"Maybe we can figure out something else," Emma murmured, moving along to the rumpus room that Logan had been sharing with Trystan until Emma had married Reid and moved out of the room she'd been using upstairs.

The basement had yet to benefit from the updates upstairs. Everything was tidy, but dated. In here, there was a distressed dresser, a television with slots for VHS and DVDs, and a sofa that turned into a bed. If Logan's muttered remarks were anything to go on, that sofabed was a medieval torture device.

"Logan was going to set up his desk in here but hasn't found the time or the right place. This room is too small for his desk once the bed is pulled out. I was planning for the kids to stay in here. Trystan stays in my old room on his nights with Storm, which is actually the room he used to share with Logan," Emma said with a chuckle. "He's mostly on the *Storm Ridge* now, but I'll need it for Mom. I guess Logan will be on the bed in Storm's room when he's on shift."

"They arrive this weekend, don't they? Have you decided whether you're going to Vancouver to meet them?"

"I am." Conflict had her squinching up her nose. "I hate to leave Storm, but I'm excited to see the kids. I've missed them so much."

Emma didn't say she missed much from her life in New Zealand, but her niece and nephew were the top of the list when she did.

She frowned with concern. "I also have to ease Mom into the idea of all this without, you know, putting Storm in her arms from the jump. That dinosaur exhibit you suggested hasn't started yet, by the way. We'll try to catch it on the way back, but we're going to the suspension bridge and the aquarium. Then we'll fly here, mess around for a few days, go on the boat tour with Trystan, another few days here, then back to Vancouver before they fly home. It will go fast."

"Maybe from your perspective. Logan's going to be at my house most of that time." Sophie quickly waved off her acrimony. "I'm just having a whinge." Having Logan under her roof would stir up old feelings, ones she didn't want to allow.

"Do you want to tell me what happened?" Emma searched her expression.

"No. It makes me feel too stupid."

"Been there," Emma said with a faint smile of empathy. She planted her hands on her hips and looked to the stairs. "We thought about making our walk-in closet into a temporary nursery, but that's a lot of work and once Storm is in there, she might not want to go back to her old room."

"Honestly, Em, it's fine." Sophie gave in to the inevitable. She hadn't come here to plead her case anyway. She was far more concerned about what would happen to Storm and thus Emma.

Before she could pry any further on how Emma was coping, Emma asked, "Did you ask Biyen if he'd like to play with Immy and Coop while they're here?" Imogen was Biyen's age and Cooper had just turned five.

"He does, but he's supposed to go camping with Nolan as soon as school finishes."

"Oh? I thought…"

"I know. They usually go later in the summer, after Biyen's birthday, but Nolan and Karma aren't getting along."

"Metaphysically?" Emma lifted intrigued brows.

"Yes?" Sophie brought her shoulders up to her ears. "Karma is his girlfriend."

"Oh right."

"But Nolan has never bought into the idea of cause and effect. Most people understand that if you move in with your girlfriend, but never pay rent, eventually she'll kick you out. That blindsides him every time."

"How does *she* pay rent? I thought she sold oils and crystals and such."

"She does. She also works for BC Ferries. She wants to quit and open a store. I'm getting all this through Biyen, reading between the lines. She thinks Nolan should get on with the ferries and support her while she opens her own business, rather than, you know, him doing odd jobs for beer money and smoking weed all day."

"Maybe she should have consulted her runes before she let him move in."

"She should have consulted *me*," Sophie said out of the side of her mouth, but they were both chuckling. God, she loved Emma for those deadpan dunks of hers.

"Does Nolan smoke pot around Biyen?" Emma tucked her chin with concern.

"No," Sophie said firmly. "That's a red line and he knows it. But it's legal now and he used to bring it to Mom when she was in treatment so I can't be too judgmental about him using it on his own time. Biyen knows what it is. I've talked to him about it and why I don't want him to try it."

Infuriatingly, Nolan was not a bad father. He might be lousy at paying taxes or even buying a cup of coffee if he could bum one, but he showed up regularly to take Biyen fishing or hiking or kite-flying. It might only be an afternoon, but his time with Biyen was almost always one-on-one, nurturing Biyen's love of nature and sense of self-worth.

"Tell you what," Emma said brightly. "After Mom and the kids leave, you and Biyen can move in here. Logan can stay with Art. Would that work?"

"I don't hate that idea, but you might want to ask your husband first."

"I'm just going to tell him. I want to see his face."

They both knew Reid well enough that the mere idea had them bursting into laughter.

As Logan sat down with Reid, Trystan, and Emma, Emma said wistfully, "Our last dinner as a family for a while."

She had roasted a prime rib, maybe to turn it into a bit of an occasion. Reid was pouring wine, looking for anyone else who wanted a glass.

"You sound like Glenda." Trystan was offering spoonfuls of pureed carrot to Storm, but she was more interested in squashing the banana pieces on her tray.

"Because she called us a family?" Reid pointed a warning finger at Logan. "Do not accuse me of marrying your mother."

"Okay, Dad."

"Glenda offered to come stay while I'm away," Emma said as she passed the mashed potatoes.

"To look after us?" Logan asked dryly.

"Wait a minute. Are you *our* nanny?" Trystan circled his finger to indicate all three men. "Guys, we've had this all wrong."

"To look after Storm," Emma said impassively, ignoring their silliness.

"I'm insulted. Are you insulted?" Logan asked Reid.

"I feel my ability to parent has been slighted, yes," Reid agreed.

"Trys?"

"Glenda knows I won't be here. Obviously, her faith in the two of you is somewhere below sea level."

"She offered to clean the house and make some food so I could spend my time visiting with my family instead of cooking, but I'll leave all of that in your capable hands, then." Emma raised her brows at Logan in a silent, *Ha*. "Seeing as you don't feel a need for assistance."

"That is exactly something Mom would say," Logan noted, curling his lip in annoyance.

"I take that as a compliment. I adore her." Now Emma's eyes were sparkling, her teeth flashing as she closed her smile over her fork.

"She'd probably like to meet your mom," Reid said.

"She told me she would." Emma nodded. "I explained

we won't have any spare beds once my family gets here."

"She stayed with Art and Sophie when she was here for Dad's service. They'd have her, wouldn't they?"

Trystan's cheeks went hollow. Emma gave the end of her nose a rub.

"What," Reid demanded, looking at each of them in turn, ending up at Logan.

He refused to be a coward about it.

"Art invited me to stay with them while Emma's family is here so there's no room at that inn, either."

Reid's expression hardened. He slowly turned his attention back to Emma. "What does Sophie say about that?"

"Not much." Emma shrugged.

"It's nice that you all care so much about Sophie's tender feelings but can we all take one step out of my private life and remember that it's been *eight years* since Sophie and I—" Logan cut himself off as all eyes turned to look at him.

Even Storm turned her innocent, curious blue gaze onto him.

He refused to kiss and tell, but it was painfully obvious that Sophie wished him dead. He had thought she would have lightened up on her mad by now, but nope. That woman had a strong grip when it came to a grudge.

"Can we move on?" he said.

"She's your direct report," Reid said without heat. "Moving into her home is a recipe for an HR issue."

"Raven's Cove is one long HR issue." The hiring pool was microscopic. Even when they managed to recruit from afar, the isolation took a toll. Attrition was rampant, but hiring locals also had pitfalls. Firing someone who didn't work out impacted their ability to pay rent, creating a domino effect through the community. Outside of work, affairs and personal conflicts were rife. "David Attenborough himself hasn't seen this much raw, animal behavior."

"You should set one of your episodes here, Trys," Emma said with a wink.

"Too dangerous," Trys assured her.

"There's nothing else to rent," Logan said, since Reid was continuing to glare at him. "You know what this place is like."

"I know what Dad was like."

"Says the guy who slept with our fucking nanny," Logan shot back. "That apple fell right at the base of the tree, didn't it?"

"As family dinners go, I'm starting to feel right at home," Emma said with false brightness. "How are preparations coming for your first tour, Trys?"

Reid kept his gaze locked with Logan's. "You'll notice I married her."

"Reid." Emma touched his wrist. "Sophie is a grown-up. If she felt threatened by Logan being there, she would say so. Art wouldn't put her in the way of harm."

"Everything is done that can be done," Trystan answered Emma. "Now we need to launch and work out the kinks. I'm glad we'll have your bunch on board for one of our early trials. You'll be more forgiving. And maybe do the dishes?"

Reid finally looked away, turning his attention to

Trystan. He began quizzing him about staff. He was a big brother in the Orwellian sense sometimes, micromanaging in ways that drove Logan and Trystan nuts.

But as his brothers hashed out some fine points, Logan caught Emma watching him. Calm, sweet, compassionate Emma.

She didn't say it, but he heard her all the same.

Watch your step, mate, or the next roast in my pan will be carved out of your sorry gut.

Chapter Three

Sophie wound up working Sunday, of course. A tug broke down and a cabin cruiser had to be pulled out for a new drive shaft. She could have counted inventory in the hardware store, but she left that tedious job to Logan since he was the one who had hired the kid who had screwed it up.

By Sunday afternoon, she was down to the final 10 percent on her internal battery, promising herself a glass of wine while she made dinner if she could just get through helping Biyen clean out the playroom.

"What about this one?" Biyen asked, holding up a LEGO creation.

"Buddy, you have to make these decisions yourself. If you want to keep it, you can put it on the shelf. If you're ready to take it apart, it goes in the bin." She was trying to make up the guest bed. Why did she always grab the wrong corner of a fitted sheet? It was like a gift.

"But what if Cooper breaks it? You said he's little. He might not know to be careful."

"If Cooper comes over to play, you'll have the bin in your room. That's why we're taking it in there."

"But what if he gets up? At night?"

"Buddy, do you think Cooper is sleeping here?" She pointed at the bed.

Biyen's distinct dark brows quirked in a quizzical way. He'd been doing it since he was a baby and it always made her want to laugh with joy.

"Yes?" he hazarded.

"No." She shook her head. "Logan will be sleeping here."

"Logan Fraser?" Biyen stood taller, as if even at his age, the Fraser name had the ability to put him at attention.

At that moment, the knob on the door at the bottom of the stairs gave its distinctive *squeak-clunk*. The stair treads began croaking under a heavy step.

This homestead had started as a two-room cabin with a cellar dug by hand, one that had been accessed through a trapdoor in the floor back in the day. When children had come along, the enterprising family had added a second floor. The stairs were accessed through a door beside the one that led onto the back porch. A small octagonal window illuminated the railed landing between the two bedrooms up here.

Around 1950, electricity had arrived with indoor plumbing. A stove and a refrigerator had been added, too. That's when the kitchen had been moved and a fourth bedroom had been added downstairs. That one was over a proper concrete basement, but the original cellar was still in the floor under the kitchen table. Biyen liked to play there in the summer sometimes.

Sophie's mother had made further updates while running the house as a B and B, giving it a new roof and proper insulation. Gramps continued to take care of small repairs like leveling a door or replacing a rotting post on the porch. The house was seaworthy, in his words, despite its noises of complaint.

Logan arrived in the open doorway. He wore shorts and a T-shirt and had a duffel slung over his shoulder.

"Hi." His gaze touched her, Biyen, then skimmed the slant-ceilinged room and the plethora of toys on nearly every surface from the window ledge to the desk to the highboy dresser.

The room shrank, becoming claustrophobic. Sophie cleared her throat.

"I was just explaining to Biyen that you're staying here so Cooper can have your bed at Storm's house."

"That makes *way* more sense." Biyen gave himself a face-palm. "I thought Cooper was staying with *us*. Then he would play with my toys while I was away with Dad and that's *okay*. I can *share*. But some of them are special."

"Cooper and Imogen are staying with Reid and Emma and their grandma," Sophie clarified. "*Logan* will be playing with any toys you leave in here."

"I won't break any. I promise. Is that one special?" Logan dropped his duffel to the floor and crouched while Biyen took him through the wings and mismatched wheels on his creation, explaining how it traveled back to the Triassic period.

Aside from the occasional friendly greeting at the marina when Biyen checked in with her on his walk home from school, Sophie had never seen Logan interact with her son. All her protective instincts went to high alert while she listened.

At the same time, she grew self-conscious as she finished making the bed. It was shoved into a corner so it was impossible to tuck in a sheet or plump a pillow without crawling across the mattress. Very graceful.

"You can leave these in here if you want to. I'll be careful," Logan said.

"Thanks!" Biyen moved to add his sculpture to the ones already at the window.

"I didn't expect you until after dinner." Sophie breathlessly found her feet and moved to tuck the bedspread down against the footboard.

"I was sent to invite you all to dinner. Reid's barbecuing burgers. Emma's mom is making some kind of salad that everyone loves. The kids are excited to meet *you*." He pointed at Biyen.

"I'm a vegetarian," Biyen said.

"I think they'll still be excited," Logan said matter-of-factly.

"We'll take one of your veggie burgers." Sophie smoothed the rooster tail on Biyen's crown. "But why don't we take some of your outside toys over? The ring toss, maybe."

"And the bubble tub?"

"Sure. Wait," she commanded as he started for the door. "Logan needs somewhere to put his stuff. Clear the desk and the night table." She picked up the bin full of

LEGO bricks and pointed. "Shelf or bin?"

His excitement at the prospect of meeting new kids overrode sentiment. Everything was unceremoniously dumped into the bin.

"Thank you," she said to Biyen's back as he brushed past Logan and clomped down the stairs.

"Art moved just as fast when I told him there was a barbecue waiting for him," Logan said.

She snorted. Gramps did enjoy a free meal.

"You'll have to come in here so I can take this to his room." There wasn't enough space to swing a cat on the landing, but there wasn't enough air in this room once he stepped inside and tried to shift out of her way.

She slipped by him and shouldered into Biyen's room, leaving the bin in a corner of the floor by his dresser.

When she came back to the door of the bedroom, Logan was studying the rest of Biyen's keepers on the shelf.

"I kind of wanted the LEGO bin to stay in here," he said.

"Have at 'er, champ. Biyen will be dragging me over to Emma's in—"

"Mo-om!" The door clunked open at the bottom of the stairs. "When can we leave?"

She bit back a sigh. "I haven't had my shower, yet," she leaned to call down the stairs.

He made a pained noise and slammed the door.

"I'll walk him over. You can take your time," Logan offered.

Everything in her pumped the breaks. Nolan was forever introducing Biyen to new women. Sophie was damned careful about confusing him with her own romantic interests. Of which there were none.

Logan was definitely *not that*. He was a houseguest who was offering a friendly gesture. Nevertheless, "You don't have to. I'll only be ten minutes."

The door squeaked and Biyen's steps *clomp, clomp, clomped* up to the top of the stairs.

"Mom," he panted. "Gramps is putting the toys in his Gator. I'm going to ride over with him."

"Okay. Did you get your burger from the freezer?"

"No." *Clomp, clomp, clomp* as he descended. "Gramps!" The stair door banged again, followed by the door to the porch.

"I emptied the top two drawers." Sophie pointed at the dresser. "Towels are in the closet downstairs, across from the bathroom. There's a second toilet and sink in the shop. What else might you need?" She glanced around.

"Mom!" *Clomp, clomp.* Biyen stopped halfway up the stairs. "Gramps says buy more beer tomorrow because he's taking the six pack from our fridge."

"Roger that."

Clomp, clomp, slam.

"Sometimes I envy people who do all of their communicating over text," she said with a bemused smile. It was as close as she would come to apologizing for the chaos. If Logan didn't like it, he could leave.

"Reid texts me so often, I want to slit my throat with my own smartphone. The grass is always greener."

She had to give that one a small smirk.

Usually, on the rare occasions when Biyen and Art were both out, she reveled in the bliss of having the house to herself. Today, she was really, really aware that she was alone in the house with Logan. That she was heading into the shower where she would stand naked while he…

"I guess I'll meet you over there? Er… I mean, unpack first if you want to." She waved at the dresser again. "I'll give you a key, not that we ever lock up. Gramps is always here and…" She shrugged. It was Raven's Cove. If a local walked into your house, they needed what they came for and left a note telling you what they had borrowed. By the time strangers showed up in the summer, she was leaving all her windows open anyway, trying to catch a breeze.

Also, Gramps and Biyen were the only things Sophie truly valued. So long as they were safe, she didn't care who stole her refurbished laptop or took the company four-by-four for a joyride.

"Thanks." Logan moved his duffel to the bed and opened it. "I'll get the beer tomorrow when I pick up my groceries."

That made her feel churlish, especially when she was being invited to eat with his family today.

"There's no sense cooking two meals," she grumbled. "The dishes alone will become a nuisance. We don't have a dishwasher. Buy whatever you plan to make and we'll take turns."

"If that works for you, sure."

"It does." God, this was going to be awful. She could

tell. "I'll see you over there."

"Copy that."

She thumped down the stairs and hit the shower. A cold one.

SOPHIE LEFT HER hair down to dry and smeared on sunscreen that Emma had given her. It doubled as a moisturizer, was reef safe, and didn't feel like a coat of paint, which was the reason she had always resisted wearing sunscreen in the past—and wound up lobster red beneath her freckles as a result.

She pulled on her best pair of shorts and a ribbed tank top, then tied a flannel around her waist, anticipating the temperature would drop with the sun.

As she came out to the kitchen, she found Logan rinsing the draining tray after putting away the dishes.

"What are you doing?"

"Crew not cargo, baby."

"Heh. That comes straight out of your dad's Handbook for Evaluating Humans," she said with a wistful chuckle.

She missed Wilf Fraser. A lot. He had been a very flawed man, one who had never made a politically correct joke in his life. In his view, if he had hired a woman, he couldn't possibly be sexist. One of his son's mothers was Indigenous, so how could he be racist?

Wilf had dreamed bigger than he could accomplish with his limited education and complete disregard for the reality of his finances. He had started more jobs than any one person could finish in a lifetime, and he had never, ever cleaned up after himself. Back when the boys were young, he would say, *That's why I had three sons.*

Boy oh boy, had that brag come home to roost.

Working for him had been a challenge on many fronts, especially after Tiffany moved in with him, but Wilf had earned Sophie's undying loyalty after he had hired her with only one year of apprentice training under her belt. She hadn't even had to ask him for a job. He'd offered it. That had allowed her to leave Nolan and get on her feet as a single parent.

Wilf had also said, "You're a smart girl, Soph. I never understood how you wound up rowing around cargo like that piece of shit." Wilf had paid for the rest of her certification and, after Gramps had retired, left the running of the marina largely in her hands. Every time she asked for a raise, he gave her one without any quibbling.

"Ready?" Logan folded the tea towel over the rail at the end of the counter.

"Yeah." She kicked into her flip-flops and closed the door without locking it.

They started up the path that crossed in front of the garden. This track through the long grass had been worn into the hill back when Glenda and Janine had been running back and forth to borrow sugar and exchange gossip. Nowadays, it was well trampled by Sophie and Emma.

Sophie's agreement with Logan to not speak about anything personal, and to only speak about work *at* work, left a gaping silence between them as they walked.

Trystan had become Sophie's go-to for the inside scoop if Emma wasn't being forthcoming, but he had left on his first tour in the *Storm Ridge*.

"Emma didn't say much about what's going on with Storm's aunt," Sophie said when she couldn't stand the silence, or her concerned curiosity, any longer. "I don't want to pry, but should I be worried? Are you?"

"When has worrying ever solved anything?" Logan asked dryly.

"Okay, *I'm* worried. I can't help it. Emma is Storm's mom. Can you reassure me that she won't lose her?"

His profile hardened. "I'd like to."

"But?" She stopped. Her breath rushed out as his aggrieved expression seemed to plunge a knife into her belly. "How could they even think of giving her to Tiffany's sister? She's a criminal or something, isn't she?"

"That was our initial impression. We were told she was in police custody, but she's actually in *protective* custody. Once she finishes testifying, she could potentially ask to be Storm's guardian. At that point, it would be a matter of who can provide the best care. Right now, that's weighted to Reid and Emma, especially with Trystan and me here to support them. Plus, this is Storm's home. Those are all things, we're told, that make a difference in our favor. But nothing's guaranteed," he added with aggravation.

"Poor Emma." Sophie's heart went out to her so hard it was a physical sensation of being stretched and pulled. "I've worried about a lot of things as a mom, but never whether someone would take my kid."

"Yeah, this blows." Logan *was* worried.

As he should be, but it was a small shock for Sophie to see how affected he was. All he'd done since he'd arrived was give off vibes about how inconvenienced he was by his little sister. He had learned to be a decent caregiver, capable of changing a diaper and being a quick-draw on a bottle of formula, but when Reid and Emma had married, he'd been chipper as hell, starting to talk about heading back to Florida and his life there.

"Biyen's dad never fought you for custody?" he asked with curiosity.

"Not really."

"What does that mean?" He sent her a side-eye of puzzlement.

She hesitated, conflicted about revealing anything to him, especially something so personal.

"I didn't really intend to leave him," she admitted. "I came to visit Gramps. It was supposed to be for a week. You know, check on him, put a few casseroles in the freezer. When I saw your dad, he asked me when I was going to come back and work for him. The guy who had replaced Gramps after he retired was ready to retire himself. I had dropped out of my apprenticeship once I had Biyen and was serving in a pub. The money was okay, but I wasn't getting ahead." She had been supporting her son and her son's father and had been deeply unhappy, but she hadn't seen a way out until Wilf made her that offer.

"There was a spot available in the daycare so I said I would try it for a week," she continued. "Your dad kept offering me more money to stay another week. Biyen liked it here and Gramps wanted us to stay so, after a couple of months, Nolan called to ask when I was coming home. I said I wasn't."

She felt Logan's full attention swing onto her.

She didn't mention this had all happened shortly after she'd seen him at Glenda's wedding four years ago, when she had recognized two things: that she didn't love Nolan and that she still reacted strongly to Logan Fraser—fueled by dislike, she assured herself.

"He didn't want to join you two here?"

"I didn't ask him to. I sent him money for back rent, which was the reason for his call, and told him I already had a child to look after. If he wanted us to be a couple, I needed him to be an adult. He showed up a few weeks later, expecting to move in with us, but Gramps said his stuff had to stay on the lawn unless he started paying support and rent."

"Art doesn't mince words, does he?" Logan grinned.

"Where do you think I get it from? I wound up telling Nolan he didn't have to pay support if he let me have primary custody. He loves Biyen. I've never doubted that, but having a child is more responsibility than he ever planned to shoulder. We have an arrangement that works for us. Once or twice a year, usually around Christmas and Easter, I go see your mom in Port Hardy. Nolan's mom lives there so Biyen spends time with his family, and I get my Glenda fix. Through the rest of the year, Nolan comes here and either sleeps on a friend's couch while he hangs out with Biyen during the day or he takes him camping, which they both love." Sophie hated camping so it was a win-win all around.

"And he's—" Logan cut himself off, mouth going flat.

"What?"

"I don't want to piss you off as we're going into the party." He lifted his chin toward the house where the lively voices of the kids were already carrying from the back lawn.

She halted and so did he. The suspicion in his eyes told her what he wanted to ask. She sighed.

"Nolan is definitely Biyen's father." She tried not to be defensive or angry or wistful, even though she had hoped back then, with a heart-wrenching type of despair, that her baby had been conceived with Logan. "Nolan asked for a paternity test. Biyen is definitely his." Why else would she let him have so much access?

Did Logan flinch? It was hard to tell. He turned away, nodding, carrying on to circle around the house, wordless.

She absently rubbed at the scored sensation between her breasts, already regretting saying as much as she had. Did he think her pathetic? Slutty? Even *Nolan* had doubted he was Biyen's father, which said everything about how she had been behaving at the time.

Voices rose in greeting as they appeared. Sophie found a smile and did her best to shed whatever leftover desire she had for Logan Fraser's good opinion of her. It had never served her well and she needed it even less now.

Chapter Four

"HOW ARE YOUR drinks?" Logan checked in with Art and Emma's mother, Delta. They were seated in lawn chairs, watching the children throw hoops at pegs.

"Would you put water in this for me, please, Logan?" Delta handed him her empty wine glass. "I'll be asleep before dinner if I have more wine."

She was an older version of Emma, a little plumper, a little more formally dressed, with a distinctively stronger New Zealander accent.

He filled her glass with ice water and fetched himself a beer from the downstairs fridge, bringing one for Sophie who was too busy playing with the children to take it. He brought it up to where Reid stood at the barbecue on the deck off the kitchen.

"Thanks." Reid drained the one in his hand and cracked the new one.

"Tough day?"

"No, it's fu—Freaking hot standing here." He sent a glance to the kids below, but they were too wound up with excitement to hear his almost curse.

"Where's Em?" Logan looked toward the kitchen.

"Changing Storm."

"She calmed down yet?"

"Still pretty clingy."

"Which one are we talking about?"

"Yup." The corner of Reid's mouth kicked up in affection as he took another gulp of beer.

It was hard to tell who had missed whom the most. Storm had been cranky the last few days, fully aware that her favorite human was absent. Reid had been, too.

Logan had brought the baby down to the wharf when the seabus from Bella Bella had come into the cove a couple of hours ago, joining Reid who had poorly disguised his eagerness to see his wife and meet her family.

Reid had restrained himself to a kiss, but the moment Storm saw Emma, she had burst into tears. Emma had done the same as she gathered up her defacto daughter and kissed her cheeks as though she planned to eat her for lunch.

"Oh, moppet, I missed you, too," Emma had sniffled as she rubbed the baby's back. "I'm sorry I left. Meet your nana and cousins."

Storm had clung to Emma's neck, refusing to look at new people. She had only picked up her head once to give Emma the most hilarious scold of a sad face before hugging her again.

Since Reid was busy trying to make a good impression on his new mother-in-law, Logan took control of the luggage, getting everything into the company vehicle. He let Reid drive Emma and her mother up to the house with Storm while he walked the two kids up the drive. They were a riot, speaking in their broad Kiwi accents.

"You guys sound just like your Auntie Em, you know that?"

"Auntie Em sounds funny," Imogen assured him. "More like you."

Delta seemed pleasant enough, if given to tensing her upper lip in judgment while she took in the home her daughter had chosen over returning to New Zealand.

It was a hell of a lot nicer than it had been when Logan and his brothers had arrived in April, Logan wanted to tell her. Between them, they'd put in a new kitchen, refinished, refloored, repainted, and repaired everything that needed it, not necessarily in that order. They'd knocked out the trees impeding the view and got the moss off the roof and out of the cracks between the tiles on the patio where Delta currently sat.

They'd done all of that believing they would sell this house along with the resort. Then, for Storm's sake, Reid and Emma had decided to marry and stay here until the adoption went through. Since they all considered it Storm's home, Logan and Trystan endorsed their living here.

It would have eventually worked out, providing Storm exactly the same strong financial start that Wilf had given his sons, but this news about Tiffany's sister had thrown everything into flux. He wished they could at least learn her intentions. The uncertainty was stressful for all of them.

"Hey, you're back." Emma came out with Storm on her hip, placemats in her other hand. "Can you take her while I set the table?"

Storm turned her face away from him when he reached for her and snuggled tighter into Emma.

"I guess I'm setting the table," Logan said wryly as he took the placemats. "You go visit with your family."

"Thanks." She seemed to hesitate briefly, expression pensive, then went down the stairs where she pulled up a chair near Art and her mother.

"Problem?" Logan asked Reid in a low voice.

"Her mother is being weird about the adoption," Reid said under his breath. "Didn't appreciate being called Storm's 'nana.'"

"Oh Christ. Can't her family let her be happy?"

Reid's brows lifted in a silent *amen*.

Emma was enjoying her niece and nephew, though. The next time Logan came outside, Storm was in Sophie's arms—the little traitor—while Emma played tag with the kids, laughing it up.

"Did you get that inventory straightened out?" Reid asked.

"Hmm? Oh yeah, but I don't know what I'm going to do about that store. Anyone can ring through a purchase and stack shelves. Even Kenneth," Logan insisted when Reid sent him a look. "This is his first job. He's gonna screw up, but he's keen, and he *shows* up."

Reid nodded acknowledgment of what a feat that was for some.

"The bigger issue is that I spend all day walking down there to talk to someone who wants to save money by doing the repair themselves but treats me like their personal

YouTube tutorial. We need someone in the store who has a clue what all the parts are for and can give tips on how to make quick fixes."

A metaphoric light bulb went off between them. They both stepped up to the rail and peered down at Art.

"You think?" Reid asked.

"No harm in asking," Logan said.

Reid nodded and opened the lid on the barbecue, then went back to the rail, calling down, "Who wants cheese on their burger?"

"I'm a vegetarian," Biyen stopped playing to say.

"Yeah, I know, bud. Your mushroom burger is here. You want cheese on it?"

"Yes, please."

"Okay. You kids want to come and get your buns ready?"

"What's a vegetarian?" Cooper asked as he trailed Biyen up the stairs.

"I don't eat meat that comes from animals," Biyen explained. "Only fish if me and my dad catch it ourselves. Except, one time, Trystan gave me some sausage made from a bear. My dad said that's okay because it was hunted responsibly."

"You ate part of a bear?" Imogen's face twisted into incredulous revulsion.

"Just one time."

"Is your dad a vegetarian?" Logan asked Biyen as he came to the table.

"Uh-huh. But we have eggs if they come from happy

chickens."

Sophie was still holding Storm as she came up the stairs behind the kids. She sent him a cool look.

Logan got the message and dropped it, but he was really curious how she'd wound up with someone who seemed so different from her.

"Who needs help with their bun?" Logan asked. "Cooper? What do you like on your burger?"

Gramps was known for accepting any dinner invitation and for leaving almost immediately after he'd eaten. He drove home in his Gator while Sophie was helping Emma in the kitchen.

Delta was still shaking off the cross-Pacific travel so she retired to her room to unpack and have an early night. Reid and Logan were splitting their attention between sports highlights and Storm on her mat with her toys. The bigger kids came in from outside as Sophie put the last dry dish in the cupboard.

"Can we have screen time, Auntie Em?" Imogen asked. "I want to show Biyen something really funny."

"I'm sorry, sweetie. It'll have to wait," Sophie said before Emma could respond. "It's a school night for Biyen. We have to get home and get ready for bed."

"Awuh." Biyen stuck his lip out.

"I know," Sophie commiserated. "You should ask Mrs. Yuki if you can bring Imogen and Cooper one day. They might think it's interesting to see a Canadian classroom."

"We didn't bring our uniforms," Imogen said.

"Kids here don't wear uniforms," Emma told her. "Some schools have them, but it's not as common as at home. Look." Emma pointed at the fridge, inviting Biyen to view the kids' school photos stuck there beneath magnets shaped like ladybugs.

"Isn't it Fun Day this week, buddy?" Sophie recalled. "When it gets to be end of year, they have a day outside where they play silly games like an egg and spoon race," she explained to the other kids. "Everyone gets an ice cream and a sunburn. I think I'm supposed to be a volunteer," she recalled with a sense of mild panic. Quinley Banks, head of the Parent Advisory Committee, would never let her hear the end of it if she missed it. Over her shoulder, she said, "Logan, I need a day off, but I don't know which one."

"We don't give days off. You know that." He rose and stretched, then swept up his baby sister. "Nighty night, nutty nut."

Storm shoved her slobber-coated teething ring against his mouth, but he only made a slight face of disgust before kissing her cheek and plopping her onto Reid's lap.

Sophie had a brief flash of, *This could have been our life.* It was a very domestic moment, with everyone saying good night and Reid and Emma negotiating a bathing rotation for all the children as they left.

The walk home might have become awkward at that point, but Biyen chattered the whole way, providing a diary of his run up to summer.

"And then on Friday, Dad will come and take me camping in Rum Runner Cove. That's where the smugglers went when—what's it called, Mom?"

"Prohibition."

"Right. When alcohol was illegal. I found a fossil there, once. It was just a fern. Er, a palm frond? I have it in my bedroom and can show you. Did you ever go camping there when you were my age?"

"What age is that? Sometimes I think you're older than I am," Logan said.

"Mom says that, too." Biyen snickered and stuck his hand in hers, definitely still her little boy for a little longer. "Did you?"

"Go camping? No, we didn't do things like that. Too much work to be done around here." His voice was even, his profile difficult to read in the light of the half moon.

"Trystan did. He told me," Biyen said.

"Trystan went camping with his mother and her relatives. I always stayed here with my mom and dad. You know Glenda, don't you? She's my mom and she used to be married to our dad, Wilf."

"Uh-huh. I know."

Sophie's heart panged as she had a flashback to those times when Reid and Trystan were absent, visiting their mothers. Logan had always struck her as very lonely at those times, relegated to painting at the lodge or sweeping in the machine shop or filling potholes with gravel, struggling under the weight of a shovel.

"Sometimes I wish my mom and dad lived together,"

Biyen said.

Sophie's breath rushed out as that knife went in.

"You were only joking about not giving Mom a day off for Fun Day, right?"

"I was joking, yes," Logan confirmed.

"Good. I'll get the fossil to show you." He ran into the house as they neared the porch.

"Does he ever wind down?" Logan asked wryly.

"You wanted to stay in that playroom. You're free to make other choices."

"I wasn't complaining, just asking."

Biyen's crashing entry had woken Gramps where he had fallen asleep in his recliner.

"You're back." He patted a yawn.

"We are. Did you take your blood pressure pill, Gramps?" Sophie checked the pill dispenser marked with the days of the week and found his pill inside the section marked Sunday.

She brought it to him with a glass of water, then interrupted Biyen who was determined to leaf through every page of his fossil book.

"You can show Logan the rest tomorrow, champ. You need to hit the shower. Your feet are filthy enough to grow potatoes between your toes."

"Peas," he corrected. "My toes are too little for potatoes."

"And then the vines would climb all over you!" She came up behind him and attacked with tickling hands down his front, making him wiggle and giggle.

When she released him, he slapped the book closed and went into the bathroom, turning to yell from the door, "Are my shark bajamas clean?"

He still called them bajamas with a *b*.

"I'll get them." She ran down to the basement for the basket of fresh laundry and came back to set his pajamas on the lid of the closed toilet, catching him singing George Ezra's *Shotgun*.

When she came back to the kitchen, she overheard Gramps saying, "Hell, no. I'm not climbing into a bilge at my age."

"I was thinking the hardware store."

"Sophie said you hired Eunice Houstie's grandson."

"We did. He's keen, but green. We need someone to train him."

"I'm no help with computers, son."

"No, the practical stuff. He can read a label and find parts on a shelf, but he doesn't know what they're for. We need someone who can tell a customer, 'Yeah, that will work,' or 'No, you need a three-eighths.' It doesn't have to be full-time. Any hours you could spare would be a big help."

Gramps took off his glasses to give them a polish with the cloth he kept beside him. "What are you paying?"

"What do you want?

"Cash."

"That could be arranged," Logan said dryly.

"What do you think?" Gramps slipped his glasses back on and looked over them to where Sophie was folding laundry on the kitchen table.

She thought it sounded like a healthy way to get him out of the house. Sometimes it seemed like he didn't leave his chair all day.

"You know locals will start treating the shop like a drop-in center," she warned Logan. "The old-timers will come in to jaw-wag with him, but won't buy anything."

"More chance for him to be there when he's needed." Logan shrugged that off.

"Why don't you try it and see if you like it?" she suggested to Gramps.

"I'll have to leave in time to be here for Biyen, when he gets home from school."

"He can meet you at the shop and catch a lift in your rig. Hell, put him to work," Logan said. "How old were any of us when you set us to sorting nuts from bolts?"

"You little shits were trouble. You needed something to do."

"That's a true fact," Logan agreed. "Is there any chance you could come in for an hour tomorrow, though? I have to do Reid's rounds at the lodge while he takes Emma's family around the island."

"An hour's not worth leaving the house for," Gramps scoffed. "I'll be there when I get there and leave when I'm ready."

"Perfect." They shook on it.

Chapter Five

LOGAN WAS NOT a nostalgic person, especially for his childhood, but there was something quaint and familiar in the morning scramble in the Hughes-Marshall household. Socks had to be located and a sack lunch prepared. There was yelling up and down the stair well and the smell of burnt toast and Art sitting in his chair, watching the morning news with the volume a little too high.

"Did you take your morning pill?" Sophie asked as she brought Art a cup of coffee.

"I did," he assured her.

Logan noticed she checked the dispenser on the shelf over the coffeemaker anyway.

"Leave the dishes, Logan," Art urged him. "I'll do them before I come to the store. You all get going or the boy'll be late for school."

Logan turned off the water, suspecting Art was looking forward to peace and quiet.

The house was only a little farther from the marina than the one Logan had grown up in. He walked with Sophie and Biyen down the long driveway to the lane that led past the bottom of his own driveway and across the grounds of the resort—what they all called the village—

past the pub and around to the boatyard and the side entrance to the marina building.

Logan imagined the walk felt longer in the rain, but this morning the sky was bright with the promise of a fine summer day. The air smelled like salt and school almost out and long days in the marina about to start. That, too, had an odd sort of appeal.

Biyen chattered the whole way, telling him dinosaur facts and a story about his friend's little sister who put a crayon up her nose.

"Color me surprised," Logan said.

It went over Biyen's head, but Sophie sent him a look of mild admonishment for the pun.

"They had to go to the clinic in Bella Bella to get it removed," Biyen continued. "So then we all had to come back the next weekend for JayJay's birthday party *again*."

"The lesson I'm getting from that is not to have a little sister. Sheesh, buddy, you could have warned me before I got one for myself," Logan said.

"Now you know, though. Pro. Tip." Biyen tapped his nose.

Who the hell was this kid, saying hilarious shit like that? Logan shook his head in amusement and reached for the door to the stairs that led up to the marina office.

"Have fun at school today," Logan told him.

"I will. Love you, Mom."

"Love you, too, bud." She gave him a hug and kissed the top of his head.

He started up the hill.

Sophie faltered as she realized Logan had waited and watched them. Maybe it was his holding the door for her that made her cheeks go pink with self-consciousness.

"Thanks," she murmured, starting to walk through it.

Logan was being polite, not chivalrous, but now it felt weird.

Thankfully, Biyen called out to him.

"Hey, Logan!"

They both stepped back outside to look up to where Biyen stood on the road going up the hill.

"Remember that time you barfed by that tree?" Biyen pointed.

Sophie made a choking noise in her throat.

Awesome.

"I do. What about it?" Logan asked.

"I don't know. I just remembered." He shrugged. "Can I play with Imogen and Cooper after school?"

"I'll check with Emma. I'm sure they'd like that," Sophie said.

"Okay. Bye!" He finished running up the hill.

"You barfed by that tree?" Sophie smirked as she walked past him.

"The day after we got here. I guess my mother was right. A first impression is a lasting one." He followed her up the stairs.

"When has Glenda ever been wrong?"

"Just the one time, when she agreed to let Wilf Fraser buy her a drink."

Sophie snorted and took her coveralls off the hook by

the door, carrying them into the office. She gave them a shake, then stepped into them. Rather than push her arms into the sleeves, she tied them around her waist, leaving the heavy cotton bagging around her hips while she pulled off her sneakers and stepped into her work boots.

Don't ogle. He forced himself to start the pot of coffee they would nurse the rest of the day.

"I'm going to try to get these invoices entered before the phone starts to ring." Sophie stood in front of the desk they shared, absently holding the bronze water pump that had weighed down a red folder. Wilf had been old school, still doing everything with hard copies. Logan had insisted they move everything online, but some of their vendors were being slow to transition.

Fuck, she was cute right now with her coveralls hanging like hip waders off the indent of her waist. Her beige bra strap was showing on one side from beneath her green tank top. Her hair was up in its tangle, like a snag of red gill net, and her mouth pouted in concentration while she read a note left by accounting.

"Did you see—What?" She caught him staring.

"Nothing." He looked at the coffeemaker, an old drip thing full of limescale. "This should have been replaced ten years ago. Are these barnacles?"

"That's what gives the coffee its unique, chewy texture. I don't actually drink anything that comes out of it. I've been wondering why you do."

"Death wish, obviously." Storm, was the real answer. Between his nights with her and various worries over her future, this business, and his own, he had lost a lot of sleep in the last two months. "Art always had a pot going. I thought that's what we still did."

"Yeah, he's not allowed to drink that much coffee anymore. Thank you, by the way, for asking him to work at the store. Even if he decides not to do it, it's nice for him to feel needed. Losing your dad hit him really hard."

A cold, hollow sensation scraped behind Logan's sternum. He pivoted away from it and poured the first cup of what was truly rancid coffee.

"Is his health okay?" He was thinking of her diligence in making sure Art took his many pills.

"If he went to the doctor, I could answer that," she said with exasperation. "He's eighty-four. Every time he goes, they tell him something else needs watching. Blood pressure, thyroid, cholesterol, blood sugar…." She shrugged. "He gets bummed about his limitations. Hopefully, being in the store gives him a sense of purpose. I kind of wish I'd thought of it, to be honest." She circled her desk and tapped to wake up her computer, then pulled the folder closer. "Did you see the fuel surcharge on this one?" She waved an invoice at him. "High seas piracy."

They were done with personal talk, Logan surmised.

"Lemme see." He took it and sipped his coffee, then spit it back into his cup. "I can't do it. I'm going to the coffee shop for a red eye. You want one?"

"No, thanks."

By the time he got back, she'd been called down to a charter yacht with an oil leak.

It was a typical Monday where everything went sideways and time disappeared before Sophie knew where it had gone. She briefly saw Gramps in the store, when she stopped in for a part. Otherwise, she'd been run off her feet all day with repairs, big and small.

By the time she climbed the stairs to the marina office again, planning to sit down at her desk and finish those invoices, Biyen was there, talking to Logan. He was at the desk working through the invoices himself. Or trying to.

"Some dinosaurs lived for three hundred years," Biyen informed him.

"You're fibbing me."

"No. It's in my book. I'll show you when we get home."

"You sure love dinosaurs. Why is that?"

"That's a good question." Biyen pinched his chin as he deliberated. "I don't think I've ever thought about it."

Logan looked at Sophie, expression bemused.

Biyen provoked that reaction a lot. Some people called kids like him an old soul, but Sophie liked to think he was just a bright kid who hadn't been devastated by life yet. He led with his heart because it hadn't been broken.

"Hi, Mom. Did you ask Emma?" were the first words out of his mouth.

"Rats. I forgot." She came to the desk, hit the button for speakerphone, then the speed dial button labeled WILF HOME.

"G'day," Emma answered after one ring.

"It's me. Biyen is wondering if the kids want to play?"

"They've been asking about him all day. Send him over."

"He just got off school. He hasn't had a snack."

"I'll start a box of mac and cheese."

"You're a lifesaver."

"No worries."

"Thanks, Mom." Biyen dumped his backpack on the floor and ran down the stairs.

"I'll take that home myself, then?" she said to the door he'd left open.

She didn't mind too much. She worked a lot in the summer and felt less guilty about it when Biyen was playing with friends. Also, he hadn't eaten his apple. She washed it along with her hands and crunched into it.

While she ate, she perched on the stool by the other computer and began filling out work orders, matching her hours to vessel names and registrations so accounting could bill for them.

"Busy day?" Logan asked.

"Mm. I should tell you about this one nugget…" She spun on the stool. "Since he might complain. He called me down first thing with low oil pressure. I pretended we didn't have the part on hand because he was solidly drunk. He reeked and could barely stand upright. I said he'd have to wait for it to come in tomorrow, but he staggered up here and of course Kenneth sold it to him. Gramps wasn't there yet. Anyway, he tried to install it himself and made it worse."

"'Course." Logan nodded.

"So I genuinely did have to machine something at that point. I kept it under a hundred dollars, but he was super pissed. I left him trying to install it and warned the dock master that he shouldn't be piloting anything until he sobers up, but…" She shrugged. It was the coast guard's job to fine him if he was drunk on the water, not hers.

"See, I thought I had won Prick of the Day with a contractor who literally told me to fuck myself."

"You hear that so often, you think it's a term of endearment," she scoffed, then couldn't help continuing the joke. "Seriously, if you think that earns you a beer, I owe you one for every day you've been back. I say it all the time. Usually under my breath, but still."

"Are you vying for Employee of the Month?" he asked, cocking his head and narrowing his eyes in suspicion.

"Ooh, why have we never had that?" she asked with excited discovery.

Prick of the Day was a longstanding tradition. Wilf had often bought a beer for whichever employee had the worst run in with a snotty tourist or grumpy fisherman. As far as Sophie could figure, it had been Wilf's attempt to get someone to buy him a beer, but it had also been a way to let off steam and bond with other marina and resort staff while venting a crummy experience.

It wasn't always a customer or tourist who ruined your day, though.

"Did you know there was a woman working in the grocery store last year who was drinking from the bottles of liquor behind the counter? She topped them up with water, then *sold* them. She never did it to locals, but someone called from Alaska to say they'd just opened a bottle of gin that was pure water. She's the employee to beat. I don't think I can do it, sadly."

"Come on, Soph," Logan chided. "I believe in you. Apply yourself."

"Don't tempt me." The saucy phrase turned their easy banter into something more like flirting. Which made her blush so she shut up and spun back to the computer and got back to billing out her day. She thought she could feel Logan continuing to watch her, but she ignored him.

When she started to unlace her boots, Logan closed the folder of invoices.

"Pub, then?"

"No, thanks." She waved off his offer. "I have too much to do."

"I'm bringing beer home, anyway. You can have one there, when your day is done." He worked an elastic band around the folder.

"You're funny. My day is never done. But you don't have to get beer." She skimmed out of her coveralls and shook them, then stepped outside the door to hang them. "I bought some and gave it to Gramps to take home in his Gator." She came back to put on her shoes.

"Why?" Logan looked up from pushing his chair into place under the desk. He was ridiculously tidy. "I said I'd do it."

"You might have forgotten. Gramps likes to have one before dinner so..." She shrugged. "Buy some more. It doesn't go bad. Not at the rate you drink it."

"Are you serious? You didn't trust me to buy *beer*?"

"Oh my God, Logan. Are *you* serious?" His affront lit her temper. "I'm not three men and a nanny looking after one baby. Between work, Biyen, and Gramps, I'm going flat out at all times. I don't have the luxury of trusting that someone else is doing anything. If it needs doing, I do it. It's done. Happy day for you. Go home and have a cold one."

"Wow." His head had recoiled at her outburst. "You really do owe me a lot of beer."

She pinched her mouth flat, refusing to take back that diss against him and his brothers. She hooked Biyen's backpack over her shoulder and looked around for anything else she had to do before she left.

"I'll make dinner," Logan offered. "What else can I help with tonight?"

"I wasn't complaining. I was stating a fact."

"Sophie—"

"Fine. Look at the fan in the bathroom if you want to. It sounds like it has a bent blade. Gramps will get on a chair and try to pull it down himself if he notices so I can't leave it, but I have to water the garden, get gas for the lawnmower, and mow; otherwise Gramps gets hay fever. Then I have to shower and check the delivery on Biyen's birthday present. Also, I was supposed to reorder one of Gramps's prescriptions today and forgot, damn it. Let me make a note of that."

She came to the desk and found the sticky notes in the drawer. She scrawled the reminder and stuck it to the black screen of the monitor.

The phone rang.

Fuck. This was how her life had been going even before Wilf died, but she was only one person.

Logan snatched up the receiver.

"Hi, Kenneth." He listened. "Uh-huh. Yeah. No, she's gone for the day." He jerked his head at her, telling her to leave. "I'll come down." He hung up. "The drunk says you're a shitty mechanic, but also, he made it worse."

"Shocking," she muttered and headed for her coveralls. "I'm going."

"You don't have to. But if you could call Emma and tell her to send Biyen home—"

"Sophie. *Go.* I'll make sure his boat stays tied up."

"Really?" She kind of hated him more when he wasn't being an asshole than when he was. "Thank you."

Chapter Six

LOGAN FINISHED THE repair, told the skipper he had warned the coast guard about him, then went to the grocery store. He picked up a call from his mother while he was walking home.

"Hi, Mom. What's up?"

"I'm just wondering how everything is going with Emma's family."

If that was true, she would have called Emma, but he played along.

"Good. Reid drove them around the island today." There were only a handful of logging roads so it hadn't taken more than an hour.

"When do they leave on their cruise with Trystan?"

"Wednesday, back Sunday." The tours were staggered so the other one left Saturday and returned Wednesday.

"Have they decided whether they'll take Storm?"

"They're not." Emma was reluctant to leave her again, but everyone agreed that an infant on a boat could be less than ideal. Storm wasn't crawling, but she would still need a life preserver. "In a small space like that, if she isn't happy, everyone will know it. Reid offered to stay home with her, but I told him to go. It's not exactly a honeymoon, but it's the best we can do for now."

"I agree. And Emma's mother will want to get to know him."

"Exactly." Also, Emma could use a wingman. She hadn't said anything, but she had looked relieved when Reid had agreed to come with her. Logan only knew a little about the way her family had walked all over her in the past but wasn't prepared to let it happen again if he could help it.

"That leaves you with Storm and work, though. How will you manage that?"

"Storm's a Fraser. Crew not cargo. She comes to work with me."

"You have her scraping barnacles already? Your father would be so proud."

"She actually runs the place. I wish I was joking," he added as she chuckled.

"Be serious now. That's not ideal. You trying to work while you have her full-time? My real reason for calling—"

Here we go. He'd known she would have an ulterior motive.

"—is to say I'll come up. I want to meet Emma's family anyway. I was waiting to find out when the children's end of year assembly will be held." She was very involved with her husband Tan's grandkids, which was a boon for Logan. It kept the pressure off him to provide her with any. "That's Wednesday so I can come on the Thursday ferry. I'll stay the night at Barb's and come over in the morning."

Barb lived close to the ferry slip in Bella Bella and ran

a B and B. She picked up and delivered guests all through the summer so it didn't bother her that the ferry landed at midnight. It was just a fact of life here so it wasn't the reason Logan protested, either.

"Mom, I've got it." He was still stinging from Sophie's lecture about three men and a nanny. "I'm given to understand that single parents handle their own shit without help all the time."

I don't have the luxury of trusting that someone else is doing anything.

He had wanted to make some caustic remark about, *Whose fault is that?* seeing as she had been so reluctant to let him do anything.

"Also, I'm staying with Art and Sophie. There isn't actually a bed for you, not once Reid and Emma get back from the cruise."

He waited for her to take issue with his staying at Sophie's, but she only said, "There's always a bed for me. Biyen will be camping with Nolan. I'll sleep in his."

How many spies did she have on this island?

"Are you coming to check on me and Storm? Or me and Sophie?" he asked with suspicion.

"Do you need to be checked on?"

"No."

"Then I'm coming to visit my son and offering to help with the baby."

"You know you don't have to keep taking care of Dad's kids, right?" Wilf's marriage to Reid's mom had fallen apart because of his affair with Glenda, but when Miriam hadn't been able to keep Reid, Glenda had insisted Reid come live with them. Seeing as she already had Wilf's third son from yet another affair in her house, that had seemed like a perfectly rational solution to everyone except Logan.

"You know you don't have to stay angry with me for wanting to, don't you?" his mother said mildly.

"I'm not." He was so angry with her for it.

The sound of a mower started up in the distance. He set his grocery bag beside the washtub at the end of Art's driveway where the deer had chewed the flowers down to green stubble.

"I shouldn't have become involved with your father. Is that what you need to hear?" His mother said in his ear. "I was wrong to sleep with a married man who had a new baby at home. God knows Miriam was set up for failure, dragged into isolation with a newborn. You have a taste of parenting now so you can begin to understand how much stress that puts on a person."

Miriam's mental health struggles hadn't been properly diagnosed yet, either. Everyone had more compassion for her these days, but thirty years ago, the prevailing opinion had been that Wilf was the victim, married to an unreasonable woman. His affair with Glenda had been shrugged off as justified.

"I should have supported Miriam, not him," his mother continued. "But I refuse to say I regret having you. Or that I regret staying married to him as long as I did. I loved him, Logan."

"I know." Maybe he did, too, beneath his resentment.

"And Pauline, goodness, she was a child," she said, mentioning Trystan's mother. "I could have killed him for taking advantage of her, but I couldn't judge her for being the other woman, could I? Not when I'd been one myself. Trystan deserved to know his father and brother, same as you. His living with us while Pauline finished her degree made perfect sense."

It made for a cheap soap opera, in Logan's opinion, but one of his earliest memories was crying in Trystan's bed because Trystan had left for Christmas with his mom. He had never admitted that to anyone and never would.

"And Reid? What was I supposed to do? Let him go into foster care when Miriam was so unwell? I was the reason for their divorce. I contributed to her troubles. He needed stability so I did what I could to provide it for him."

"I know, Mom." Logan looked to the sky, having heard all of this before, but for the first time, he saw the decisions she had made through a different lens—that of a pseudo parent.

He understood how she could feel an obligation to a child she hadn't made because he hadn't made his little sister, yet felt responsible for her. Storm was so freaking helpless. She hadn't asked for her mom and dad to die. She couldn't speak or walk or even feed herself. *Someone* had to look out for her.

Much as it sounded like a convenient solution for Tiffany's sister to swoop in and take her, Logan couldn't stomach it. How would he know whether Storm was clean and dry and fed unless he was there to ensure it?

"I'm not mad, Mom," he said on a sigh. "Really."

There would always be this jagged hole of disillusion behind his breastbone, one formed by his father's behavior, but he couldn't blame Glenda for it. She had only done what she thought was right.

Reid had come to live with them when Logan was seven. He'd been a year older than Logan, sullen, and had brought a PlayStation he very begrudgingly shared. The tougher adjustment for Logan had been the way their offbeat blended family had become the talk of the town. That's when Logan had learned his mother was a homewrecker, his father a cheat.

Why did she stay with him? had been the question that had dogged him through his teens, especially when his father was so hard on all of them.

She had done it for them, was what she had always said. For him, he realized now. So he would grow up with his brothers, little as he had appreciated that.

Turning her away right now, when she was only trying to be herself—supportive and maternal—would be ungrateful in the extreme. God knew Sophie would have nothing but contempt for him if he refused to see his mother.

Hell, his mother would mother *her* while she was here, which was reason enough to accept her offer.

"If you really want to come, I'd appreciate it," he said. "Art would like to see you, I'm sure."

"Good. I'll see you Friday, then. I love you."

"Love you, too, Mom." He ended the call and picked up his groceries to continue walking toward the house.

Sophie was pushing the mower and Biyen was raking. He waved at Logan and Logan waved back.

What kind of person would Biyen be if Logan *had* been his father, Logan couldn't help wondering. What kind of life would they all have?

The question hit him with a lash of shame. There was nothing wrong with this life Sophie and Biyen were living. Its location in untouched rainforest made it pretty damned special, but it was modest. If Sophie had come with him when she'd wanted to, would he have still gone to Italy? Would she have become one of those rich, high-maintenance wives he'd met on Florida's party circuit, the ones with fake boobs and fake nails?

He couldn't see it. And kids? He had never wanted any. Would she have buckled to his wishes? Because she was a great mom. He had no doubt she'd been through hard times as a single, working parent, but he could tell she wouldn't trade Biyen for anything. Not even a life with him.

That caused a weird pang inside him. He ought to be thinking he'd done her a favor, but he felt pushed out. Unnecessary and forgotten.

As he should be. He'd been deeply self-involved when he had come back to help Glenda leave Wilf. Reid and Trystan hadn't been here. His mother hadn't asked for help from any of them and none had wanted to see their dad. Logan had barely spoken to him, mostly showing up as a giant fuck-you to his old man.

But there had been Sophie, stepping out of the gangly teenager she'd been and into the confidence of young adulthood. She'd been starry-eyed for her future, funny as ever, and just as quick to build up his ego.

He was three years older than her. At the time, that might as well have been decades. When she had asked him to be her first, he should have said no. He had rationalized it as a favor to a friend. Who else would be so careful with her? Who else would stop if she changed her mind?

Who else would he *want* it to be?

No one. He wanted it to be him.

He really was a selfish prick exactly like his father. He had definitely suffered the same delusion that sex didn't have consequences. That it didn't mean anything if you didn't want it to.

Maybe it didn't. Maybe he was still full of himself, thinking Sophie becoming pregnant right after he left had something to do with him. He didn't slut-shame. She'd been a very passionate person. He had left days after their affair started. He had no right to feel kicked in the gut by her moving on to someone else so quickly.

She obviously still blamed him to some extent, though. Why? He wasn't the only reason her life had been turned upside down. She had dropped out of school to nurse her sick Mom, then moved back here to look after her grandfather. Those things had nothing to do with him. She had had choices.

Hadn't she?

He walked into the kitchen to see dinner dishes in the sink. Art was snoring in his recliner. There was a packet of birthday invitations on the kitchen table, waiting to be addressed. When he put the groceries away, he found a wrapped plate of food in the refrigerator with his name written on it in Biyen's uneven scrawl.

Logan had missed lunch and was starving, but he went to look at the fan in the bathroom first.

PERVERSELY, WHEN LOGAN moved back to the Fraser house to look after Storm, Sophie missed him.

He'd only been here three days. Like at work, they did their best to stay out of each other's way. They crossed paths in the morning as they all used the bathroom and walked with Biyen into the village. They put in their time, then Logan had a beer with Gramps when he got home, before helping with whatever chores needed doing. After his shower, she listened to his floor creaking overhead. She tried not to think about whether he slept naked when she was in her own bed.

No, it was her son she missed, she insisted to herself. Biyen had left with Nolan this morning, grinning ear to ear over his new sleeping bag with dinosaurs on it.

"They glow in the *dark*?" He'd been agog with excitement.

Glenda was arriving tomorrow so it wasn't as though this house would be quiet for long. Sophie ought to be enjoying the peace, but she was lying here awake, mentally running through her day tomorrow. She had to strip and wash Biyen's sheets before Glenda got here. She would count the canning jars while she was down in the basement. Gramps had been freezing salmon, anticipating they would can it. Maybe Glenda would help with that. Sophie would buy lids tomorrow. Oh. And paint for the porch. Gramps wanted to—

The phone rang, startling her into sitting up.

It wouldn't be Nolan. There was no service on that side of the island. Not many sailed at night so it wouldn't be a work call.

On the second ring, she threw off her sheet and padded down to the kitchen, snatching up the landline from its cradle on the wall.

"Hello?"

"It's me," Logan said over a crying Storm. "Can you come over?"

"What? No. Why? I'm in bed." She folded one bare foot over the other.

"Storm's sick. I thought she was missing Emma, but she's hot and threw up her bottle." She'd never heard him so anxious. "I don't know what to do."

"I'll be right there." She hung up and got herself into jeans with a long-sleeved shirt, then shook Gramps awake enough to say, "Storm's sick. I'm going over to help Logan."

"All right." He rolled over and probably wouldn't remember. He was snoring again by the time she found the flashlight and her shoes.

The moon was waning, the sky was clear. She arrived at the house breathless from jogging up the hill.

Logan opened the door before she knocked, obviously watching for her flashlight. He was shirtless, wearing only trackpants hanging low on his hips. His hair was mussed, his cheeks stubbled, his brows glued together with worry.

"Hey, sweet pea," Sophie said, touching the back of Storm's neck.

She turned her face away, crying wretchedly into Logan's shoulder.

"Did you take her temperature?"

"The thermometer is there." He pointed to the kitchen island. "I didn't know how to do it." He grimaced.

"You put it in her armpit."

"Oh shit. Yeah, I thought I had to—This is why I called you."

She hid her smile at how discomfited he was and set her box of supplies on the counter. It was full of all the things she reached for when Biyen was sick, but Emma was equally prepared. There was already a plastic tub with a thermometer and teething gel along with a bottle of infant Tylenol and a dosing syringe.

Logan shifted Storm so he could tug open the snaps of her sleeper and bared her arm. She wasn't having it. She cried even harder when he gently pinned her arm down for the minute the thermometer needed to get its reading.

It finally beeped and Sophie read, "A smidge over one hundred. Let's see if this brings it down." She gave the grape flavored medication a shake, then read the dosage schedule. "How much does she weigh?"

They double-checked the concentration and each other's math, finally squirting a small measure of the syrup into Storm's mouth.

She stopped crying as she decided whether she liked the taste or not, then fell back onto Logan, crying it out again.

"Let's get a damp cloth and cool her off a little. Oh! Em has Popsicles for the kids, doesn't she?" They had all had one the other night. Sophie opened the freezer. "They're not ideal for rehydration, but it might calm her down and cool her off."

It helped. Storm knew exactly what it was and reached for Sophie when she saw it.

"Do you mind holding her?" Logan asked. "I still smell like barf and have to clean her crib."

"Of course. Come on, pumpkin." Sophie carried her to the couch and sat with Storm sniffling in her lap. Storm kept one hand on Sophie's to keep the orange Popsicle against her unhappy mouth.

Logan went up the stairs, then came back a few minutes later to carry a basket down to the basement. He returned wearing a blue T-shirt and brought a damp cloth.

Storm didn't like the cloth on her hair. She promptly rejected Sophie with a wail and a reach for big brother.

"All right," Logan murmured as he gathered her up. He paced and rubbed her back. "This is what happens when you get into Dad's rye. I hope you've learned your lesson."

"Something all the Fraser children learn the hard way, I

presume," Sophie said, setting the melting Popsicle on its wrapper.

"Oh, we never learn. We got into it a couple of weeks ago like a bunch of amateurs." He touched his lips and dipped his chin to indicate Storm's eyelids were drooping.

Sophie sat quietly, lulled by the sight of him soothing Storm to sleep.

The handful of times Sophie had played What-if with herself, wondering how Logan would have handled fatherhood, she had taken a dark comfort in believing he would have been terrible at it. He was as selfish as Nolan, but in different ways. He wouldn't have left the payment of rent up to her, but he would have been single-minded about his own pursuits, not generous with himself or his time.

At least, that's what she had always believed. Now, she wasn't as sure. He was capable of holding a baby with tenderness and waiting patiently while she drifted off. He cupped Storm's neck, set the backs of his fingers against her cheeks, and seemed satisfied that her temperature had come down.

He slipped upstairs and came back with a baby monitor.

"Where's that Popsicle?" He looked around.

"I put it in the sink."

"I would have finished it."

"Do you want Storm's plague?"

"Good point. You want one?" He went to the freezer for a fresh one.

"I'll have an ice cream bar." She'd seen the high-grade

dark chocolate and almond-coated treats when she had retrieved the Popsicle.

He brought it to her and unwrapped a green Popsicle for himself.

"Thanks for coming. She had a fever after her shots, but it wasn't serious, and Em handled it. I was ready to call a medivac."

"I don't think you're there yet. If she gets worse or she's still feverish in the morning, call across to the clinic in Bella Bella. See what they say."

"What do you think it is? Flu?"

"She's a baby. It could be anything. A virus or something she ate. She's at an age where she's putting everything she touches into her mouth. When Biyen was one, I caught him chewing a slug. He was mad as hell when I pried his teeth open and got it out."

"That is the grossest story I have ever heard. And I've watched my brother eat bugs on his show." He pointed his Popsicle at her.

"Toughen up. Parenting is not for the squeamish."

"Exactly why I don't want to be one."

Well, that certainly slammed a door on this conversation.

She dropped her gaze and focused on finishing the ice cream she no longer wanted. She used the damp cloth to wipe her fingers when she was done.

"I'll—"

"How did you do it?" he asked at the same time, voice pitched quiet enough she had to say, "What?"

"This." He waved at the house. "Juggling a baby and work. How did you do it with your mom and everything?"

She couldn't take that near awe in his gaze. She dropped her attention to a bruise on her knuckle she couldn't remember getting. A pipe wrench in a small engine room, probably.

"I wasn't working while she was sick. I should have found a job as soon as I realized I was pregnant. Then I would have been eligible for maternity benefits, but I stuck out my second semester at school. Mom didn't have much left of the settlement from losing my dad, but it was enough for her to live on while she was in treatment. She left me what she could, and I lived off that until Biyen was a year old."

"I guess Biyen's father was there to take him when you needed to be with your mom."

"Not really." She felt the shakiness of emotion that entered her voice when she revisited that time. "Biyen didn't take a bottle so I couldn't leave him with anyone. Sometimes I wonder how he turned out so easygoing when he was drinking pure anxiety as an infant," she joked faintly. "I'll always be happy I was able to share him with her, though. We had so many laughs over my new mom adventures." Her throat was growing raw. So was her chest.

"Janine was very funny. I always remember that about her. Whenever I was sent to the store for milk or whatever, she would make some crack about something, and I'd leave chuckling. I know Mom really misses her."

"Me, too." Seven years later, the grief could still rise up

so intensely it threatened to swallow her whole. But wallowing in her private agony had been yet another luxury she hadn't been able to afford. "Having Biyen forced me to get on with things after she was gone. It probably could have gone either way, but he kept me from sinking into depression. He's so delighted by simple things. I miss him when he's with Nolan, but he'll come home in a week and tell me with great pride that he pooped in a hole he dug himself. It puts all of my agonies and aspirations into perspective."

He snorted. "No kidding. Hashtag mental health hack."

"Right?" She chuckled, embracing her love of her son to ward off all those other, difficult to bear emotions.

"Is his dad like that?" Logan asked curiously. "Is that why you fell for him?"

"Nolan keeps his life very simple, yes." She cautioned herself not to be bitter with disappointment. "But I didn't love him. He's a guy I brought home from the bar because he seemed harmless, and things got complicated when I became pregnant." She closed the wrapper from her ice cream bar over the sticky stick.

"Since when did you bring home men from the bar?" Logan's brows crashed together.

"That smells a lot like judgment when I know for a fact that at nineteen, you spent your weekends in the bar, picking up girls. Trystan told me that's what you told him you were doing when I asked him if you were enjoying university. Sauce for the goose."

"*Trying* is the operative word that he missed when he relayed that information," Logan said through his teeth.

Trystan had been *trying* to help her shake off her long and useless crush. She had not appreciated him for it.

"Either way, I'm guessing that behavior continued more or less nonstop until you got the call that Wilf was gone and had to leave your condoms on your yacht while you moved in with your brothers. So I'll say a polite fuck-you and fuck your double standards." She rose. "What did you want me to do, Logan? Sit here and pine for you some more?"

"No." His jaw was locked, his mouth grim. "I'm saying it seems out of character to the woman I knew."

The one who had saved herself for him. As if he had ever really known her or cared one way or another what she did.

"I was getting over you, Logan." Screw him and his stirring up of all her old baggage. Now her tortured, angry emotions were leaking everywhere, especially out of her mouth. "I fucked around in empty hookups because I thought that's how I deserved to be treated. Because that's how *you* treated me."

"Sophie." He pressed back in his chair with shock.

"I *hate* you for the way you treated me," she spat, letting the poison squeeze out at last. "But I hate myself more for allowing it. For spending so many years waiting for you. For not seeing that you never actually gave a shit about me."

"That is not true." He shot to his feet. "I gave a shit. I

have always cared about you."

"Oh fuck off." She shook her head and flung out a hand, rejecting his bullshit. "You didn't care about anyone but yourself, but *I* don't care about that. I'm furious with myself because *I* treated myself badly. I punished myself for being stupid over you, and I wound up derailing my future. That's not your fault. I did that to myself." She tapped her breastbone where it was throbbing as though fractured all the way through. "But I won't do it again, Logan. I won't do this." She motioned between them. "I won't have cozy chats with you where I share my feelings and you convince me I matter. Never again. Understand?"

He stood very still, fists clenched as though he were withstanding something unbearable.

"We work together. For Storm's sake, I'll help you with her if you need it. Stay in my house and wash my dishes and give Gramps a laugh. He needs it. But we both know you're leaving as soon as you can. We are not friends. We never were and we never will be."

Chapter Seven

STORM WAS FEELING better when she woke the next morning, but was still discontent that Emma was absent. She was moaning a nonstop, "Mumumumum."

Logan strapped her to his chest and went down to the wharf to greet his mom as she came off the seabus.

"Hello, little love." Glenda swooped straight for Storm, cupping her cheeks and smiling gooily at her.

"Now I understand how women feel. My eyes are up here," Logan told her.

"Oh poor you." She touched his arm so he would dip his head enough that she could kiss his cheek. "You brought the truck? I've been making food since Emma told me her family was coming."

"Of course you have." And of course he brought the truck. This was not his first rodeo. Still, even though he had expected her to bring food, he was exasperated by the growing pile of insulated boxes being transferred onto the wharf. "You should work for the Red Cross. Here. Take Storm. This will be a few trips."

Storm went to her without complaint. His mother inspired immediate trust in everyone, especially children. She carried her up to where the truck was parked at the top of the ramp.

As Logan was starting up with his second stack of boxes, Sophie came down the ramp with a length of air hose coiled over her shoulder. She was dragging the portable air compressor behind her. Her coveralls disguised her figure, but it was a warm day so she had left them open at her throat. She'd rolled the sleeves back to reveal her wrists and had a pair of worn leather work gloves sticking out of her pocket.

Pull it together, he ordered himself, dragging his gaze off her collarbone as he stepped aside to let her pass.

He'd been tied up in Reid's office all day yesterday so he asked, "Anything happening that I should know about?"

"Nope."

"You know where to find me if you need me."

"Yup."

They were back to keeping things strictly about work. It sucked. He hadn't stopped feeling as though a primal scream was lodged in his throat, but what the hell could he do about it?

"Oh hey," he called to her back. "Mom will be cooking tonight if you and Art want to join us."

"I'm busy, but Gramps is at the store. She's gone to ask him." She kept walking.

Another day in paradise.

Logan got his mother's boxes into the truck, then collected her and Storm from the store, driving them up to the house where he unloaded everything into the basement.

"Can you get all of this put away yourself? Storm and I

have to get back to work." He set the sling on the top of the washer, starting to buckle her into it, but thought to check her diaper first. It was okay for now.

"Leave her with me," his mother chided.

He was tempted. Covering for Reid meant Sophie was covering for him and she already had her hands full because Randy was still away.

"She was sick the other night and she's grumpy with so many of us gone. I'll keep her with me for now and bring her back when she's ready for her nap." He checked all the straps as he buckled Storm to his chest, glancing up in time to catch an expression on his mother's face that said, *Look how cute my boy is, caring for his baby sister.*

Ugh.

"Also, the contractors are less inclined to swear at me when I have her. I'm using her as a human shield, really."

Her look admonished him, then grew more serious.

"Sophie's not coming for dinner. Are you two still fine?" She knew they weren't. He could hear the suspicion underlying the bland interest in her tone.

He drew a breath that felt loaded with fiberglass. He and Sophie had never been fine. Not since he had left her at the ferry slip eight years ago. He had known it then, but he knew it even more unequivocally now.

I punished myself.

"She told me..." He absently set his hands under Storm's feet, allowing her to push against them. Beyond the basement window, the backyard fell away, leaving a view of treetops and cloud-skudded sky.

His regret was like that. Endless. He couldn't even see the horizon of it.

"What do you know about how she was after you and I left here that summer?" he asked.

Her brows went up and her lashes went down, hiding whatever was in her eyes. Her mouth pursed briefly as though she considered her words very carefully. When she spoke, there was no inflection.

"According to Janine, she went on a tear. She was in the pub every night and didn't come home except to shower and go to work. Janine hoped she would settle down once she was at school in Nanaimo, but it seemed to be more of the same until she came home at Christmas and told Janine she was pregnant. She settled back into school for another semester, but Janine was diagnosed. She moved to be closer to Sophie and treatment. Once Biyen arrived, Sophie withdrew from the program and spent as much time as she could with Janine."

I fucked around in empty hookups because I thought that's how I deserved to be treated. Because that's how you *treated me.*

Such a heavy ache sat on his lungs he could hardly draw breath.

"And Biyen's father?" he asked gruffly. "What's he like?"

"A stray dog." His mother pursed her mouth again, perhaps regretting such a blunt statement. "I think Nolan was a warm body to sleep against when she needed it. He's immature in many ways so of course he makes a wonderful friend for Biyen, but what I see in them is a relationship like Reid had with his mother. A boy parenting his parent. Sophie rose to the challenge, though." Glenda worked the lid off one of the insulated boxes, making the foam squeak against itself. "She tried to make it work with Nolan for Biyen's sake, after Janine was gone, but she knew when to cut her line. It couldn't have been easy, coming back here to all the talk about how she had behaved before she left. Being here has been good for all of them, though. Biyen and Art, especially. I'm proud of her."

So was Logan. And grateful. The marina's books would be a lot more dire if they hadn't had someone so invested, historically and emotionally, managing things.

"I don't know how to tell her I'm sorry," he admitted in a low voice.

His mother lifted her gaze to meet his and it was hard to allow it. She didn't scold or reveal disappointment. Somehow that was worse. He swallowed the lump in his throat and looked away.

"You could start by saying it to her instead of me." She said with her quiet, frustratingly simple logic.

"Yeah." His voice felt as though it passed over gravel all the way up his chest.

"Storm's yawning. Give her to me and I'll call you when she wakes."

SOPHIE WAS ON the wharf Sunday afternoon, chewing the

fat with a couple of trawlers, when she saw the *Storm Ridge* coming into the cove. As it neared the wharf, Reid came on deck to drop the fender buoys off the port side.

She moved down to catch the bow line he threw to her. He moved to the stern and leapt to the wharf when they were close enough, bringing that line with him and leaning back to draw the cruiser in.

"How was it?" she asked him, looking for Emma among the guests gathering on the deck.

"Great. Definitely good value for the cost. We could be charging more." He stepped aboard to take the steps from where they'd been stowed and set them for the guests to disembark.

Sophie moved forward to help take the bags he handed off and set them on the wharf for people to collect on their way to the lodge and the rest of their travel plans.

"Sophie!" Imogen came topside and grabbed the rail. She wore a windbreaker and a life preserver over her shorts. "Where's Biyen?"

"Still camping with his dad."

"Oh." She pouted.

"He'll be home in a few days. Did you have fun?"

"We saw bears!" Her eyes went as big as dinner plates. "They were catching fish. And otters."

"The bears were catching otters? I've never seen that!"

"No." She giggled. "We *saw* otters. They were so cute."

"There's nothing cuter than otters, is there?"

"One had a *baby*."

"I stand corrected. Baby otters are definitely the cutest."

Imogen nodded enthusiastic agreement.

"There you are, Imogen." Delta came out to the rail with Cooper's hand firm in her own. "Did you find your hairbrush? Put it in your backpack and bring it up." She sighed as the girl disappeared. "It was a relaxing trip until thirty minutes ago, when we all realized it was over. Thank you, Reid."

Delta accepted his hand as he helped her onto the wharf.

Cooper pulled free and stayed at the top of the steps.

"Uncle Reid!" Cooper lifted his arms and grinned with anticipation.

Reid grabbed him and lifted him high, then lowered him halfway to the wharf.

"Why are you so wobbly? Why can't you stand?" He joggled him so his feet swayed. "You got a bad case of sea legs?"

"I'm not down! You have to put me down," Cooper said through his giggles, clinging to Reid's arms as his feet cycled, searching for the solidness of the wharf.

"What? Oh. I thought you were taller." He finally set Cooper on his feet.

Sophie almost fell in the water, never having seen Reid act so silly with anyone, particularly someone else's child.

"Can you be a super-helper and take this bag up to the truck?" Reid draped what looked like a beach bag with long handles over Cooper's shoulder. "See where Logan is?"

Sophie stubbornly refused to turn and look. Things had been *very* awkward since the night she'd helped with

Storm. She ought to be glad that he was keeping his distance, but she mostly alternated between hating herself for revealing how badly he'd hurt her and hating him for taking her at her word that they would never be friends.

"Hey!" Emma greeted her with a wide smile as she came on deck beside Imogen.

"Hi. Was it a good trip?"

"So good—Oh, there she is." Emma didn't even pause to hug Sophie as she leapt off the boat and hurried past her.

Sophie wasn't insulted. Her coveralls were filthy and the squeal from Storm behind her was irresistible enough that Sophie did turn then, watching Storm try to launch herself from Logan's arms to get to Emma.

"Tag, you're it," Logan said as he left the wiggling baby in Emma's arms. "I'll get all the luggage, Delta. You can walk the kids up to the house and relax. Mom is there, putting out snacks. She has something for you guys, too." He gave each child's head a light pat.

Of course, she did, Sophie thought with affection. Glenda always had coloring books or bubble wands or something that won the hearts of children and kept them busy being kids.

"Thank you, Logan. Imogen, leave your life preserver— There we go." Delta smiled her thanks as Sophie took the bright-orange vest from her. "Let's go, moppets. A walk will help us find our land legs, won't it?"

"Glenda is here?" Reid asked Logan as they gathered luggage, preparing to carry it up to the truck.

"Yeah. She moved into Sophie's this afternoon and

leaves tomorrow night. She's got salads and everything ready to barbecue for dinner tonight."

"Always the lifesaver," Reid said. "Em will appreciate that. She's done most of the cooking while we've been aboard. You're coming for dinner, Soph?" Reid asked as he started past her.

"We'll see. I just finished my second callout on my day off so it's been like that." She shrugged.

"It's July." He frowned. "Isn't Randy finished school?"

"He had a family wedding back east. Not great timing, but the bride rudely didn't ask me which dates would be convenient for her brother to attend."

"Brides." Reid shook his head with disgust.

"Right? It was actually your dad who told him he could go. It's been planned since last year."

"Hmph. Well, you don't want to cook, do you? Come up." Reid glanced at Logan, maybe looking for him to encourage her, too.

She was still refusing to look at Logan so she didn't know what was on his face. Whatever it was made Reid's mouth tighten.

"Try to make it if you can." He followed Logan up the wharf to the truck.

Sophie stepped aboard the *Storm Ridge* and opened the hold labeled LIFE PRESERVERS.

"Thanks." Trystan came down from the pilothouse with some dishes he took into the galley.

Trystan was arguably the most handsome of the Fraser boys.

Reid had the severely tailored, clean-shaven stockbroker vibe nailed down flat. He was not hard to look at, but he could be hard. He set impossible standards of perfection for himself and everyone around him, but that made him easy to trust as a leader.

Logan was more of a sexy playboy. His taste in clothing was less buttoned-down, but always very smart and flattering. His hair was a sun-streaked brush cut that was invariably tousled by the wind off the water and his weapon of choice was his disarming smile. He was the most like Wilf in that regard, not that she would ever say so to his face. She didn't mind throwing out a few insults when appropriate, but she didn't want to actually kill him.

Reid and Logan were a year apart, Trystan coming along three years later. He might have been significantly younger than his brothers, but he was a student of animal behavior. He had read the rec room as soon as Reid arrived in it. While Reid and Logan had begun jockeying for dominance, Trystan had walked his own path, one that took him away from the fray and everyone else. That's how he'd become an online sensation with his wilderness survival series, by excelling at being alone.

He wouldn't have become a star without his star power, though. He was definitely a looker with his shiny black hair and rugged build and his perma-tanned complexion. He also possessed that Hollywood "it" factor, an inexplicable, compelling presence that mesmerized. Whether he was in person or on screen, he made it seem as though he was talking directly to *you*. He could be covered in mosquito bites, or eating grubs, or boiling water he'd distilled from his own urine, and women would fill his comment section with offers to carry his baby.

Judging by his patience with his little sister, he would be an incredible father if he ever decided to go down that road.

If Sophie had wanted a Fraser boy, Trystan was the one she should have set her sights on. He had never once betrayed her. If she had had a dollar for every time her mother or anyone else had nudged her toward Trystan instead of Logan, she would have a nice mansion in LA because Trystan had made himself a very tidy fortune with his series and bought one. Then sold it recently, maybe to pour money into Raven's Cove? It was hard to say because he didn't say much, which was also part of his enigmatic charm.

She adored Trystan, but they had enjoyed too many fart jokes when they were six for her to see him as a romantic interest. He'd seen too many longing looks from her toward his brother to want to compete, either. He liked her. She would dare to say he loved her the way he loved his cousins and stepsiblings, but the one time they had kissed over spin the bottle, they had laughed themselves weak over how wrong it had felt.

They had landed on being very good friends. Often that was from a distance. Sophie didn't resent that distance because she knew that's what Trystan preferred. Her understanding of him made their friendship as strong as it was. For his part, he gave her his nonjudgmental support, no matter how rashly, or irrationally, she behaved.

He was the second person after her mom who she'd told she was pregnant.

What do you need? had been his response.

I need you to tell me I'll be a good mom.

You'll be a great mom. He'd sounded so sure, not hesitating for a second, she couldn't help but believe him.

He'd been away a lot through the years, but he had often called to say, *I'm heading off-grid. I wanted to make sure you're doing okay before I go.*

He meant money and she had never asked him for any, but she knew she could and that meant a lot. It was that kind of friendship. The handful of times they'd crossed paths, when he had been in the area to visit relatives, he always made a point of having a coffee and catch up with her and Gramps and Biyen.

So she helped him tidy up the *Storm Ridge* without being asked. She moved through the various decks collecting garbage, not filling the silence with chatter because it was enough to be around him. When she brought all the litter to the galley, he was in the saloon, stuffing bedding into a commercial laundry bag that was already full.

"Ready to go straight into the bush?" she guessed.

"Straight there, never coming back."

"How did an introvert get saddled with tourism?"

"I opened my big mouth. Reid said we should sell these tubs. I said they were a solid addition to the business. He said, *Prove it*, and here I am."

"Rookie."

"Yup."

Trystan would prove it, though. He wasn't the bull-headed force that Reid was, or the relentless charmer that Logan was, but he was absolutely as tenacious and driven to achieve.

These ecotours fed directly into what had provoked him to make his wilderness series. He wanted people to see and value the environment so they would understand why delicate natural ecosystems needed to be preserved. Economically, these cruises were good for the resort and local businesses, bringing money from afar. They also gave the local First Nations people a chance to tell their side of history.

"It's not that bad," he admitted. "My steward and first mate both like to chat so they usually carry the social load. I gave them the week off so Reid and Em could have their cabin and Em was great. She made sure all the guests were happy and Reid gets shit done without being asked, but having Emma's mom aboard meant I had to be more engaged. And Reid had so many hot takes. Why don't you do it this way? Why don't you take us over there? He's exhausting. Take the wheel if you think you can do better."

Sophie bit her lip, far too amused when something got under Trystan's skin because so little did. His brothers were always a guaranteed culprit, though.

"You both came back alive," she noted. "He said it was a good trip and that you should be charging more."

"Probably," he conceded. "Delta seemed to enjoy it. That made Emma happy, which made Reid happy."

"Look at you, making the world a better place one cruise at a time." She angled her elbow toward him.

"My work here is done, then. You want to refuel this beast so I can get lost?"

"I hate to tell you, sport, but Glenda is cooking dinner at the house."

"Logan couldn't hack it and had to call his mom?" His lip curled with smug amusement.

"To be fair, Randy is away and Storm got sick. We needed backup."

"What happened?" His head came up in concern.

"Just a little fever. She's fine now. But you know how Glenda likes to see her kids all together, playing nice."

"You'll be there, too, then?" His brows lifted in challenge.

"We'll see how my time is." She hooked the band that held a curtain open, brushing the bottom so the skirt of it fell nicely. "I need to catch up the weeding in the garden. If I don't, Glenda will be out there tomorrow, and my conscience can't hack that. Not with her back the way it is."

"I will tattle so fast if you can't find a better excuse than weeding."

"You *child*." She planted her hands on her hips. "Okay, what if I help you turn this place over, then you come weed with me? I promise not to talk to you."

"I've heard that before," he said pithily. "But sure. Let's do that."

Chapter Eight

LOGAN WAS PUZZLED when Trystan arrived with Art, riding in the Gator with him as Art puttered it up the drive.

Logan drew a couple of cans of beer from the ice-filled cooler and offered them in greeting.

"Thanks, son." Art accepted a can and took it to the nearest lawn chair in the shade.

"I thought you were still on the *Storm Ridge*," Logan said to Trystan.

"I was helping Sophie in her garden."

"Why?"

Trystan narrowed his eyes at Logan's tone.

"Because it needed weeding." He popped the beer he held and took a couple of gulps. "Then Nolan brought Biyen home. Biyen got stung by a wasp. He's fine." Trystan waved off Logan's frown of concern. "Sophie thinks he knew the kids were back and he wanted to see them. They're still getting cleaned up. They'll be over soon."

"That's good. Mom was worried she wasn't going to see Biyen this trip." He glanced toward the trail to Sophie's house. "Is—" He hesitated, not sure he wanted an answer to this question. "Is Sophie bringing... What's his name?"

He knew damned well what it was. Trystan had just said it, but Logan would be damned if he would let it pass his lips. It was like saying Beetlejuice three times. He didn't want to summon the bastard.

"Nolan," Trystan provided with a twitch at the corner of his mouth. "I don't know if she has a choice. That guy is like a bear. He can smell a free meal from a mile away. You might find him sleeping in your bed when you get back there tonight."

As long as he wasn't sleeping in hers, Logan thought with more acrid dislike than he was entitled to.

"I told her I could help pull weeds after work this week." Logan was annoyed she had asked Trystan for help. He hadn't found the right time or place to apologize and had thought the garden while Biyen was away camping might give him the chance he needed to clear the air with her.

"She wanted to get it done before Glenda got into it. On that topic…"

"No." Logan forestalled the sparkle that had come into Trystan's eye. "Before you start riding me about Mom being here, she insisted on coming. Even with her here, it's been really busy with Storm and covering for Reid. Sophie has been run off her feet so I was doing it as much for her as anyone else."

"Uh-huh. Keep telling yourself that."

"She's been asking for you, by the way."

"Storm? I figured I'd let Em have first crack at her."

"Hilarious. Storm could care less about anyone but Em.

She's taken root on her hip."

"There's my favorite skunk cabbage," Trystan said, handing Logan his beer and breaking out one of his rarely used wide smiles. "Are you going to come see me?"

Storm kicked and grinned and buried her face in Emma's neck, making Emma wince as she grabbed a handful of Em's hair, but she was chuckling at how excited Storm was.

"Say hi to Trystan, you silly goose," Emma urged the baby.

Storm abruptly twisted to reach for Trystan, making a *tsking* noise against her teeth.

"Are you trying to say my name, you little ball of yarn?" He lifted her over his head, making her chortle, then he brought her down for growly kisses against her neck.

"I'm going to hit the toilet while she's distracted," Emma said under her breath and hurried inside.

While Trystan cruised Storm around the yard like an airplane, Logan stuck his brother's beer back on ice and let himself be drawn into playing ringtoss with the kids.

Sophie arrived a short while later and she did bring What's-his-name. She wore cut-off jeans and a pale-pink T-shirt. Her hair was still drying from her shower so it was falling around her face in red-gold curlicues that he hardly ever saw loose like that. He found them extra fascinating and really wanted to touch them.

"Delta, this is Biyen's dad, Nolan." She stopped where Delta had joined Art in the shade.

Logan would have listened more closely, but Biyen ran

up to him. "Logan, look. I got stung by a wasp."

"You sure did." He touched under the boy's chin to tilt his face and examine his puffy cheek. "Does it hurt?"

"Not anymore. Dad put ice on it, but I wanted to see Mom. She said I'll live. Gramps said we can camp on the yard instead, since Auntie Glenda is visiting and needs my bed."

"That all works out, doesn't it?"

"Yup. Hey, Dad. Do you want to play ringtoss with us?"

"Sure, dude. Hey, man. I'm Nolan," he drawled with a heavy vocal fry as he came across and offered his hand to Logan.

"Logan. I think we met at my mother's wedding a few years ago." He offered the toy rings he held rather than a handshake.

"Yeah, that was a fun night." Nolan's clothes gave off a vague aroma of campfire, but his hair was wet and combed off his tanned, bearded face. A face that bore a distinct resemblance to Biyen's.

"Let me get you a beer," Logan said as an excuse to walk away. "Sophie?"

"I'll find a glass of water first." She went up the outside stairs to the kitchen.

Logan relayed the beer to Biyen's father and checked in with Delta and Art who didn't need refreshing yet.

"Uncle Reid," Cooper called up to where Reid was cleaning the barbecue on the deck off the kitchen. "Will you be on my team? Immy doesn't want to play anymore."

Imogen had fallen for the Trystan Effect. She was following him and Storm around the yard, asking questions about sea otters and orcas and owl pellets.

"Sure thing, buddy." Reid looked to Logan. "Will you finish this for me?"

Logan nodded and passed him on the stairs.

"Oh, you want to be on our team, too?" Reid asked as he walked by Trystan and Storm reached for him. "That might be an unfair advantage, but sure."

Trystan gave her up and crouched beside Imogen, pointing up to the treetops, then down at the ground as he explained some wonder of nature to her.

Reid looked like the quintessential dad, cradling Storm in one arm while he helped Cooper hone his ringtoss technique, giving Biyen and his father a run for their money.

Logan stood at the rail of the upper deck, looking down at all those men in their fatherly roles. He had always looked down on that role because he'd looked down on his own father, but for once he felt differently about it.

Reid was really trying to do better than their father had. Logan had to admire him for it. Trys was Trys, naturally good in any one-on-one role, especially with a kid. Even Biyen's father couldn't be faulted, praising Biyen for a, "Good try, bud. Take my turn. See if you can get it this time."

Logan had no faith in himself as a father. He presumed he would be terrible at it, like his own, which was why he had never wanted to be one.

A gritty, tarred sensation invaded his chest as he wondered, really wondered, if he could ever be even half as good at it as those men were. As far as responsibility went, shaping the life of a child was monumental.

"Logan."

Sophie's voice cut into him like a blade, making him jolt with a strange mix of culpability and defensiveness.

She wasn't looking at him. She clapped her glass of water onto the table and shaded her eyes. "Something's going on with the *Missionary II*."

Logan followed her gaze to where the tour boat was coming into the cove. Built in the early 1900s as a floating hospital, the vessel had been converted by a couple out of Campbell River into a tour boat ten years ago. It carried sea kayakers along the coast, coming into Raven's Cove a few times each summer. Its name was a source of adolescent amusement among the locals. Everyone knew what the first missionary position was. What was the second?

Logan swore as he saw the smoke. The people on board were scrambling and the boat seemed to lose power.

"They've cut the engine."

They were likely radioing for help, but Logan clapped the barbecue shut and turned off the knobs, whistling down to his brothers.

"Fire on the water."

He clattered down the stairs. Reid handed Storm to Delta and leapt behind the wheel of the truck. Sophie came in beside Logan while Trystan rode shotgun. Minutes later, they were running down the wharf, hurrying to launch the

Storm Ridge along with half the other boats moored alongside them. The fire brigade from the fueling station was headed out there, too.

As they approached, kayaks were being dropped into the water along with lifeboats. People in life preservers were scrambling to get down ladders, but more than one fell into the water or jumped.

The powerful engine of the *Storm Ridge* allowed them to be one of the first on scene. Trystan slowed as they approached, trying to keep his wash to a minimum.

"Man overboard, starboard," he called down, cutting their engine.

Logan spotted the man clumsily trying to swim in his life preserver. He threw a ring for him and Reid joined him at the rail, helping him pull the rope to haul the man closer.

Alarms and a bullhorn were sounding all around them. The fire boat was pouring water on the *Missionary II* while smaller boats buzzed closer, trying to help without running over those who were in kayaks or in the water.

Sophie came up on Logan's right, starting to hook up the recovery harness and ladder. She wore her own life preserver and hurried to secure each side before she removed a section of rail.

"Do you need help?" she called down to the man.

He shook his head, but he was clearly struggling against shock, needing two tries to grasp at the rubber rungs of the ladder before he very shakily climbed up.

"We've got you," Logan assured him, going onto his

belly so he could reach down and grab hold of the man's life preserver. Reid did the same and they dragged the man up, landing him like a two-hundred-pound tarpon onto the deck where he lay shaking and gasping.

Sophie was over on the port side calling, "Come around to the ladder."

Two pairs of double kayaks paddled around the bow. An older woman in the front position of the first one was crying. She held a paddle, but didn't seem capable of using it, or even knowing what to do beyond making a panicked grab for a rung on the ladder.

"I'll come down and stabilize it for you," Sophie said, starting to swing her leg down to the ladder.

"You will not." Logan caught the waistband of her shorts in a fist.

"You guys are stronger," she pointed out impatiently and brushed his hand away. "You need to pull her up. I'm wearing a life jacket."

She lowered herself down the ladder and, with one hand and foot on the flexible rungs, stepped her other foot onto the kayak, keeping it close. The second woman in the kayak took the paddle and Sophie guided the first woman onto the ladder.

"There you go. That's it. You're doing it. Keep going."

The ladder quivered under the wobbling scramble of the terrified woman. Sophie swung precariously outward as the kayak shifted beneath her foot. The second woman in the kayak was anxiously pushing forward so she could also climb the ladder.

Logan swore, heart swerving as Sophie grasped on with two hands and worked to secure her footing.

They got the two women aboard, both shaking with reaction.

Trystan guided each out of the way, wrapping them in blankets before he came to help with the second couple.

Once they were aboard, Trystan went down the ladder to help Sophie recover the kayaks and paddles. They guided them up and Logan stowed them out of the way while Sophie and Trystan came back on deck.

Reid closed the rail while they all scanned for anyone else still in the water.

Sophie was safe, Logan told himself, waiting for his heart rate to settle. He didn't have to worry she was in the water, floating out of reach, but damn her for almost letting it happen.

SOPHIE COLLECTED THE names of their passengers and radioed that they were aboard the *Storm Ridge*.

A few minutes later, the captain of the *Missionary II* announced everyone was accounted for. While the fire brigade continued to put out the fire, Trystan steered the *Storm Ridge* back to shore.

They all breathed a huge sigh of relief. That could have been so much worse!

"You'll help with salvage," Reid instructed Logan who nodded curtly. "I'll open a tab at the pub to feed everyone."

"People are going to need beds," Sophie said. According to the information she'd just received, "There are twenty passengers, plus crew."

"We can sleep twelve here. Fourteen if we drop the settee," Reid said.

They continued making logistical decisions as they came ashore. Locals were already gathered at the top of the wharf, ready to offer blankets, beds, and meals.

Reid took charge, herding everyone to the pub for food and drink, bed assignments, and medical assessment by the resort's first aid attendants.

Sophie hung back, planning to help Trystan make up the beds with the fresh linens he'd picked up from the lodge a few hours ago.

As she gathered up the damp blankets people had discarded, Logan came striding back into the saloon.

"I thought you were going out with the tug," she said, surprised to see him.

"I am, but—" He came right up to her and hooked his hand behind her neck, planting a hard kiss on her lips.

Her hands automatically came up to his chest, but she didn't push him away. This was too hungry a kiss. Too infused with raw need.

His gaze was angry as he held hers, but he stopped short of bruising, swiping his hot lips across hers in a message of desperation, one that made her heart crash around in her rib cage.

Heat, an old, fierce, furnace of heat, burst to life inside her, melting her bones and sinew and willpower.

As her eyes started to flutter closed in surrender, he abruptly released her.

"Don't you ever do anything so reckless again. You have a son to think about." He passed Trystan on his way topside. "Not one fucking word."

Trystan watched him go, brows up, then turned his bemused look onto Sophie.

She was still trying to press the sizzle from her lips. *Be mad*, she told herself, but her head and heart were bonking into each other, incapable of outrage, still trying to make sense of what had just happened.

With her cheeks stinging, she picked up the blanket she had dropped when Logan had grabbed her.

"It *was* pretty stupid," Trystan said. "Going down that ladder like that without a line."

"You did it, too! You weren't even wearing a life preserver."

"It was stupid of me, too." He pulled a retractable clothesline with three wires from one post to another across the saloon and secured it. "Maybe if I had a son, he would have kissed me, too."

"Oh shut up." She threw the wet blanket at his smirking face.

HE SHOULDN'T HAVE kissed her.

He hadn't meant to. One second, he had been on his way to the tug; the next he'd been in the saloon. Angry, anxious words had been in his throat, but a far greater need had overwhelmed him. He'd had to touch her. He had needed to feel that she was real and safe. He had had to transmit in the most basic way that she mattered and shouldn't scare him like that ever again.

So stupid. He was her boss. Her houseguest. Acting like a damned Neanderthal did nothing to improve her opinion of him. He had just been so fucking scared. Not just by those tense minutes while she had been hanging over the water, but by everything she had told him that he couldn't undo.

I was punishing myself.

He couldn't stop thinking about her saying that, going over and over it without ever finding a way to travel back into the past and fix what he'd broken.

Not that he had time for ruminations or building a freaking time machine. The next two days were hairy as the boat was salvaged, the kayakers were reunited with their belongings, and the travelers scrambled to find a way home after their vacations were cut short. Some were understanding about the late-night ferry schedules. Some bummed their way onto vessels going whichever direction they were headed. A handful of passengers pressured the captain of the *Missionary II* to charter a plane, annoyed there were no direct commercial flights back to Vancouver.

The commercial flights left from Bella Bella, which was only a seabus ride away, but the plane was small and usually booked out well in advance. The airstrip here in Raven's Cove was overdue for some TLC, but a bush Otter was secured, and they were flown to Victoria the next afternoon.

"What a bunch of babies," Sophie muttered, coming back into the marina office from driving those passengers to the airstrip. She clattered the keys for the company truck onto the desk. "Welcome to Canada. It's big. Things are far apart. It takes time to get from here to there. Gawd."

"Thanks for doing that," Logan said. "Give yourself some danger pay."

Danger pay was a meal voucher for the pub, usually offered by the beleaguered lodge staff to resort customers who were particularly grumpy or inconvenienced.

"Bitching about it is its own reward, but I'll take a free lunch. Thanks."

"I wish everyone had your sunny attitude. Will you look at these numbers? It's a ballpark estimate for the insurance claim."

She came to stand beside him where he sat behind the desk that he had mostly appropriated from her. She studied the spreadsheet on his screen where he'd listed the major expenses and his best guestimate of cost for a rough and dirty calculation.

While she read, he took stock of the collared resort T-shirt she had pulled on for her civilian duty of driving people up to the airstrip. She usually wore bicycle shorts under her coveralls, the kind that hugged her hips and thighs, but today wore cargo shorts that fell almost to her knees, showing only her muscled calves above her slouched socks and heavy work boots. *So* cute.

"Maybe include a fiberglass option?" she suggested.

He forced his gaze up to her freckled face.

"The original hull is wood. The charm and value is in its construction."

"Right. The labor looks accurate, and we can source the lumber here, but the shipping charge on a new engine? I'd double the fuel surcharge on that. They are killing us right now. Remind the captain to add lost revenue to their claim, too. The *Missionary II* is definitely out for the season. What?"

She caught him staring at her mouth. Apparently, he was just as turned on when she talked about fuel surcharges as when she physically changed out an oil filter.

"Nothing." He swallowed. "When—"

He'd been about to ask when Biyen's father was leaving, but Trystan walked in with Storm doing her wiggle dance in the sling.

"Are you lost?" Logan asked.

"Reid said to find you." He texted as he spoke. "He wants to talk to us."

"About?"

"That's all the information I have." His phone dinged and he glanced at it. "He'll be here in a sec."

"Good. I want to talk about our emergency procedures." Logan sat back and couldn't stop himself from cutting a glance at Sophie, still mad at her for putting herself at risk. "That rescue was a shit show. We're lucky it turned out as well as it did. We had too many hands on deck, not enough coordination from shore."

Sophie sniffed and walked away, slipping onto the stool at the other computer and turning to tap its keyboard.

"It wasn't great," Trystan allowed.

"No, it wasn't. I've had a look at the safety manual. The procedures are reasonably up to date, but we need to run a few drills. Reid will have to rewrite some for the new lodge and the rest of the new construction."

"Sounds like you guys have it under control. We love it when the heroes do all the work, don't we, Storm?" Trystan let her grasp onto his fingers so he could bring her arms over her head like a champion.

"You're not off the hook. Your purview will be lost hikers and wildfire response. Anything that happens to our guests on land outside our lease is your jurisdiction."

"Since when?"

"Maybe be careful with that one?" Sophie pivoted on her stool. "I've always found it good practice to check in with the tribal council office in Bella Bella before sending a team offsite. That way we're not trampling up a sensitive wetland or other meaningful place."

"Absolutely we should coordinate with them," Logan agreed. "But let's not be dicks. We can't put it on them to rescue our guests."

"I'll touch base with them, see how they want to handle it," Trystan said.

"Handle what?" Reid asked as he came in on the tail of Trystan's statement.

Logan caught him up.

"I actually had a reminder in my calendar to run a fire

drill before the cruise. It fell off my radar, but it's top priority now." Reid looked around. "I forgot what a dim little place this is. Why don't you wash that window?"

"I've hosed it down four times since I've been here. It doesn't stay clean," Logan said.

"There's an exhaust from the repair shop below," Sophie pointed out. "It kicks up dust off the embankment."

"Move the exhaust," Reid said with a shrug that said, *Problem solved.*

"Is that the best use of your money?" Sophie asked. "Because I can exhaust it to the other side of the island if money is no object, but the view out that window is a muddy hillside. I sit with my back to it. Fresh air is nice when I want it, but what do I care whether I can see out the glass?"

Reid looked to Logan.

"This is my life," Logan said. "I tell her how to spend our money and she tells me how to save it. It's kind of annoying. Tell him what you said yesterday about the *Missionary II*," he prompted Sophie.

She blinked. "I thought the consensus was that it was even more boring than regular. You just watch TV and go to bed."

Reid choked and pinched the bridge of his nose.

"You did not just say that to your boss*es*," Logan said, because that was not what he had meant. *At all.*

"I thought it was an action movie," Trystan confided to Reid.

"It's not a lunar launch?" Reid asked with mock surprise.

"That wasn't even dirty!" Sophie defended. "You should have heard some of the things my old boss said to *me* before you three came along."

"Please don't drag us into that workplace harassment claim," Reid said smoothly. "And thank you for the laugh. I needed it."

"She suggested we buy it," Logan said of the damaged vessel.

"That was off the cuff," Sophie said with a dismissive wave. "Two of the crew from the *Missionary II* would have stayed if they could have found a place to live. I just said to Logan that it's too bad we couldn't have kept it as a floating staff house, especially for the summer months."

"See? It's a solid suggestion," Logan said. "The fire damage is mostly in the engine room and replacing the engine will be very spendy. If we bought it as is, repaired the hull, and parked it, we would instantly gain two-dozen bunks."

"We don't need that many rooms for staff. Once the renos are finished, we won't have so many contractors on site, either." Reid was skeptical.

"It could be a cheaper option for the sports fishermen who still want to come here, but don't want to pay the higher price at the renovated lodge," Trystan pointed out.

"We could book it out for private parties. Family reunions. Weddings," Logan added.

"I don't hate the idea," Reid said. "We definitely need more accommodation available in summer months. Adding it into the lodge reservation system would be simple enough. Put some hard numbers together and a plan for the remodel. Let's circle back on that." He nodded at Logan. "Right now, we have a more pressing matter. But thank you, Sophie. That was a great suggestion."

"Sure. Do you want me to leave?"

Reid looked briefly conflicted, then waved at her to stay where she was.

"Em will tell you anyway so you might as well hear it. We just got a call that Tiffany's sister has been released from protective custody. There's no indication that she's coming here, but I wanted you two to know that it could happen and keep your ears open."

Logan swore. Trystan set his hand on Storm's belly. Storm chewed her teething beads, oblivious to the blanket of concern that had descended over the room.

"What does that mean?" Sophie asked tentatively.

"I don't know." Reid's voice held all the frustration that Logan felt. It was reflected in Trystan's face as well. "We know that she knows about Storm and was planning to come here, but wound up in trouble with the law. Now she's loose. If she wanted to call and arrange a visit or something, I think we'd figure something out."

Reid looked to Logan and Trystan. They each jerked their shoulders in *maybe*.

"But if she challenged us for custody, then no," Reid said firmly. "That's a war we need to be prepared to win."

"How's Em?" Sophie asked.

"Freaking out and pretending she's not." Reid gave his

jaw a rub. "I said I'd bring Storm home. Do you mind?" he asked Trystan.

"I have to finish getting the *Storm Ridge* ready to sail anyway." He unbuckled the sling, as somber as the rest of them.

Reid took Storm but pulled her out of the sling. He let the contraption dangle off his elbow while he held the baby securely against his chest.

Hold on to her. Hold on tight, Logan wanted to insist. His own arms felt weak and useless, his chest hollow.

"Maybe it's nothing," Reid said, but he didn't sound convinced or convincing.

"Maybe," Trystan echoed in a hollow tone.

Until they *knew* that it was nothing, they would all fear the worst.

Chapter Nine

LIVE ENTERTAINMENT IN Raven's Cove was almost nonexistent. A local DJ played three nights a week in the summer for any tourists who happened to be moored here. Locals often ended their busy week with a few drinks, but no one made a point of going to the pub for music.

Therefore, when an actual band turned up, it was an event. The act could be a yodeler with a pan flute and the entire community would show up.

Almost the entire community. Somebody had to watch the kids and Emma's mother offered, including Biyen so "you lot" can have a night out. Biyen could have stayed with Gramps, but he was even more excited than Sophie for this special treat. He was going to eat popcorn and watch a movie with Imogen and Cooper and have a sleepover in the rumpus room at the Fraser house. Could life get any better?

Storm was already down for the night when Sophie arrived with him. Delta waved off any concerns.

"I'll text Emma if anything comes up, but Biyen is good as gold and Storm knows me now. She won't play strange if she wakes and I go in to her. Have fun."

"Your mom is warming up to Storm," Sophie noted

when she was walking down the drive alongside Emma and Reid. From below, they could hear the muffled voice of someone introducing the band inside the pub.

"I think Glenda shamed her into it," Emma said wryly. "If Glenda is big enough to dote on her ex's baby, surely Mom could open her heart to her daughter's adopted daughter."

"I thought it was because Imogen got Storm to say 'Nana,'" Reid said.

"Pretty sure that was a fluke," Emma said wryly. Storm was only eight months and babbling nonsense most of the time.

"We still need to keep an eye on that girl, or she'll put Storm in her suitcase when she leaves," Reid said.

Sophie wondered if seeing how anxious Emma was over the prospect of Tiffany's sister turning up here might have impacted Delta's attitude. She was very reserved and Emma seemed incredibly sensitive to the slightest criticism from her mother. From what Emma had told Sophie of her relationship with her family, it had nearly strained past its breaking point through her divorce. When she had first arrived here, she'd barely been speaking to any of them. She and her mother had become more relaxed with each other as this visit had worn on, though, which was nice to see.

Tonight wasn't the time to get into that, though. The band was finishing up a lively rendition of "One Week" by the Barenaked Ladies as they arrived at the door.

"That's not the real band, is it?" Emma asked.

Reid paused in opening the door to point at the poster

showing a half-dozen musicians in toques, holding maple syrup, poutine, and a stuffed beaver under a maple-leaf-shaped logo that read, CANADIAN CONTENT.

The band helpfully introduced themselves as they entered the crowded pub. The tables were full, and the bar was elbow to elbow with people trying to order drinks. Two servers were holding trays of shots as they wove between the clusters of patrons.

"Thanks for coming out, Raven's Cove," the lead singer said. "We are Canadian Content. We cover Canadian bands and something we hear all the time is, 'I didn't know that song was Canadian.' We turned it into a drinking game. If you want to play along, the rule is, if you say, 'I didn't know this band or song is Canadian,' you have to buy a round of shots for your table. Ready, Raven's Cove? Let's parteeeee."

A cheer went up and the band rolled into "New Orleans Is Sinking" by the Tragically Hip.

"Oh, I like this one!" Emma began rocking her hips. She glanced for Reid, but he was wedging himself into a space at the bar. "Dance?"

Sophie nodded and they started toward the dance floor.

"I didn't know this song was by a Canadian—" Emma had leaned toward Sophie to be heard over the music, but stopped herself, eyes going wide as she slapped her hand over her laughing mouth.

"No!" Sophie went back and tugged on Reid's shirt. "Shots on her!" She thumbed at Emma.

"Really?" Reid mouthed and shook his head, amused.

He nodded and waved to get the bartender's attention.

They danced through Arcade Fire, Arkells, and a Shania Twain medley before going to find Reid.

He was on the patio with Logan, who had been sent ahead to secure them a table. They were at one of the high tops, and one of the contractors was sitting with them. A pitcher of water and one of margueritas sat on the table with four glasses. There were also two full shot glasses, two empty ones, and each man held a beer.

"Hi, Cameron," Sophie greeted the contractor.

"You clean up well, Soph," Cameron said, nodding at her dress. "You always look great, Emma."

"Thank you." Emma took the chair Reid held for her.

"Yeah, thanks," Sophie said dryly. "Charmer."

"I just got myself kicked off the cool table, didn't I? I have to go read the riot act to a couple of my guys anyway. I can see they're going hard tonight. You want to dance later, you come find me." He pointed at Sophie as he vacated his chair for her.

Logan slid his gaze down Sophie's summer dress as she swiveled into place. She had purchased this for Glenda's wedding four years ago and had worn it maybe twice since. As dresses went, it was comfortable with its A line and stretchy fabric, and flattering with its simple white flowers on wine red, but it felt fussy when Logan sat so close and took notice of it.

"Good call on the water," Sophie said, helping herself to the pitcher.

"Those are yours," Reid said, pointing at the shots. "Be

more careful."

"I will," Emma promised. She tapped hers to Sophie's and they threw them back.

With perfect timing, the crowd started singing along with the band's rendition of "Ironic."

"Is Alanis Morissette Canadian?" Emma asked with surprise.

"*Nooo*," Sophie and Reid cried.

"No, she's not or…? Oh." Emma wrinkled her nose, grinning sheepishly. "Sorry."

"We're going to need a Kiwi exception, or we'll all be too drunk to walk home." Reid waved at Quinley who carried over a tray of B-52s.

After her second shot, Sophie ignored the margarita and stuck with water. The alcohol was making her feel loose and sexy, far too aware of Logan beside her smelling all showered and fresh, looking sharp in his snazzy shorts and crisp short-sleeved button-down shirt.

"Good turnout," she said as an excuse to turn her back on him and look at the crowd.

When he leaned forward to speak next to her ear, his breath disturbed the fine hairs on the back of her neck.

"Why is he still here?"

"Who?" She looked over her shoulder and he was *right there*, his mouth way too close to her own.

He had kissed her! She kept trying to pretend he hadn't, and she kept running into the reality that the spark had still sizzled between them, as amazing as she remembered it, which made the whole thing way too unsettling.

He wasn't looking at her mouth right now, though. She followed his gaze to where Nolan was sitting with a handful of locals.

"He wanted to stay for Biyen's birthday party tomorrow." And Biyen was having fun camping in the yard with him. Sophie didn't mind. It was nice that Biyen was having a good time with his father, but was still under her nose where she got to see him every morning.

"Sopheeeee!" Randy burst from the crowd.

"Randy!" she cried. "You're back!"

Randy was a chunky guy with a heavy beard and hair that needed cutting. He ignored both his employers as he held his fists in the air and released a very loud and triumphant, "I passed my final exaaaaam!"

"What? Ahh!" Sophie threw herself off the chair and hugged him, finding herself picked up and spun in a circle while she clung to his bulky shoulders.

"Dance with me!"

He didn't give her a choice, basically carrying her to the dance floor where the band started "The Safety Dance."

They both sang along, leaving behind the friends who didn't dance because they were "no friends of mine."

"You're drunk," she accused as the song ended.

"So drunk," he agreed, dancing wildly.

His exuberance was infectious, especially because this news meant he was back full-time. The work load on her would lighten considerably and that was definitely a reason to celebrate.

She danced with him through "I'm Like a Bird" and

"Everybody Wants to Be Like You," then left him chest-bumping with Kenneth while she threaded her way back to the table in time to see Emma lead Reid onto the floor.

Traitor.

"That's good news," Logan said as Sophie retook her chair. "About Randy."

"Is it ever. Your dad would have loved this band." She cocked an ear as they shifted into a Guess Who/BTO medley. "It was all seventies, all the time, in the office. It drove Randy nuts. He's more of a Drake fan."

"Is Drake Can—That's a *joke*," Logan insisted when she flung him a look of outrage. "I know he's Canadian. I've met him." His brows went up in self-deprecation at his own brag.

"Really. When? How?"

"A party." He shrugged it off. "I'm sure he forgot my name the second he heard it. Everyone was trying to talk to him."

"You didn't play the Canadian card?"

"Nah, I was the boat guy." He took a pull off his beer.

"What do you mean?"

His mouth went sideways, rueful and maybe reluctant to say.

"Some of those ballers in Florida have so much money, they literally don't know what to do with it. After I designed a cabin cruiser for one, he started inviting me to parties on it. He liked me to help him tour his guests so I could give all the technical details. He was really happy with it, so that part felt good, but he was always pushing people to hire me to build them their own boat. That was awkward sometimes. I got business out of it, but it turned into people saying, 'Right. You're the boat guy.'" His tone became flat and dismissive.

"Oof. You should have got yourself a T-shirt. Stay ahead of it."

"At least it gave me something to talk about at those things. I always thought parties like that would be more fun. They were actually…" He trailed off.

"What?" She drained her water and tipped a splash of marguerita into her glass.

"I don't know. Empty?" He didn't look entirely comfortable admitting it. "I liked my clients. They were great, but we were friendly, not friends. When I was out with them, it wasn't like this, where I look around and *know* people, not just recognize them. By the way, since when is Tamara into guys?" He nodded toward the receptionist from the lodge. She had her head tilted toward a young man as the man shaped his words with his hands.

"That's her cousin. Supposedly he's just visiting, but I hear he's tired of the rat race in Surrey *and* has an HVAC ticket. Maybe buy him a beer."

"Good recon."

"Right? Randy has a girl in Nanaimo, by the way," she warned.

"We sponsored his apprenticeship. He has to give us three years or reimburse us for his tuition."

"Something he could do on city wages so I suggest you give him a very nice bump in his hourly rate and feel him out on where her skill set lies. I suspect it's nursing so that could be tricky." They absolutely needed more health care here, but positions were filled by the health authority with temporary contracts. There wasn't much opportunity for permanent full-time.

"Hmm." He frowned.

"Yeah."

Sophie suddenly realized that, as they had spoken, they had leaned in close to each other. Their shoulders were almost touching. She drew back but had to stay close enough to talk over the music.

"Is this really what you were missing when you were drinking champagne on a superyacht of your own design? Labor problems and your employee's love life?"

His gaze shifted restlessly across the crowd then came back to her face where she felt his study almost like a physical touch. She expected him to offer a laconic comeback, but he looked very serious.

"That's not exactly what I was missing, but I definitely felt like something was. I should have been as stoked as Randy. I worked hard to get to that level. Being 'the boat guy,' getting contracts where cost is no object is a dream come true. I loved that and I haven't been able to take on any new ones since I've been here so that's driving me nuts. I loved the sun, too." He shook his head with mild disgust at the changeable, damp coastal weather here. "But the rest of my life was pretty hollow."

"Oh no." She poked the top of his chest near his shoulder, understanding exactly what had happened. "You're starting to love your little sister. Aren't you?"

"So?" He gave her a cross look, smirking behind it. "It's Stockholm Syndrome." He wet his lips with his beer. "Babies are very sneaky. They break you down with sleep deprivation, then act like you're a god because you disappear and reappear with your *own hands*."

"I know, right?" She chuckled. "Wait until she's talking. They say the funniest things." She smiled wistfully at the memory of Biyen learning to talk, trying to make sense of his world. "Watching them grow up is such a bittersweet balance of celebrating every little milestone and saying good-bye to the child they were. I love who Biyen is now, and I *really* love how independent he is, but I miss the boy who fit in my lap and believed I had all the answers."

Logan's grin faded and his gaze dropped into the amber ale he was nursing. Was he realizing he might not be here when Storm was too big for his lap? Or worried that Storm wouldn't be?

"Do you ever think about having another baby?" he asked curiously, lifting his gaze to hers. "Not asking as your employer," he clarified dryly.

"Now that Randy's back, you think I'm liable to go on mat leave? Tempting." She was being facetious. "I thought about it a lot in those first couple of years. I wanted Biyen to have a sibling, but things were already hard, not having Mom and Nolan being so…" She shook her head, glancing at her ex. "He didn't want another baby and my life was complicated enough without bringing a new man and another baby into it."

She was doing it again—confiding in Logan, but maybe he needed to hear it.

"I often wish I'd given Biyen a brother or sister by now. Growing up, I was really envious of anyone with siblings, even you boys who acted like you hated each other." She gave him a pointed look. *Appreciate what you've got.* "Maybe your childhood wasn't all that it could have been, but you went through it together and there's value in that. Reid and Trystan understand you in a way no one else does."

"I guess." His head tilted as he considered that. "But as someone who was gifted a baby sister at twenty-nine, I am pleased to inform you that it's never too late to give someone a sibling. Too early? Definitely," he said as Reid and Emma came back. "But never too late."

"What?" Emma asked as Sophie rolled her eyes.

"Logan is being his warm and loving self. Is the band on intermiss—No, Emma," she said sternly as Quinley set four shots on their table.

"It wasn't me. It was Reid."

"Did you know "Rockstar" is by Nickelback?" Reid asked Logan.

"If I didn't, I wouldn't admit it. I'm embarrassed for you, I really am." Logan picked up one of the shots.

"I've been living in Alberta," Reid defended. "Ask me about country music."

"Nickelback are from Alberta," Sophie cried with exasperation. "Turn in your passport and let's make a pact that this is our last one."

They lifted their glasses in agreement and shot them.

It was not the last one, but they danced off the alcohol in the second set, ending with a rousing shout of "Life Is a Highway," which had the whole place singing along.

"We like to end with this Leonard Cohen song," the lead singer said. "It's called "Closing Time," and it's not the one by Semisonic so no need to order any shots unless you want them. Find the one you're going home with and cuddle up for your last dance."

Emma went into Reid's arms.

Sophie started to leave the floor, but a very bleary-eyed drywaller stepped in front of her.

"You're the most alive person I've ever seen," he said.

Sophie had thought she'd heard all the two a.m. come-ons. Hell, she'd fallen for plenty of them way back when, but this was so corny she could only blink with bemusement.

"Has that ever worked? Ever?" she asked.

"No dice, champ." Logan slid his arm around her and turned her into his chest, drawing her into the lazy rhythm of the song. "Unless you wanted to dance with him?" he asked as he created a small space so he could see her face.

His shirt was damp from all their dancing. His hands on her waist were heavy and hot enough to scald.

"No, but I should get home." Her feet shuffled into the slow beat, though, so she swayed in time with him. Their bodies brushed and she let herself lean a little closer.

The band sang a lyric about the gates of love budging an inch and she kept her gaze pinned on the hollow at the base of his throat.

Leave, she told herself, but she stayed in a state of heaven and hell, thinking of all the times she had left with the wrong guy, wishing Logan had been the one taking her home. He would be tonight, but not in the way that mattered. Not forever.

He had called his life in Florida hollow. Hers had been so full all these years it was often too full, but there was a pocket of emptiness in it, too. It was a Logan-shaped hole that she had packed with graveled resentment and hostility, then papered over with Never Again.

Those sorts of patches never stuck, though. It was splitting and spilling and she could feel that empty space growing inside her again.

The last notes petered out and the lights went up and all the couples broke apart.

Sophie felt sweaty and melancholy as they trailed outside to begin walking home by the flashlights on their phones.

"Did you get your credit card?" Emma asked Reid.

"I told them to put all our drinks on Logan's tab. They'll settle up with him next time he's in."

"Joke's on you. I'm going to expense it," Logan said.

"The joke is on them." Sophie thumbed at Reid and Emma. "They have a houseful of kids to wake up to. Thank you for that, by the way. Oh wait. The joke is on *me*," she realized with a groan. "I have a nine-year-old's birthday party tomorrow. That's going to be loud."

"We have played this so smart, Em." Reid looped his

arm around his wife. "It's Logan's day with Storm. See you at seven, bro. Oh wait. I'll still be in bed."

"We promised the kids you'd make pancakes," Emma said over her shoulder. "But Imogen is a great helper. She hardly ever gets eggshell in the batter anymore."

"Yeah, yeah," Logan said as they reached the spot where the Fraser driveway split off from the lane that led to Sophie's driveway and the rest of the houses along the flats behind the bluff. "You kids go home and have some of that loud sex you like to have. I'm sure Delta has learned to sleep through it."

"Why does he have to ruin everything?" Reid asked Emma as they started up the hill.

She said something that made him chuckle, but Sophie didn't catch it.

The night closed in around her and Logan as they continued along the lane.

Despite the glow off her phone, Sophie staggered when her foot turned on a small, round rock.

"Okay?" Logan caught her elbow.

"Why do I get the feeling you're not as drunk as me?"

"I outweigh you by fifty pounds and I train for nights like this."

He didn't actually drink that much. He often had a beer with Gramps at the end of the day, but not always. If he did, it was usually just the one. As far as she could tell, he didn't drink at all if it was his shift with Storm.

"How drunk are you?" he asked in a tone that instantly made her cautious.

"Not sober enough for whatever you're thinking about suggesting."

"I don't want sex." He sounded insulted. "I wondered if you were going to remember something if I say it."

"Do you want me to?"

"Yes."

"What?"

He stopped and turned off his flashlight. Her own glowed in a circle around her feet as she stopped to look at his silhouette.

"I'm sorry." His voice was low, but firm and sincere. Powerful enough to shake the ground beneath her feet.

"For?" She braced herself, not sure she wanted to know. Not sure she wanted to go all the way back to that. Not now. Not ever.

He drew a breath and slowly blew it out. His head turned so he looked out to where the wind was coming in off the water and the sound of waves washing against the shore was a steady rush.

"For hurting you. For taking advantage of the way you felt about me. It's no excuse to say that I needed to reinvent myself away from here, but that's what it was. That's why I didn't want you to come with me. My screwed-up relationship with my father—with my whole family—was never yours to fix so I shouldn't have turned to you when I was looking for ways to avoid him back then. That was childish and selfish."

"It was." She folded her arms, trying to tamp down on the ache that was rising in her chest like a breaching orca.

"It was *him*," he said in a rasp. "I knew that's how he behaved. He never thought through to the fact that he was hurting someone, but I went ahead and did it myself. To you. I told myself our situation was different because..."

She stopped breathing, instinctually bracing against whatever he was about to say.

"I didn't believe what you felt for me was love."

That went into her heart like a hot, sharp blade.

"How could it be?" He continued softly. "You were young and too removed from the real world to know there were far better people out there. I didn't feel lovable, Soph. Not good enough for any kind of love, especially not the kind you were offering." He squeezed the back of his neck. "So I let myself believe your feelings were immature and superficial. That way, hurting you wasn't such a cruel thing to do."

She definitely didn't want to hear this. Her lungs ached and her throat was so tight, she couldn't speak. She clicked off her own phone so they were in the dark. Only the dim moonlight obscured by clouds provided a faint illumination.

"I only realized that what you felt was really love when it was gone." His voice was thick with regret. "Even at Mom's wedding, I thought you were just mad. Making a point. I didn't want to believe that you could hate me, either. Isn't that ironic? But the more I realized that you were never going to forgive me, the more I realized what I had killed. I am so sorry for that."

A huge chasm stretched from the back of her throat

down behind her breastbone, open and aching, leaving her exposed. She was right back to standing on that ferry slip all over again, feeling immature and insecure and wronged. Raw. The hot sting of betrayal and loss and self-contempt sat behind her eyes in scalding heat.

"If..." He swallowed. "If you wanted to hurt me by hurting yourself, you did. Don't do that again. I'm not worth it."

Her lips were so unsteady, she had to iron them straight by pressing them together before she could find words in the cavern of her chest and bring them up.

"You did me a favor," she said, voice strained. "If I had gone with you, I wouldn't have Biyen. I would have spent all that time with you instead of Mom because I would have been too afraid of losing you to make her my priority. You taught me that *no* man is worth gutting myself over. No man is going to come along and save me, either. I learned to look after myself and I do. So thank you for that."

She wasn't trying to sound bitter, but his breath sucked in as though she'd landed an unexpected knee to his gut.

"Thank you for the apology. I appreciate it. I do," she said sincerely. "But I hope you understand that it doesn't change how I feel about you."

Chapter Ten

"I KNOW," LOGAN said, feeling sick. What had he expected, though? Forgiveness?

She clicked on her flashlight and continued up the path.

Logan followed, stomach as weighted as his feet. He had been wanting to say all of that, but now he was cycling back through every word, trying to work out if there had been a better way to... What? Reach her? Inch her back toward friendship?

As they approached the porch, they had to pass Nolan's domed tent where it was planted in the grass near the garden. Noises were coming from inside it. Very distinct groans and pants and movements.

"Wait," a female voice said as the porch boards creaked under their feet. "I heard someone."

"It's my ex. She doesn't care," Nolan said.

Sophie snorted as they entered the kitchen and closed the door behind them.

"I really don't," she said. The light over the sink glowed, but otherwise the room was empty and dark.

"Water?" she offered, going to the sink.

"Sure, but should we be quiet?" He glanced to the chair

where Art usually sat.

"Gramps wears earplugs." She pointed to a closed door where snores were resounding.

"Thanks." He took the glass she filled for him. "Can I ask you one more thing?"

"You're determined to ruin the runner's high I got off all that dancing, aren't you?"

"It can wait."

"No, go ahead." She poured her own glass and turned her back to the sink, same as him, so they stood side by side, sipping their water.

"When you said you didn't think it was likely you'd have more kids... I can't help wondering if that's my fault, too. That I made you too mistrustful of men."

"Please don't take this as me lashing out, but not everything is about you, Logan." She gave him a look of exasperated patience, then nodded vaguely at the open space between kitchen and living room. "It took a lot for me to get this far, where I'm still busy as hell, but my son is flourishing and so is my bank account. It's not a fortune, but it's enough. All of that changes if I stop work to have another baby. The simple privilege of sleeping through the night is gone for *years*."

"It's such a simple concept," he noted dryly. "Sleep and you'll feel better. Why don't babies *get* that?"

"They're monsters," she agreed. "And this might come as news, but pregnancy and childbirth suck. They say you don't remember, but I remember. My back hurt all the time. Labor was horrendous."

"You're a good mom, though. You obviously love Biyen a lot. If you wanted another baby..." He pumped the brakes as her eyes widened.

She leaned away from him, wary.

"That's not an offer," he assured her, feeling a sting on his cheeks that he hoped she couldn't see in the shadowy light. "I was only trying to say..." Hell, maybe he was more drunk than he realized because he didn't know what he was trying to say. "I think it's a shame that more kids don't have a mom like you." Yeah. That.

"You did. Glenda's pretty great. After my own mom, she's probably the person who influences me the most in how I parent Biyen."

"I guess." He was in a very introspective mood tonight. He didn't know how to wear it. It felt like he'd put his clothes on backward.

"Do you ever think about being a father?" She took off her earrings and set them behind her on the counter.

"My answer to that has always been a hard no, but if Reid and Emma weren't taking Storm..."

"You would?" She seemed shocked.

"I can't say I wouldn't," he allowed. "And what you said earlier about how quickly kids grow up keeps coming back to me." He drained his water. "I know I'll be involved in Storm's life forever, come hell or high water. I'm also realizing that being a brother-uncle figure is a different role than a parent. I never saw myself as a dad, but then I look at how much Reid has stepped up. Did you ever imagine he could act so—"

"*No.* I mean, it's cute. Don't get me wrong. I love it. And Emma deserves a good guy who wants to give her a family because that's something she has always wanted, but I thought Reid was basically Spock. Super logical and finds us humans kind of tiresome."

"Right? I genuinely believed Dad broke our ability to be a decent father, but if Reid can do it, I can." He heard his own arrogance and shrugged it off.

"Why are you so competitive with him?" she asked with a chuckle of disbelief. "Still, at this age? Over something like *that*? Fatherhood isn't a contest."

"Everything is a contest with Reid." Had she not met the man? "And my need to compete is exactly what you just said about him. He acts so superior to the rest of us." It made him tired to think of it. "He always has. Man needs to be kept in check."

"Okay," Sophie snorted. "But maybe look in a mirror?"

"Hey." He scowled at her. "I'm not as bad as he is."

"You are exactly, equally, not any more or any less as bad."

"God, you're mean sometimes." He hid his grin with the lip of his glass.

"The truth hurts, my friend."

God that word hurt. *Friend.* So out of reach.

Her gaze was sparkling with amusement, though, making him almost believe it was possible. Her smile… That smile she tilted up to him—to *him*—was so precious he wanted to frame her face with his hands and just gaze on it.

He wanted the right to touch her. To feel her lips under his and—

Don't.

He yanked his gaze away to Art's empty chair and the half glass of water beside it.

If Sophie was willing to call him her friend, he would take it. And he would *not* screw it up this time.

"All right." He turned to rinse his glass. "You have a big day tomorrow. You should hit the sack."

There was a pulse of silence where she didn't move. Then she said briskly, "Sure. Good night. Close your window on your way to bed."

"It's too hot—Oh gross." He groaned as he realized.

"Yeah. They're right below you. Sleep tight."

TECHNICALLY, IT WAS Sophie's day off. Logan was on call so she could host Biyen's birthday party.

Logan was already at the Fraser house, taking his shift with Storm, when a call from the pub got Sophie out of bed. They needed a toilet fill valve after their busy night. Could she open the hardware store?

Gramps happily seized the excuse to get out of the house even though it was spitting rain. He trucked his Gator up to the store, made the transaction with the pub, then circled past the Fraser house for the lawn toys. He brought them back to where Sophie was making slow but steady progress on setting up for the party.

Nolan's hookup from last night left when Sophie conscripted him into erecting a tarp over the picnic table and cleaning the barbecue. He agreed to cook, too, even though she was including classic wieners and smokies along with tofu dogs.

She was setting condiments on the picnic table with bags of cut buns, hangover finally receding, when she caught sight of Logan walking toward her with the older children.

Damned if her ovaries didn't spontaneously burst like dandelions when she saw him carrying Cooper on his back, Imogen and Biyen happily skipping alongside him.

"Hi, Dad. Hi, Mom!" Biyen ran up to hug her waist.

"Hi, bud. Happy birthday." She smoothed his rooster tail. "Did you have fun last night?"

"Uh-huh. Logan made blueberry pancakes for breakfast. With whip cream. Storm ate so many blueberries, he said her bum will be purple for a week."

"That sounds about right. Where is Storm?" Sophie forced herself to look at Logan. This was her first face-to-face with him after his apology last night and their disturbing conversation about having more children.

His expression was remote, his attention on Nolan.

"Napping." He tilted sideways to lower Cooper to the ground. "Emma said to call if you need her help, otherwise she'll come down with Reid and Delta once Storm wakes up."

"I think we have everything under control. Do you kids want to put the goody bags together? All the stuff is on the porch. Put the filled bags into the empty box. We need fourteen so don't eat any of the candy until you've filled the bags."

They all ran to where Gramps had come to sit in his lawn chair behind the rail.

"Fourteen?" Logan repeated with a horrified grimace.

"What can I say? Biyen is an inclusive kid. He invites the whole school. We have a big yard, though, and the shed if it starts to pour. I don't do many parent things at the school so this is my contribution. Now that the kids are out of school and bored at home, I give them something to do for an afternoon."

"Do the parents come?"

"A few might." She shrugged.

"You don't really hang out with the other parents, do you?" he said with a frown of realization. "Is that because you work so much? You and Quinley were always friends, weren't you? Her son is Biyen's age, I thought."

He didn't recall that she and Quinley had been rivals for his affections?

"People around here all have something to say about something. I can't be bothered trying to straighten them out. I keep my distance and they keep theirs."

"What kinds of things are they talking about?" he asked with suspicion.

"You staying in my house. Nolan staying on my lawn."

"Oh for fu—" He stopped himself from swearing and glanced at the kids. "Really? Why didn't you say something?"

"I did," she assured him with a blithe bat of her lashes.

"That's why they send their kids here without setting foot on my lawn."

"Oh?" His mouth twitched. "I'm not actually surprised by that. What happened?" He folded his arms, enjoying this, she could tell.

"I might have had a teeny-weeny tantrum at a bake sale my first year back. Not my best day," she admitted, wrinkling her nose in self-disgust. "I mean, if certain people didn't have gossip, they wouldn't have anything at all, right? I should feel sorry for them. Instead, I set fire to a few bridges over a couple of remarks that weren't untrue, just hypocritical. Hypercritical, in my opinion. Then I paid for the cake I had thrown on the floor and left."

He was trying to stifle his laughter with his fist. "How have I never heard about this?"

"Because Quinley Banks knows I'm a crazy bitch who will murder a cake if she talks smack about me again."

"Oh shi—eesh." His shoulders were shaking.

"The boys play sometimes, but we keep to our corners."

"And you don't let her come to his party because you're worried she'll retaliate? Throw Biyen's cake on the grass?"

"I paid a lot for the vegan, T-rex decal that I had to fix myself because they spelled his name wrong. Again."

Over at the porch, laughter went up and Biyen said, "We *can't*."

"Of course, you can," Gramps insisted, leaning forward in his chair to point at the little packages of jelly beans. "Take the black ones out and put the rest in the goody bags."

"You can have this one," Imogen said helpfully. "I counted. It's extra." She held up a package that Sophie knew held half a dozen jelly beans. "It has a black one."

"I don't like the other colors, only the black ones. Fetch the scissors, Biyen." Gramps was having as much fun as the kids with this performance. "We'll nip the corner off each of these and I'll take the black one. I'll eat them before the kids get here. No one will ever know."

"No!" The kids were all giggling. "They'll fall *out*."

"So?"

"You can't have sugar, Gramps," Biyen reminded him.

"You came back for Art, didn't you?" Logan said.

While she'd been grinning at the shenanigans on the porch, he'd been watching her. A sense of transparency had her folding her arms.

"He was missing Mom as much as I was. I thought I'd visit for a week or so, but I could see how much he'd aged." A tiny tremor entered her voice as she accepted her grandfather would not be here forever. "I came pretty close to quitting when Tiffany started turning this place upside down, though. Gramps or no Gramps. Then Em showed up and she's been such a good friend, I couldn't abandon her."

"Yeah, Em's pretty great."

"But I'm worried about Gramps. He's been… I thought it was grief over your dad, but he's… I don't know. Tired, I guess. Can I ask you a favor?"

"Of course." He sobered with concern.

"I'm going to make him a doctor appointment. He always says he doesn't want to put me out, because I'm always busy with work and Biyen. Maybe if you said you were going over to Bella Bella anyway? Then he wouldn't have an excuse not to go."

"Done," he assured her.

"Thanks. Oh. Here we go." She nodded at the kids walking up the driveway, all carrying wrapped gifts. "Fasten your seatbelt and put your tray table up."

THE CHAOS OF sugar-saturated children reigned for two hours.

Logan helped get hot dogs into them, then sparked a tantrum in Storm when he wouldn't let her have a bite of his.

"I put hot mustard on it," he argued, but no, he had betrayed her with his selfishness. He would not be forgiven. Ever.

"Umm-umma," she cried pitifully and reached for Emma.

"Poor thing. Come sit with me. Look, I brought your cereal," she said of the toasted O's she produced from the diaper bag.

Storm settled between Emma's legs on a blanket and chased spilled O's while everyone sang "Happy Birthday" to Biyen and his cake was served.

The kids all sat on the grass to eat while they watched

Biyen open his presents. They were a predictable assortment of LEGO kits and dinosaurs, books and a stuffed spirit bear that the Kiwi kids had picked up while away on their cruise.

"Cooper. Imogen," Emma called softly, waving them closer.

They came over very distracted, watching over their shoulder for the last present to be unveiled.

Emma whispered something to them.

Imogen's eyes popped wide. "*Yes.*"

"Okay, shh. Go give this to him. It's a secret, Cooper." Emma touched her lips.

He nodded, but his eyes were alight with excitement. Both children moved to sit right in front of Biyen.

"You already gave me the bear." He took the mysterious little box. It didn't rattle or jangle, though he gave it a shake to see if it would.

Sophie seemed to know what it was because she was watching closely, anticipation playing around her smile.

Cooper looked over at Emma. Emma touched her lips again in a reminder.

Logan was silently urging the kid to hurry up because his curiosity was getting the better of him.

Biyen tore the wrapping and revealed a box of baby swabs. His brow quirked up in puzzlement.

"That's not a real box. Is it, Auntie Em?" Imogen asked.

"No, look inside, Biyen."

"Is it a secret message?" He slid the drawer of the box

and withdrew a rolled-up piece of paper with a ribbon on it.

"Read it," Sophie urged.

"Do you want to come to Vancouver with us and see the dinosaur ex-hi…"

"Exhibition," Sophie provided.

"Really?" Biyen didn't know where to look. His head almost snapped off as he looked between his mom and Emma and the kids. "*When?*"

Logan felt a chuckle of pure enjoyment fill his chest. That was about the greatest thing ever, to see a kid get that excited.

"This weekend," Reid provided. "I decided to go with Emma when she takes everyone to catch their flight. There's room on the plane so we thought you might like to come, too."

"And stay at a hotel," Imogen said with suitable awe. "Do you want to?"

Biyen looked up at Sophie. "*Can* I?"

"Your dad and I already talked about it and agree, yes, if you want to. Do you?" She was beaming at him, enjoying his thrill as if it were her own.

"*Yes.* Wait, are you coming?" he asked Sophie.

"I have to work."

"Dad?"

"Just you, little dude."

Logan opened his mouth, ready to find a way to send Sophie if necessary, but Biyen shrugged.

"That's okay. I'll still have fun."

"You will," Sophie agreed. "It's a pretty cool present, isn't it? What do you say to the kids? And Reid and Emma?"

"Thank you." He shyly hugged everyone.

"When did you cook this up?" Logan asked Reid as the kids went back to playing.

"Yesterday. Emma wasn't feeling good about leaving Storm again. I said I'd go with them so we could bring her. Then she asked me if I would take the kids to the dinosaur thing in case Storm wasn't loving it. Cooper mentioned Biyen had been wanting to go so Em called Sophie. We didn't want to tell the kids until Sophie had cleared it with Nolan and Em had checked with Delta."

Reid sent a brief side-eye to where his mother-in-law sat next to Art on the porch.

"She likes having Biyen around," Reid said with fatalistic lift of his brow. "The kids bicker when it's just the two of them, but that boy has a career in diplomacy if the paleontology thing doesn't work out."

"True that. So I'm covering for you again?"

"Only on Friday. The weekend should be quiet. You'll have the house to yourself, too. No parties. Hear me?" He held up a warning finger.

"Between last night and this, I'm done with parties for a while." He wasn't so much hungover as lacking sleep, definitely looking forward to some quiet time after all this socializing.

Apparently, the birthday party had run its course. Sophie called out, "Okay, everyone. Biyen is going to hand out your goody bags before you walk home."

"Subtle," Reid said with a smirk. "I heard from the owners of the *Missionary II*, by the way. They're talking to the insurance company about it. When will you have a proposal put together? And how are the designs coming along?"

I need a space to work, Logan would have said, but he noticed Emma had started chatting to one of the other kid's moms. Storm was trying to scale Emma's thigh to go after Emma's abandoned plate of cake. Logan stepped closer to the blanket and leaned his hands down.

"Come see me?" he invited.

Storm looked up at him and grinned, their disagreement over the hot dog forgotten. Her arms came up so he could grasp her torso and gather her into his chest as he straightened.

"Thanks," Emma said absently and began collecting gift wrap and other litter from the blanket. Reid helped Delta take leftover watermelon and hot dogs into the house, and within a few minutes, nearly everyone had left, including Delta who was being chauffeured home in Art's Gator.

"Immy, Coop," Emma called. "Time to walk home."

"Biyen wants them to come to the beach with us," Sophie said. "You guys go home and put your feet up. I'll bring them home later. Thanks for coming."

She waved and turned back to whatever Nolan was saying to her.

Logan wasn't trying to eavesdrop. He only moved closer because he was picking up the diaper bag, but he heard Nolan say, "...and said not to come back. I'd rather move here anyway. If I could stay until—"

"No," Sophie said, quiet but firm. "It's Gramps's house, not mine. He said only until Biyen's birthday. Plus, it would be confusing for Biyen. He would think you and I are together." She glanced for Biyen, who was playing tag over by the shed with Imogen and Cooper. She stiffened as she realized Logan had come close enough to overhear them.

Nolan looked at him, too.

"Art let *him* move in." He cocked his head at Logan. "Does Biyen think you two are together? *Are* you?"

Perhaps he wasn't a clueless as he seemed, if he could sense the possessive hackles that were rising across Logan's shoulders.

"Logan pays rent," Sophie said flatly. "If you need a loan for a damage deposit so you can get a new place, I can front you that, but no. You can't move in with us. I'll ask Gramps if you can stay on the lawn until Biyen leaves with Reid and Emma this weekend, but that's it."

"Come on, Soph."

She didn't even shake her head. Only stood with her shoulders straight and her face impassive.

"This was fun," Logan said with firm cheer as Storm tried to crawl from his arm onto his shoulder. "Thanks for having us."

"Uncle Logan." Imogen came running up. "Are you going? Can Storm come to the beach with us?"

That sounded like a recipe for sand from scalp to diaper, but he said, "She'd probably like that. Are you ready to go?" he asked Sophie, offering her a reason to walk away from Nolan.

"Let me get the rest of the food put away. One minute."

Chapter Eleven

A LARGE PORTION of Sophie's Monday was spent kneeling in bilge water, working to get a pleasure cruiser on its way.

When she was done, she threw her filthy coveralls into the soiled laundry and had a quick shower in the cubicle off the locker room next to the machine shop. She dressed in a clean tank, cycling shorts, and the old boots she kept in her locker for exactly this situation. She grabbed clean covvies from the rack and carried them up to the hook by the office, hoping she wouldn't need them until tomorrow, but they were there if she got another call to the wharf.

When she pushed into the office, she found Logan in the middle of the room, hands on his hips. He was staring at the wall. Not at the nautical map of the central coast that hung over the coffeepot and not at the computer where she and Randy logged work orders. He was staring at the empty space between those two things.

He glanced at her and the clash happened, the one where she felt his presence down to her toes. His gaze went from her bare shoulders and arms, down to her bare legs, and landed on her heavy boots.

In all these weeks since his return to Raven's Cove, her

antipathy toward him had acted as a force field, allowing her to deflect this intense awareness of him, but that protection had been eroded by his apology. She couldn't seem to hate him as much as she used to. That meant all those other feelings—the old infatuation and her newer, growing admiration for the way he was stepping up here at work and with his sister—were surfacing. It made her movements feel uncoordinated and filled her with a suffocated, restless sensation.

"That valve replacement turned into a bubble bath in the bowels of hell," she said as explanation for her wardrobe change. She moved in front of him and slipped onto the stool to log her time. "What are you doing? Practicing how to be mad?"

"Reid said we're likely to make a deal on the *Missionary II*."

"That's cool." She swung around on the stool. "How were you thinking of approaching the restoration?"

"As a rule, the right way. Invariably, that's the expensive way. I need to run some numbers, but I need an office. I've been trying to do my design work off my laptop since I got here and it's hell on my eyes. I bought a desk and a couple of extra monitors, but there's nowhere at the house to set it up. I keep getting kicked out. I'd rather work here."

"I sense an eviction coming. Are you going to send me back to doing paperwork behind the counter in the hardware store? Because that's a lot of interruptions, which means mistakes. Also, sometimes people are listening to calls they shouldn't be privy to."

"No, you and I talk too much about day-to-day stuff. I don't want to have to walk downstairs every time I want your two cents."

"I have a solution for that." She waved at the desk. "We have these things called telephones. They're a primitive technology, but they still work in a pinch."

"So you don't mind walking upstairs every time I call and tell you I need to talk to you?"

She walked up and down those stairs a thousand times a day, but point taken. She would kill him if he called her more than once a week.

"What did you have in mind?" She glanced around. "Taking out that coffee shelf isn't going to give you much room for your own desk."

"No, but there's a supply closet on the other side of that wall. It's for all those reams of paper no one uses anymore."

"And a photocopier that's been broken for years."

"It doesn't even work?"

"The fax machine part does."

"That's useful," he snorted.

"There's a recycle place in Bella Bella. I've been suggesting for ages that it would make a good school fundraiser for the company to cover the cost of shipping a pallet over. No one wants to pack their old TV across on the seabus, but they'll pay a few bucks to add it to a pile of electronics that's already going."

"That's a good idea. Make it happen."

"Awesome." She had a broken VCR she'd been trying to get out of the house for years. She turned back to finish logging her hours.

He stretched out his arms in a rough measure of six feet.

"I am compelled to point out"—she spun around again—"if your goal is to add expense to the restoration, an office reno definitely nails it."

"As always, I appreciate your input." He didn't look appreciative.

"Well, it seems like a lot of effort unless you're planning to stick around longer than the end of summer?" Why did that thought unfurl such a sense of promise inside her?

"It's a workspace, not a homestead." He pulled the tacks from the corners of the map and started rolling it.

"What's really eating you?" she asked.

"I need a space that's *mine*." He set the map aside. "I'm leaving your place at the end of the week to go back to a room that wasn't even mine when I was a kid."

He retrieved the sledgehammer she used as a doorstop.

"Logan! You have to warn accounting. You'll scare the hell out them if you crash through that wall like the Kool-Aid guy. You're not even wearing your goggles. What if there's electrical inside that wall? Safety first!"

He sent her a deadpan look as he lay the hammer in the middle of the floor, perpendicular to the wall. He stood and stretched out his arms, measuring a rough six feet again, then nudged the hammer a little farther, providing a sense of how far a wall might come out.

"Oh."

"What do you think? We could put a wall here to separate my desk from yours and a door here. That computer goes into the nook it creates over there."

"I can see it." They discussed a few other fine points.

"There's a window from Dad's we could reuse. That would give me some natural light and a sense of space. Also, neither of us would have to get up when we need to talk."

"You could pass me the good coffee from the break room, like I'm at a drive-thru window," she said brightly. "But back up there, slick. 'We'?"

"What else are you doing while Biyen's away this weekend? You already told Randy you'd be on call. If I'm paying you for that, I might as well put you to work."

"Being on call is a flat two hours. You know I get overtime if I do actual work," she reminded him.

"I will pay you straight time and you can bank the hours to take as paid time off later."

The yard work was mostly caught up, thanks to Logan and Trystan pitching in. What *would* she do all weekend?

"Deal," she agreed, telling herself it was about the money and had nothing to do with seeing more of Logan.

LOGAN WAS SOME kind of masochist. First thing Thursday morning, he started working alongside Sophie in the close confines of the supply closet.

Randy was handling any urgent repairs down at the wharf. Sophie had caught up the paperwork backlog yesterday while Logan and Reid had carried out the broken photocopier. Accounting had finished sorting the boxes of records that had been stored in here, sending most of it to shredding, so the shelves were empty.

Sophie was suited up in goggles and her steel-toed work boots with a snug T-shirt and baggy cargo shorts. Her arms and legs held a hint of toasted gold beneath her all-over freckles. Her hair was a skein of autumn-red twine.

She used a cordless drill to begin pulling screws from the brackets that held the shelves and Logan nearly swallowed his tongue.

"What?" she asked when he stood there like a tool.

"Nothing." He took the first shelf she freed and started a stack in the hallway.

By the time she was on the floor on her back, reaching under the lowest shelf, with one knee crooked and a light sheen of sweat sitting on her skin, he was biting back a groan of pure lust.

"You guys are making way too much noise." Reid came to the doorway, gaze landing with amusement on Sophie. "Did you pull the short straw, Soph?"

"Logan's afraid to get his clothes dirty."

"Yeah, he's—What?" Reid frowned.

Logan tried to erase whatever atavistic snarl had taken over his expression.

"Nothing. I said we'd get it done by Monday. That means starting today." He shifted to block Reid's view of

Sophie's legs and felt about fourteen years old as he did it.

"I know." Reid was wearing his *What the fuck is wrong with you?* face. For once, Logan probably deserved it. "I told everyone to leave early and work from home tomorrow so they don't have to listen to this."

"What time is it?" Sophie sat up.

"Ten thirty." Reid shifted so he could see her. "I'm heading home to help Emma get everyone packed and ready to go."

"You probably wanted to spend the morning with Biyen," Logan realized. "Why didn't you say?"

"He was tying flies with Nolan. I'll take this last shelf out, then head home, not that he could care less whether he sees me. He was packed before bed last night and is bouncing off the walls for this trip. Good luck, pal," she said to Reid.

"Do I look scared? I'll see you at the wharf in an hour." He walked away.

"Oh the hubris of a man who has never been on a school field trip." Sophie lowered down onto her back and went back to removing screws.

AN HOUR LATER, Sophie hugged Biyen on the wharf. His wiry arms squeezed her waist, then abruptly dropped away.

"'Kay. Bye Mom!" He stepped aboard the seabus.

"I'll text when we land in Vancouver," Emma promised wryly as Sophie relayed Biyen's backpack to Reid.

Logan came to stand beside her, a cardboard box full of pub fare in his hands.

"These two are for me and Sophie." He took two burgers off the top and handed the box to Reid. "You guys have fun. I'm gonna miss you kids," he told Imogen and Cooper, giving the boy a fist bump. "Gonna miss you, too, brat." He kissed Storm's cheek and nodded at Delta. "Hope to see you back here soon."

"I'm sure it will be a regular event," Delta promised with what looked like a sincere smile.

There was more waving as the seabus chugged away.

Sophie ate her burger while she watched it putter out of the cove. Logan patiently waited beside her until she crumpled her wrapper and sighed.

"Is this his first time away from you?"

"On a big trip, yeah. He's spent a night with Nolan's mom a few times, but I was always at your mom's a few streets away. I've been trying to work out how to take him to that exhibit, though. Summer is so busy here, it's impossible to get away. I'm glad he'll be able see it, and he really loves those kids. He's going to miss them."

"Mom would say it's healthy for him to learn that you only leave him with people you trust."

"She would say that to *me*." She tipped an askance look up to him. "When would she have said that to *you*?"

"When I left Storm with her while Reid and Emma were on their cruise."

"It's true." She threw her wrapper in a litter bin on the way to the ramp from the wharf up to the graveled verge.

"I should have asked if Art needed a burger. What's he doing for dinner?"

"Opening a can of soup and enjoying the silence," she said wryly. "Biyen's away, you've moved out, even Nolan's gone. I think he's secretly thrilled I'm working all weekend. He likes kids, but it's been a lot with the birthday party and everything. He needs to sit and recharge." She hoped that's all he needed.

"Did you make him a doctor appointment?" He held the door into the marina building for her.

"Next Thursday. But I'll use some of these hours I'm about to bank and take him myself. I want to hear what they say." She spoke over her shoulder as she climbed the stairs.

"Sure. Let me know if something changes."

"Oh." She paused inside the door as she stepped into the office. "You got a lot done after I went home."

He had moved the computer and file cabinet, removed the coffee shelf and covered her desk with a drop sheet. A number of tools were laid out, including a reciprocating saw.

"Ready to rumble?" He slipped on a pair of safety goggles and a dust mask.

Sophie pulled on gloves, goggles, and a dust mask, then plugged in the saw. As she did, she noticed Logan watching her.

What *was* that look? Approval? Something more…interested?

"What?" she asked, finger tracing the on switch.

"Nothing. There's an electrical outlet on the other side of the wall near here." He tapped a claw hammer into the bottom of the wall, punching small holes. He then used the claw to pull away drywall and bent to peer inside the gap he'd made. "Looks like the wires go that way." He pointed away from her and up. "You should be okay to start over there."

She followed his direction, but as she was about to set blade to wall, she realized he was watching her again.

"*What.*" There was too much anticipation in the air. More awareness than usual. Maybe because she knew the offices on the other side of this wall were empty? It made this feel really intimate, and she couldn't understand why. "Is this going to be weird? Us working together all weekend?"

"No. We just shared a house for three weeks. It was fine, wasn't it? *We're* fine. Aren't we?"

Absolutely not.

"I guess." She scratched inside her collar, then adjusted her mask, and put in some ear plugs. She turned on the high-pitched whine of the saw.

While she cut long paths down and across the drywall, he *tap-tapped*, dropping a trail of gypsum as he followed the wiring.

She caught him glancing at her several times, though.

"Am I not doing it right?" she demanded, voice hollow because she still wore her mask.

"You're doing great."

"For a girl? Don't be patronizing." She turned off the

saw and set it aside to wrangle a big section of drywall off the studs.

"I'm not."

"You're something. What is it?"

He muttered something under his breath. "Okay, look."

She stopped what she was doing and looked. Stared. Watched him lift his mask to give the golden stubble on his jaw a brief rub. He seemed genuinely uncomfortable.

"I'm trying to decide if I should tell you something. Is this a safe space? Are we friends this weekend or boss and employee or what?"

"I don't know what we are." She yanked another chunk of drywall free and stuffed it into the heavy-duty disposal bag. "Being friends doesn't seem realistic. There's too much history that's too..." *Sexual? Ugh.* "There's also too much interconnection to simply be boss and employee. Neighbors?" she suggested facetiously. "Why? Because if you have a big secret, am I really the person you want to confide in? Isn't there someone else? Maybe start a diary."

He sent her a disgruntled look, then bent to pop another dotted line with the hammer before he used the claw to join them.

"You're probably the only person I've ever really confided in," he surprised her by saying. "I think it's because you were always here. At the marina, I mean. You had a front row seat to whatever was going on with Dad or my brothers. Those were the things that really stirred me up and there was no point trying to hide any of it from you.

You never judged me for it, either. In fact... Do you realize you were the first person I ever said, 'I want to build boats' to? You said, 'I know.' *I* didn't even know until I said it out loud." His smile kicked up on one side, rueful.

"Really? It was so obvious! You love everything about boats." She broke off a few more jagged edges of drywall.

"It's still a big jump from wanting to do something and being able to do it. You believed I was capable. That was the beginning of *me* believing it."

He was watching her again. It was strange. She felt as though a huge spotlight was on her. As if she had way more importance in his life than could be real. It made her heart quiver uncertainly in her chest.

"Is that what you wanted to tell me? Because it's not exactly a secret that you like designing boats." She carried the saw to another expanse of wall, tugging the extension cord behind her.

"No, that was me working out in real time why I find you so easy to talk to, even when you hate me."

"I don't *hate* you. I just don't trust you."

And now there was another of those awkward, heavy silences.

She ran the saw a few minutes, suspecting she'd hurt his feelings. That didn't sit well. She set it aside to pull the sections away.

"What about your Mom? She's a good listener. Can't you confide in her?" she asked.

"This is not Mom conversation," he assured her dryly.

"Why not? Is it about sex?" A bubble of excited laughter rose in her throat. "What is it? *Tell me.*"

"Now you're interested in my deep dark secrets? That says more about you than it does about me, you know."

"It means I smell a reason to mock you."

"No mocking. If I tell you, it goes in the vault, and we never mention it again. Especially not to my brothers." He pointed a warning finger at her.

"Five minutes of mocking," she countered.

"I am trying to repair our relationship, Sophie. I'm offering to be *vulnerable*. It's a trust fall."

"Have my five minutes of mocking started yet? Because I can tell you're messing with me, saying shit like that."

"All right, I'll say it. You can have your fun, then we'll never mention it again."

She waited. Rolled her wrist to insist he continued.

"I think women using tools is a very sexy look."

"Are you still messing with me?" She looked down at her coveralls.

"No. I think it was all those power tool pinup calendars that Dad and Art used to hang."

"The ones with women in bikinis and leather aprons holding a belt sander? They were sexist and objectifying. The tool manufacturers had to stop making them."

"As they should. They were completely inappropriate." His disapproval was deeply insincere. "But they made an impression during my formative years."

"Why would you tell me this?" She was perplexed. Flattered? No. That would be wrong.

"I knew you would laugh at me. I'm not proud of it."

"Wait. Are you saying you get turned on when you watch me work? I should take that to HR."

"I've never acted on it. I don't stand around perving at you."

"You just did! A minute ago!"

His hammer thwack was followed by the trickling sound of gypsum falling to the floor.

"I'm not ogling. It's like when you see a pretty woman in a sexy dress. You glance over and think, *She looks hot.* Then you get on with your day."

"You think I look hot while I'm using this reciprocating saw?"

"Maybe."

What was she supposed to do with this information?

"Don't you enjoy seeing a hot guy doing sweaty work?" he challenged.

"Find me a hot guy. I'll let you know."

He gave her a very watch-me look as he replaced his mask and came to take the saw. He gave the cord a rippling snap to bring it with him to his end of the wall. The tool whined and, oh damn, his biceps flexed. His snug Raven's Cove T-shirt strained across his pecs and shifted across his shoulders. His blue jeans were faded along the top of his thighs and the demin clung to his ass as he bent.

He was undeniably hot as he worked.

He turned off the saw and cocked a brow at her.

"Maybe if you were in a bikini?"

"Budgie smugglers? That's what does it for you?" He set aside the saw, and his muscles bunched while he pulled away a huge section of drywall. He snapped it in half across his knee so it would fit into the bag.

She swallowed. "I'm more about good posture and legible penmanship."

"Really," he challenged pithily.

"No."

"What then?"

He shouldn't have to ask. He had been the strongest influence on her sexual interest during her formative years, practically imprinting her to only desire him.

"I don't know how to get turned on anymore," she dismissed, taking up the saw. "Nolan was the last guy I slept with. That was four years ago and very forgettable."

"Sophie." Logan paused, hammer dangling from his loose grip. "Are you serious?"

"Why is that shocking? Once a slut always a slut?"

"Do *not* call yourself that. You don't really believe that, do you?"

She turned on the saw, finding satisfaction in the effort required to push horizontal and vertical lines through the wall, but any toughness she felt in those moments dissipated with the noise when she turned it off. Now she just felt flimsy and transparent again.

"What is the appropriate amount of sex that I should have, Logan? And why would you even care?"

"I don't care how much sex you have. I mean, I care. I think you should have exactly as much sex as you want and that it should be great every time, but I hope you don't judge yourself over your own history. I hope you're not denying yourself so you can punish yourself. You shouldn't."

Was that what she was doing? Maybe a little.

"If a guy comes along who is worth wrecking my life over—and wrecking my son's life—I might consider it. I haven't met anyone worth the risk, though."

"That's how it seems to you? That sex would wreck your life?"

"It did before. Are you paying me to talk or work?"

His brows went up at her snark, but he picked up the saw with a pensive expression and got back to work.

Chapter Twelve

THEY WORKED WELL together, not that it surprised Logan. They had both trained under Art so they had common principles and knew how to stay out of each other's way. Before quitting for the night, they got the wall removed and the area cleaned up.

He went home physically tired, but didn't sleep well, thinking too much about Sophie.

Was this part of his father's legacy, too? Wilf had come from an abusive, neglectful home. Logan didn't know a lot about it, but his mother had told him that much in the past. Wilf had never been overtly cruel to Glenda or anyone else, but he'd been deliberately obtuse to how much he was hurting others. That's why he had led with monetary generosity. He had wanted to be loved, but he didn't know how to earn it or reciprocate it.

He hadn't loved himself.

Neither did Logan. It went deeper than his self-contempt for treating Sophie so callously. He had told her he hadn't believed she could love him and that was true. Who would? His mother had, but she had loved a man like Wilf so that only told Logan how low her standards were.

Logan had done his best to play the field once he left

for university, feeling empty doing it. He'd met smart, pretty, funny girls who should have held more attraction for him, but he hadn't understood them, and they hadn't understood him. He kept waiting for something to feel right and nothing ever had.

Then, when his mother had had enough of his father's infidelity, he came back here to help her leave him. He had wanted to hurt his father by helping, not that there'd been much evidence he'd succeeded.

Logan had been hurting, though. He'd still been resentful of his upbringing and there had been Sophie, soothing the beast inside him. She did understand him and made him laugh at himself as much as every other aspect of this miserable journey called life. She'd been thoughtful and ambitious in her modest way, and he had felt connected to her in a way that was different from anyone else.

That connection had scared the hell out of him. That was the truth. He could look back and admit that it wasn't just that he hadn't wanted to bring traces of his childhood into the life he was building away from it. It was the heavier sense that she could pull him back into something he was determined to leave, something that would anchor him to this place forever.

So he had cut things short with her and left, treating her heartlessly in some bizarre effort to prove what an unlovable shit he was.

Just like his father.

He had never felt good about it. Never looked at another woman without comparing something about her to

Sophie. He had never let himself get truly close to anyone since. His few long-term partners had always pointed that out when they ended things. He was inaccessible and incapable of real commitment.

He was. He had kept his focus on work, thinking it would bring him the fulfillment that otherwise evaded him, but even that success had failed to bring him any real satisfaction or any sense of true pride in himself.

Outside, the dawn light was increasing. Ravens started making their racket, coaxing their fledglings to fly. He gave up on sleep and rose to see one young raven on the lawn, letting out helpless, prehistoric screeches that roughly translated to *I'm lost. Where do I go?*

"I hear ya, bird."

He walked up to a silent kitchen. Usually Storm was in her chair, babbling and blowing raspberries. Someone would be making coffee. They'd all talk about what they were doing that day.

Sophie's house was equally busy with Art putting on the news and Biyen spilling his cereal and Sophie bossing everyone while taking care of them at the same time.

He used to think he was lucky that he lived alone with no one to answer to. Today, he couldn't stand his own company. He walked down to the pub where he found Cameron and joined him for breakfast before heading into the office.

Sophie was already there in her coveralls, sitting on the stool, logging hours.

"Callout?"

"Mmm. Gillnetter needed a fuel line and was trying to get on his way so I came in early." She yawned.

"I brought you a coffee from the pub."

"I went through to the break room." She picked up the mug beside her, meeting his gaze over the rim. Hers seemed wary.

"I forgot we can do that now." He kept a level tone, wondering when he was going to quit spilling cold water on whatever warmth he managed to kindle between them. Her sex life was none of his business.

Not everything is about you, Logan.

"I woke up to a long string of texts from Emma," Sophie said with amusement, tone brightening. "I guess all the travel was too much for Storm. She *hated* the playpen. Thought she'd been sentenced to baby jail and was not having it."

"She sleeps in one in Reid's office all the time. Are they all sharing a suite or…?"

"Adjoining rooms. And the funny thing is—Well, it's not funny unless it's happening to someone else, but I can picture it so clearly. When babies learn to pull themselves up to stand, they just keep doing it. They don't know how to get back down unless they fall down and that scares them so they turn into this wrecking ball of self-torture. You try to lay them down and they're standing up and screaming before you get to the door."

"I'm trying not to enjoy this, because Storm will do it to me soon enough, but this is what I'm saying about Reid. Remember how he was yesterday? 'I'm not scared,'" he mocked.

"Emma said he had to walk her all over the hotel until she fell asleep. They finally got everyone down, then it was musical beds because Cooper wet the sheets. They switched up to a girls' room and a boys' room, which got them through to five this morning when Biyen woke Reid, asking if he could call me. That's another reason I was in so early."

"Does he want to come home?" he asked with concern. "Do you need to go?"

"No," she scoffed. "As soon as he saw me on the screen, he started talking about everything they were going to do today. He just needed to know I was still here, same as always." She shook her head and chuckled, turning back to the computer to finish tapping.

"Yeah." What was wrong with him that he suffered a little fomo that he had missed all of that chaos. He didn't want any part of it. Who would?

"I have to work on the propeller for that cabin cruiser today, but I'll mud the holes from the shelves first," she said absently.

Back to work. Personal time over, he noted with a raw sensation in his throat.

"Sounds good," he said. "Thanks."

BY THE TIME Sophie was finished with her marina duties, Logan had framed in the new wall, door, and the space for the window. He'd moved the electrical outlet and, as soon as she appeared, asked her to help him set the window in place.

She did, then went down to the locker room to remove her coveralls and put on the cutoff bib overalls she liked to wear for working at home when it was hot. They were loose and had lots of pockets.

"This is going to feel a lot more functional," she said, when she came back into the office. "I thought it would feel claustrophobic, but I'll actually have more space once the filing cabinet is out from behind my chair and in your office. Plus, I might actually see sunlight." She pointed through the window to his door into the accounting hallway. The breakroom had a window that faced the cove. Sunlight shone through that window onto the floor there through the middle of the day. "It's as if you went to school to learn how to do stuff like this."

"They said going all the way to Italy for a master's degree in yacht design wouldn't pay off, but they're eating their words now, aren't they?"

"You're finally realizing your potential, is what I'm hearing. What was that like, anyway?" She had always been curious about his time there. It was such a worldly accomplishment, not something her very ordinary ambitions had ever conceived of. "Did you learn Italian?"

"Sì. Then I moved to Florida and mixed it up with all the Spanish I heard there. I'm kind of lousy at both, to be honest. It was a good experience, though. It made me realize what a young country Canada is. The colonial

Canada, obviously. We have trees that are five hundred years old. They have buildings that old. Can you—?"

She went around the window to shim from the other side.

"Thanks." He set the level and tapped another shim into place. "It was where the best school happened to be and I'm glad I went, but I don't have any sentimental attachment to Genoa."

"I'm still jealous that you've lived such a big life. I took Biyen to California for the amusement parks last year. That's as far from home as I've been. I'd like to go to Mexico, but I'd also like to redo the bathroom." She mirrored his movement on her side of the window, shifting to the other side to shim there.

"If you're going to update your place, I have ideas," he said.

"You don't think the charm of our house is its complete disregard for function?"

"Homely has two meanings and it demonstrates both of them very well." He touched the level to the window frame, checking both horizontal and vertical angles. "Perfect."

"Poor old house. I wouldn't put Gramps through a full reno, though." She came back to her desk. "He has a dinner invite tonight, by the way. I'm grabbing pizza from the pub. What do you want on your half?" She picked up the phone.

While they waited for the pizza, they carried up the new drywall, then ate in the break room, enjoying the breeze that came up from the water and through the open window.

They didn't talk much and got right back to work after. Logan seemed to have taken to heart her 'are you paying me to talk or work' remark from last night.

That bothered her. She liked their banter. Back in the day, all the girls had thrown themselves at him, but none had made him laugh as often as she had. That had been her edge—the thing that had made her feel special. The thing that had made her feel seen by him.

Yesterday, that back and forth had started trampling on some very raw nerves, especially when he'd been so shocked by her saying that sex had wrecked her life. She had knocked him back a step out of defensiveness, but did he think she had been referring to him?

Had she?

That brief week with him had been such a complicated time. She rarely tried to untangle it. It was easier to lump it all in as one long bad memory when, in fact, there had been a lot of good ones. His leaving without her had destroyed her, but the sex had been very good. Awkward and silly the first time, but nice. They'd taken a picnic blanket to a spot under a tree. The sounds of nature had been all around them while he showed her how a condom went on. He'd been so slow and thorough with the lube, she'd had a little orgasm and been embarrassed about it.

You're supposed to come. I was hoping you would. He'd kissed her again while he continued to caress her in that tender, inciting way. When he'd rolled atop her and pressed inside her, it had hardly hurt at all. He hadn't lasted long enough to make her come again, but the way he'd been shaking as he rasped, *Oh fuck, Soph. I can't wait. Oh fuck.* She had liked that a lot, being more than he could handle.

Sex had got better and better in the ensuing days as they got to know each other's bodies, learning how to draw it out, trying different positions and other salacious things. He had loved going down on her, too. There had been one time—

No. She had to stop thinking about it! She was getting turned on. He would notice. Her cheeks were probably pink and she was damp between her thighs. That would definitely put guilty lust in her face.

"Do you need both hammers?" he asked.

"Nope." She was on the floor, pulling the baseboards from the supply room side of the new office. She handed him the hammer she was using and crawled to grab the other one, then rolled onto her hip as she turned back to where she'd been.

A sharp jab went straight into her ass cheek.

"Fuck!"

"What?" He turned.

"I've been putting these finishing nails into my back pocket." She got her legs under her and stood.

"Shit. I've done that. Are you bleeding?"

"I don't think so." She rubbed the spot, dislodging the point that had still been stuck in her butt cheek. "Fuck that hurts."

"Tetanus shot up to date?"

"Last year. I think it's bleeding." She twisted, trying to see if it was staining through the denim. "That's good, right? Flushes the poison?"

"Let's have a look."

"I'm not going to show you my bum, Logan."

"I'm going to spray it with antiseptic and put a bandage on it. If you think you can do that yourself, at least let me watch because you look like a puppy chasing his tail."

She quit turning in circles.

"Umi is working from home today. Do you really want to call her in for this?" He went into the bathroom.

She heard him wash his hands before he came out with a first aid kit. It was grubby with age, but she and Randy only used it for exactly this kind of injury, something that could be cleaned and covered in a minute so they could get back to work. Anything more serious had to go through Umi who made note of it in the first aid book.

"Ugh, this is embarrassing." She turned her back on Logan and unbuckled the clips from her bib, then caught the denim, only letting it fall far enough to reveal that she wore thongs these days.

"Distract yourself by thinking about how much Biyen will enjoy hearing about this. And Trys."

"Don't you *dare*."

"Now you're just egging me on. It's a scratch. I'm going to clean it with some rubbing alcohol." A damp pat of cotton against her cheek arrived with a sharp sting. "Now some ointment." His fingertip gave two quick dabs. A bandage went over it. "All done. Unless you want me to kiss it better?"

"Oh you can definitely kiss my ass," she muttered as she buckled her bib into place.

"I gave you that one because I felt sorry for you." He smirked as he put the things away in the kit and closed it.

As he returned the kit to the bathroom and rewashed his hands, a terrible pang arrived behind her sternum. She still *liked* him, damn it. Beneath her childish crush and hero worship, there had always been a genuine affection for him and it was still here. He was funny and smart and competent and, when he wanted to be, kind.

He came out to walk wordlessly past her, all the way through to the breakroom. He came back with a ceramic coffee mug that had the resort logo on it. He offered it to her.

"Stay hydrated?" She looked inside, but the mug was empty.

"Put the nails in it. Unless you want to keep showing me your ass?" He angled his head with suspicion.

"I am never going to live this down, am I?"

"The jokes about you getting nailed are barely staying in my mouth."

"I hate you so much right now." She absolutely refused to laugh.

"That's okay. I'm starting to like it." He took up the hammer and got back to work.

THEY KNOCKED OFF at nine o'clock, having readied the new room for painting and flooring first thing tomorrow.

"That was a lot of good work today," Logan said, tired, but in a satisfied way, as they stepped outside to the darkening July sky. "We make a solid team."

Sophie flicked him a glance as she locked the marina door, maybe not comfortable with any word that suggested they were together.

"Unless I get an early call-out, I'll be in at nine. I want to have breakfast with Gramps and make sure he takes all his meds."

"Sure."

Maybe their OCD-like focus on finishing the task at hand had been an effort to keep from acknowledging that other thing. Her ass.

Why. Why had she had to hurt herself *there*? He had done everything he could to behave as professionally as a doctor. It was just skin. Just a scratch. Everyone had a bum. That one happened to be hers.

That one also happened to be spectacular. Round and firm and the shape and the freckles would be imprinted on his eyeballs for the rest of his life. He *had* wanted to kiss it.

It was Friday night so the DJ was in the pub. Other than that thumping melody, the village was quiet. As they passed the wharf, Logan sent a habitual look across the marina, always keeping a mental inventory of the vessels moored there. He was never shy about dropping by to ask for a tour if he saw something new and interesting.

Sophie clicked on her phone's flashlight as they left the

lights around the village buildings and entered the darker shadows where his driveway peeled up from the lane that led to hers.

An empty house again. Great, Logan thought glumly.

"Oh shit. Bear." Sophie grabbed his arm to halt him.

"Where?" Logan reflexively pulled her close into his side and followed the point of her finger to the boulder-sized silhouette at the side of the lane up ahead.

Two eyes glowed. It didn't seem to have the hump of a grizzly, but it was big enough to be a cranky brown bear with cubs, even though he didn't see those, either.

"We're going this way," he called out, shoving Sophie behind him as he sidled up his own driveway. "You keep doing your own thing over there."

Sophie flashed her light at it a few times while they gained the higher ground of his driveway.

The bear turned away and crashed into the bushes, going the opposite direction. They turned and hurried up to the house, not talking because they were both listening to be sure the bear didn't change its mind and come back this way.

"I'll post that on the community page." Sophie tapped her phone as soon as they were inside.

"Did someone leave garbage out?" Logan asked.

"No, there are berries there. He's just being a bear."

"I left the truck down at the shop. I can't give you a lift home."

"I'll walk in a little while."

"You will not." God, this woman sometimes. "There are several beds here. Call Art and tell him you're going to stay in one of them."

"I love how you think you're the boss of me."

"I am literally the boss of you. Do you want a beer?"

"Thanks." She brought her phone to her ear and said, "It's me. I just saw a bear at the end of our driveway so I'm at Logan's. I'll walk home—No, Gramps. I'll walk—*No. It's a bear, Gramps. Not a cougar. Okay, yes, you're right. Okay.* Logan said I could stay here. Okay? Okay. That's what I'll do, then. I love you. Good night. Oh my gawd." She ended the call. "He's on his way to bed but wanted to come get me with his Gator. That thing can't outrun Biyen, let alone a bear."

"So you had the same argument with him that I had just had with you? How did it feel?"

"Oh bite me." She accepted the beer and followed him outside where they sank into a pair of loungers facing the water and starlit sky.

"Are you afraid someone will say something about your spending the night here? Is that why you don't want to stay?"

"Afraid? No. I expect it. Which is not cool for Biyen, but I'll explain." She picked at the label on her bottle.

Right then, if he could have gone back and taken her away from this place when he'd had the chance, he would have. He hated that she couldn't escape the history he'd inadvertently caused her.

"The worst part is, I have this passive-aggressive bitchiness in me that says, *If they think I'm up here fucking you, I might as well be doing it.*" She didn't look at him, only took a long gulp from her bottle, but he sensed her side-eye.

"Wow."

"Oh, don't pretend we haven't both been thinking about it since you saw my ass earlier."

His brain briefly flatlined. He absolutely had, but he wasn't going to admit it.

"You drive me crazy, Logan. You make me absolutely fucking nuts. But what am I supposed to do? Let you use me again? Use *you* just because I haven't had sex in four years?"

"Sophie—" Did she think he was doing any better over here? "Sure. Yes. Use me. Do it. Nothing would make me happier than for you to hate-fuck me as part of a bigger fuck-you to this place."

She turned her head to stare at him.

"I'm serious. Not because I want sex." He definitely wanted sex. "But because it would mean you were hitting me back. I could quit feeling like such an asshole about what I did to you."

She looked out to the water.

"But don't do it," he said more quietly. "I am trying really hard not to fuck up this…" Civility? *Ha.* Camaraderie? "Ceasefire that we've found. I don't want you to be angry with me anymore."

"I'm not. That's what makes me so nuts. I want to hate you and I can't. No matter how hard I try."

A huge weight lifted off him, one that allowed him to take a full breath for the first time since he'd arrived back here. Cold prickles of caution danced through his blood, though. Do *not* fuck this up.

Chapter Thirteen

WAS SHE DISAPPOINTED that Logan didn't join her when she showered, or when she put on the T-shirt he loaned her and went to sleep in the bed in Storm's room?

Yes. Much to her chagrin, she was quietly devastated that he didn't even try. At least if he had made an advance, she could have shut him down. Or shared the blame with him for any weakness she showed.

Now that he was becoming noble, she had even less reason to hate him and more to like. Jerk.

After tossing and turning, she rose early and ran home through the dewy grass.

"What are you doing here?" Gramps asked when he got up to find her scrambling eggs and toasting sourdough.

"Making sure you're not eating canned peaches for breakfast."

"I'll eat them after you're gone if I want them."

"You'll be too full," she assured him, filling two plates, then pouring each of them a coffee.

"This is nice, Sophie. Thank you." He sat down with her at the table. "I don't often get you to myself. When is Biyen home?"

"Tomorrow afternoon."

"It'll be good to have him back. It was too quiet here yesterday after everyone was gone. Are you and Logan—"

"No," she stated firmly. "Just friends."

Was that what they were, though? Last night, she had cracked open a door to something more carnal and he had refused to walk through it.

The rumble that came from Gramps's chest was equally skeptical.

"He apologized," she mumbled around her eggs. "Life is too short for grudges, right?"

"I can't say holding on to one ever enriched my life. I'm glad he's making up with you. I was disappointed in him when I realized he'd hurt you, but that family"—he shook his head—"none of them had it easy, not even Wilf, so try not to judge any of them too harshly."

"I don't," she fibbed, since she absolutely had judged Logan to within an inch of his life.

She swallowed a lump of egg, but it seemed to stay lodged in her throat. The timing had never seemed right to say these words, but on the heels of what he'd just said, the opening was right there.

"Gramps, I really appreciate that you never gave me a hard time over the way I acted that summer, after Logan left. Or later, when I got pregnant and had Biyen. I am *so* grateful you opened your home to us. You're a really good influence on Biyen, too. He has Nolan, but grandads are pretty special. You've always been really important to me, and I'm very glad he has you, too."

"Are we starting our Saturday by crying in our eggs?"

"No. Gotta keep the salt down because of your blood pressure."

"Hmph." He gave her a look of disgruntled affection. "I don't suppose your mother ever told you how I reacted when *she* came home pregnant?"

"No. Why? What happened?" She closed her mouth over a scoop of eggs.

"I threw her out." He stabbed his toast crust into his ketchup, mouth tight with self-disgust.

"Gramps."

"I look back and wonder what I thought that would accomplish. Babies don't get unmade just because you disapprove. I regret it to this day, losing all that time with her, especially after she left us too early." Anguish dragged even deeper lines into a face that was as wrinkled as a dried apple, leathered by years of working in winds flowing off the salt-chuck.

"Did you not like my dad or…?"

"I didn't know him. She hardly knew him herself. She met him on a weekend in Victoria, then he went back to Ontario. When I kicked her out, she got hold of him and he flew her out there. They got married and I didn't see her again until your grandmother's funeral. I didn't know what to say to her when I saw her. You were just a little thing, barely walking. They were living on the Sunshine Coast by then. He'd started logging. I didn't even know. I was sick, absolutely sick at what I'd done. Your grandmother had never forgiven me for it, but I didn't know how to change it so I let your mother walk away again without saying a word to her. I hate myself for that, too."

"Oh, Gramps." She reached across, and he turned his hand to pinch her fingers in his.

"It wasn't until she lost your father, and I went to that funeral, that I couldn't take it anymore. I'd never seen her so heartbroken. I couldn't stomach her trying to carry on alone. I asked her to come live with me here and she did. I'm grateful for that because you were my second chance to get things right."

"I really am going to cry." She grabbed a napkin and shoved it under her wet eyes. Sniffled. "She never told me any of that."

"No, she never threw it in my face, either. You want to hear a secret, though? When you started acting out and she didn't know what to do with you, I thought, there. Now you know how it feels when your child no longer makes sense to you. It's terrifying. But I sat her down and told her not to make my mistakes."

Janine hadn't. She had told Sophie that she loved her and urged her to, *Look after yourself. Be safe.* But she had never shamed Sophie for the way she was behaving, and when Sophie had told her she was pregnant, she had hugged her and asked her what she wanted to do about it.

Sophie had thought seriously about abortion, aware that school and the rest of her future would all be impacted, but there had been something very grounding in deciding to have the baby. All the things she had thought were important, like why Logan Fraser didn't love her, had ceased to matter. She loved her baby, and when Biyen arrived, he loved her back so hard, she could barely withstand it.

"I was worried about you, same as she was, but you're so much like her," Gramps was saying. "I knew you'd clean yourself up and you did. Then we lost her and that was damned unfair on you. I was very worried about you, then. I could see that Nolan was nothing but dead air. I couldn't interfere, though. Not after what I'd done to your mother. Not until you were in my house. Then I was allowed to tell him to fuck off."

She choked slightly on her eggs, washing them down with coffee.

"It was still big of you to let me and Biyen move in. He can be a lot, bashing around here, always asking questions and eating nonstop."

"Is that what you think?" He shook his head. "All I ever think is how easy he is. A helluva lot easier than girls."

"Sexist! I am the son you always wanted, in case you haven't noticed. I can replace a coupling on a transmission shaft *and* make you breakfast. Also keep you taking your meds. I'll do that while I'm thinking of it." She rose and fetched them.

When she brought the pills to him, she gave him a quick hug and kissed his cheek. "I mean it, you know. Thank you."

"You're a good girl, Sophie." He patted her arm. "I like having you and the boy here. How would I know so much about myself, if he wasn't telling me all those dinosaur facts?"

"Ha!" She sat to eat her last bites, then took her plate to the sink, coming back to top up their coffee.

"I'll say one more thing about Logan," Gramps said somberly. "He's made mistakes and I don't condone them, but I couldn't turn my back on him, either. Even though I wanted to kick him in the ass for hurting my girl."

"I know," she murmured, sitting and taking up her mug, staring into her coffee. The way Logan had worked under Gramps all those years made *him* the son Gramps always wished he'd had.

"He was never going to get where he wanted to go by staying here, Soph."

True. Raven's Cove was a far cry from Genoa.

"They all have Wilf's sense of ambition and one-track mind." He set his hand between his eyes then knifed it forward. "They had to chase whatever it was they were chasing. They would have stagnated if they'd stayed here."

"I know. But that's why nothing will happen between me and Logan," she said with a philosophical shrug. "Eventually, he'll go off to chase more dreams and I'll still be here." Raising her son and looking after her grandfather. "We want different things."

She wasn't sure if she was clarifying it for him, or saying it aloud so she would hear it and accept it.

His mouth pursed in something that might have been disappointment, but he only said, "That's his loss and my gain, then. Isn't it?"

She doubted Logan would see it that way, but, "Sure

is."

LOGAN WAS ALREADY working when Sophie got there. Aside from a, "Morning," mumbled around a couple of nails poking out of his mouth, he didn't say anything about last night or the fact she had disappeared before he saw her this morning.

She got to work, trying to ignore this confused but shimmering awareness between them.

Nothing would make me happier than for you to hate-fuck me. Not because I want sex…

Did he want sex? She did.

Oh God. She did.

Between his kiss after the water rescue and the lessening of her anger and their intimate conversations and his touch on her ass yesterday, she was starting to think—fantasize, really—about sex with Logan. Not sex colored by hate, but with something else. Forgiveness?

She leapt on a callout to the wharf, even though it was so simple she could have sold the part to the skipper and hurried back upstairs. She installed it herself and waved off the labor charge, grateful for the break.

On her way back upstairs, she stopped at the pub and picked up a couple of bowls of mulligatawny, which she and Logan polished in short order, then got back to work.

The rest of the day was quiet enough that they were down to finishing work and a first coat of paint by five.

"I'm going to knock off and make dinner for Gramps," Sophie said with a stretch.

"Why don't you invite him to join us at the pub?"

"Honestly? The pub is great but ask me to recite the menu. I can do it, word for word."

"I hear ya," he said as he wrapped a paint roller. "I eat there so often I don't need a menu, either."

"Come join us," she offered impulsively. "I'm only making salmon patties with a salad, but Gramps will enjoy your company."

It turned into a nice evening with a good meal and some big belly laughs.

"What time does the boy get in tomorrow?" Gramps asked at one point.

"Around two."

"I'll come to get him and inspect this new office of yours while I'm there," Gramps told Logan, briefly turning melancholy as he added, "I wish Wilf could see all the work you boys are getting done. It would have made him really happy."

Sophie caught the flex of anguish on Logan's face. She *felt* it.

So did Gramps because he said, "He did the best he could, son. That's all any of us can do."

"Yeah," Logan said under his breath and ran his hands up and down his thighs.

Sophie heard his regret, his inner question as to whether *he* had done his best.

"He was really proud of you guys, though," Sophie

said. "It's not as if he thought you should have stayed here, rather than accomplish all the things you've done."

"We could have come back now and again, though," Logan said with quiet self-contempt. "I could have thanked him, just once, instead of being so angry…" He shook his head at himself, profile carved to a sharp line as he stared at his empty plate. "Such a waste of energy."

And time. And opportunity. She felt that, too, as she thought about how much she had resented Logan's presence here all these weeks, only lately coming around to forgiving him.

He swore under his breath, then shook off his mood. "Everyone done? I'll wash dishes."

While Logan did the dishes and Sophie started laundry, Gramps moved into his chair. He was snoring by the time she got back to the kitchen.

"It's really nice out," Sophie said as she came in and took up the tea towel. "The sky is pink and the tide is low. If Biyen was here, we would go down to the beach and dig for geoducks."

"He eats them?"

"No. He likes to count their rings to see how old they are. Sixty-two is the record."

"That kid," Logan said with a chuckle. Then, as he rinsed the sink, asked, "Why would you tell me that? You know how competitive I am."

"You want to go dig geoducks?"

"I was going to head back to the office and put a second coat on the walls, but yeah, let's go down to the beach for a few minutes." He dried his hands on the tea towel she still held.

When they came outside a minute later, the breeze was ribboned with the warmth off the dried grass and underlaid by cool, salty currents from the wet tideline.

They ambled down the short path to the beach, which was an eroded drop down to a handful of washed-up logs and a rocky intertidal zone. They hadn't brought a bucket or shovel which was a small shame because there were tons of holes in the sand, indicating loads of clams and geoducks.

"Why is Biyen a vegetarian? Because his dad is?"

"Yeah, Nolan is very counterculture, in case you haven't noticed. But Biyen is so nature-focused, avoiding meat is probably something he would have done regardless. It can be a hassle sometimes, but there are worse things a kid could do than make you cook him extra vegetables. That wasn't a dig," she added with a small grimace as she heard herself.

"I know." He shook his head, obviously still ruminating about Wilf.

"Oh, don't," she urged, nudging his elbow with her own. "It would be nice if we all had a crystal ball to know what was coming, but we don't."

"Precisely why we should be our best self in the moment we're in."

"That's a very lofty aspiration, but it's not very realistic." She moved to stand in front of him, drawing his pensive gaze off the distant shores onto her. "We're all going to be dumb shits sometimes. And life isn't always going to offer you a tidy choice between black and white. Sometimes you're going to wind up with regret no matter what you do. Because if you said to me that you wish you hadn't been my first, and that we didn't have *that* memory between us, I'd be really hurt."

"Ah, Soph." He dragged her into a loose embrace. "I regret everything about how I treated you that summer *except* that. If I could…" His tortured voice trailed off.

"No. That's the point. There was no winning for you that summer."

She hugged around his waist and leaned into him, allowing the simple embrace to heal some of her old wounds because there had been no winning for her, either. Even if he had taken her away with him, at some point there would have been a reckoning. She had been too immature for a serious relationship then. Her behavior after his rejection proved it.

She couldn't regret their lovemaking, though. Not when his body still made hers sing this way simply by standing against hers.

Closing her eyes, she savored the feel of him, familiar, yet new. They'd both changed, maturing physically as well as emotionally. His chest was broader and more muscled, his arms heavier on her shoulders, his presence that much more imposing and confident. His scent was deeply familiar, carrying those odd vestiges from the marina office and the purity of coastal rainforest and him. That boy who was now that man.

Her fingertips found the indent of his spine in his lower back. She tilted her face up so her chin was on his chest, caught in the murky choice between being smart and taking advantage of the opportunity before her.

"Those eyes of yours," he said with a vexed pull of his brows. "I never needed you to look after me. Do you realize that?" He cupped her face while he seemed to take great care to memorize every aspect of her features.

"You always seemed lost," she whispered. "You still do."

He didn't seem to know what to say to that. His gaze tangled with hers and her hands flattened to climb behind his shoulders. He dipped his chin and his mouth touched hers.

He hesitated.

She went up on her toes, increasing the pressure.

With a rumble in his chest, his hand slid to cup the base of her skull and he slowly dragged her into a deep, thorough kiss, one that lavished attention from one corner of her mouth to the other, plundering even as he worshiped.

Here was the razor's edge between living for today and repenting tomorrow. He was leaving and she was anchored here forever, but in this second her skin was electric and her body swamped by sensations. Heat engulfed her. The velvet brush of his tongue against hers was an erotic tease. The lazy roam of his wide hand down her back unfurled her sensuality as easily as sliding open a zip.

The sting in her nipples had her pressing tighter to

him. The hardness of his thighs brought her own up to crook against it.

Dizzy, she drew on his bottom lip, enjoying the groan she pulled out of him right before his hands hardened and he dragged his head up. He caught her ponytail in his fist. His heart was thumping hard enough for her to feel it against her breast, but maybe that was her own. Neither of them was drawing a steady breath.

"Soph."

"You have an empty house," she reminded him.

"Believe me, I know," he said grittily. "I'm still kicking myself for not doing terrible, illegal things to you last night." He released her hair and cupped the side of her neck, thumb caressing the hollow beneath her ear. "But this is where *you* drive *me* nuts. You act tough enough to make me believe it, but now I know how easy it is to hurt you and I won't do that again."

She pulled away. "I'm not eighteen anymore."

"It wasn't being young that made it easy for me to hurt you, Soph."

She bit back a gasp, surprised how deeply that struck.

"We can hurt each other," he said with a squeeze of her shoulder, as if that was some kind of consolation. "I don't want us to do that again. So I'm going to go put another coat of paint on the office. Tomorrow, I'll just be putting my desk together so unless you get a call-out, you don't have to come in."

"Sure. Thanks." She crossed her arms. "Good night."

He hovered an extra few seconds before he exhaled and walked away.

Chapter Fourteen

"MOM!" BIYEN KNEW the rule she had set from the first time they'd come to visit Raven's Cove. No standing on the seabus unless it was tied up and you were ready to get off. He was barely keeping his butt on the seat, though, as he waved hard enough, he ought to be steering it off course.

"Did I leave my sunglasses at your place last night?" Logan asked as he came to stand beside her on the wharf. He was squinting at the water. "I just looked through the office and couldn't find them."

Her heart took a lift and a dip and a swerve. Was she mad that he'd shut her down last night? Not exactly. Embarrassed? Enough that she hadn't gone upstairs when she had been called out to fix a bent rudder, staying in the machine shop.

"They're by the sink. I meant to grab them when I left this morning. I was in the garden, then I got talking to Gramps and forgot."

She had almost called Logan to take the call out. Gramps had been complaining of a headache when he got up. He hadn't been coughing or running a fever, just moving slow and looking pale. She'd offered to stay home when the phone rang, but he'd brushed her off.

"I'm going to nap in my chair. Call me when Biyen gets in. I'll come truck him home," he had said.

"I'd call Gramps to bring them, but I just called to remind him Biyen's on his way. There was no answer, so he must have left already."

"No problem. I'll walk down later. Hey," he greeted everyone as the seabus came close enough.

They both stood back to let the tourists off.

When Biyen's feet hit the wharf, he hugged Sophie so hard, he squeezed an "Oof" out of her.

"I missed you, too." Her heart finally felt as though it had settled back into its place after being stretched and searching for him all these days he'd been gone. "Did you have fun?" She smoothed his hair and planted a kiss on his head, drinking in the smell of her sweaty boy.

"Uh-huh. Except I cried a little bit when we had to say good-bye to Immy and Coop. Emma cried the most, though."

"I did," Emma admitted sheepishly, disembarking with Storm in her arms. "It was so much fun, though. Thank you for letting us bring him. It was such a nice way to end the trip for the kids. And you kept Storm entertained on the flight, didn't you?" Emma said to Biyen. "I really appreciated that."

"I just read books to her," he said with a shrug.

"Dinosaur books?" Logan guessed. He accepted luggage from Reid and set it on the wharf. "Got any new facts for me?"

"A baby has a bigger brain than most dinosaurs. Thanks." Biyen took the backpack Reid handed him and threaded his arms through the straps.

"I'm willing to bet that Storm's brain is bigger than the average adult man's," Logan said dryly.

"Speak for yourself," Reid said, stepping to the wharf with the diaper bag. He nodded out at the water beyond the cove. "Look who else is coming. That's good. I had questions for him."

"Do you mind if I take Storm home?" Emma asked. "She's ready for her nap."

Storm was rubbing her eyes.

"Yeah, I'll see you up there." Reid gave her a distracted kiss before he started quizzing Logan on whether he had anything to report.

Sophie picked up the car seat and joined the rest of them carrying luggage to the truck.

"Mom, can I see inside the *Storm Ridge*? I never did and Immy and Cooper said it's really cool."

"We'll ask Trys once all the guests are off. Gramps might like to see it, too. Then we can go see Logan's new office. It will be like a Sunday drive, except on foot. How could you have ever wanted to leave?" She asked Reid, since he happened to be beside her. "Given this level of weekend entertainment?"

"It's something I ask myself every day," Reid drawled as he set the car seat into place. "Especially now I'm back."

"Where's Gramps?" Biyen looked around.

"He should have been here by now." Sophie frowned.

"That Gator is older than he is," Logan said. "I'll drive Em home, then walk down to see what's keeping him. I need my sunglasses anyway."

Emma's brows went up and Reid turned his head to send a questioning look at Logan.

"Are you that starved for entertainment?" Logan said with significantly more bite than their idle curiosity warranted. He held out his hand to Biyen, saying more gently, "I can take that, too."

"Thanks!" He slipped free of the backpack.

Logan set it next to where Emma had strapped Storm into her seat.

As Logan drove away, Biyen gave Sophie a hopeful look. "Ice cream?"

"I don't know." She put on her most skeptical look, even though she could really use an ice cream. "Do *you* think he behaved well enough to earn an ice cream?" she asked Reid.

"I do," Reid said without hesitation. "I think I did as well."

"For outstanding valor during trying circumstances?"

"For putting down a towel and sleeping where Cooper wet the sheets."

"For being a parent, then. Fair enough. My treat."

"It was dinner," Logan grumbled the minute he was away with Em. "With her and Art. Don't turn it into more than it was." *We kissed, though. It was fantastic. She wanted to come home with me. I hate myself for saying no.*

"I didn't say anything," Emma said blandly. "You're the one acting like it was more than that."

"Because I don't want anyone making her uncomfortable when we're finally—"

"What?" She swung her attention onto him.

He parked and left the keys in the ignition, stepping out to bring in Storm, still in her carrier. She was complaining about being strapped into it, squirming and letting out squawks of frustration.

He walked her into the house and came back with the luggage in time to see Emma drawing Storm from her seat.

"She's not as tough as she acts, you know," she said, patting Storm's back. "Sophie, I mean."

Logan made a wild grab for his temper and managed to keep it.

"With respect, Em, don't ever try to tell me you know Sophie better than I do."

She huffed. "I don't want to see her hurt. That's all I'm saying."

Storm rubbed her face into Em's shoulder, making the whining sound that pitched anyone's nerves to eleven.

"Me, either. So don't put her in a position where she has to defend feeding me dinner. We're trying to be friends. I can't"—he curled his hand into a fist, conflicted—"I can't leave here again with her hating me."

"With respect, Logan," she said in a very patronizing tone. "I know what it's like to hate an ex. I wouldn't spend five minutes in a room with him, let alone work for him and have him in my house for dinner. Even Nolan stays on the lawn. If you know her as well as you say you do, then you would see some significance in that."

Storm reached the end of her patience and gave her dull, sad, tired cry.

Emma crooned something to her as she carried her upstairs.

Logan shouldered Biyen's backpack and brooded as he walked down the hill to Sophie's place, unable to see the right path forward with her. Last night, he had wanted to bring her home so badly, his entire torso had felt carved out and hollow when he had walked away from her.

He refused to take advantage of her, though. And Em's words just now confirmed how vulnerable Sophie was to him.

You always seemed lost. You still do.

That seemed like such a ridiculous thing to say when he was at home in a marina. Professionally, he had known where he wanted to be and got there. He wasn't his brothers, growing up shifting between two homes. He wasn't Reid, whose mother was troubled or Trystan, who had been brought up in two different cultures. Logan was supposed to be the well-adjusted one. Why wasn't he?

He passed the shed, noting that Art's Gator was parked inside it. Weird.

He stepped onto the porch and gave the screen a couple of taps before pulling it open with a screech of the springs.

"Art? It's me." The inside door was open. He caught

the screen so it wouldn't bang as it dropped back into place behind him and hung Biyen's backpack on a hook.

Sleeping? He was in his chair and didn't rouse as Logan came in.

Logan picked up his sunglasses and dropped them into his shirt pocket, glancing again at Art. Should he wake him?

There was such a stillness to the man, however, and such a lack of color, Logan's own heart and lungs and blood cells slowed to a halt.

No.

He walked over to see Art's eyelids were partly open, his gaze fixed. Logan touched his cold hand. No pulse in his wrist, no movement in his chest.

Nooo. Such a waft of pain went through him, he was driven to his knees. Even as he was absorbing that Art was gone, an even more agonizing reality struck.

He would have to tell Sophie. And this was going to hurt her worse than anything else he had ever done.

Chapter Fifteen

SITTING AT THE picnic table that overlooked the marina, Sophie was getting a blow-by-blow of the dinosaur exhibit, complete with Cooper wandering away at one point.

"Did you find him? Is he still lost?" Sophie lowered her cone to tease.

"He was in the gift shop." Biyen's lips were orange and black with the tiger stripe he'd ordered.

"Stopped my heart for a minute," Reid admitted, drawing out his phone and frowning at whatever text he'd just received.

He handed it across to her so she could read that it was from Logan.

Take Biyen. I have to talk to Sophie alone.

Reid looked past her so Sophie glanced over her shoulder to see Logan walking toward them. He had his sunglasses on. His expression was impossible to read, but a preternatural chill swept through her, one that raised goosebumps all over her body.

Reid took his phone back and said to Biyen, "Let's go see Trys. Logan wants to talk to your mom."

"Work?" Biyen asked, making a face.

"Probably. I'll see you in a minute." She swung her legs

out of the bench seat and stood as Logan approached the table. "What's up?"

"Do you have the keys to the store?"

"Yeah." She removed them from her pocket and offered them.

He took them and waved her to come with him.

"You're being weird." The ice cream started to feel like gravel and acid in her stomach. Her hands were going cold so she dropped the cone into the bin near the door and she followed him inside. "What's up?"

He waited until the door jangled closed behind them, then locked it, and steered her to the stool behind the cash desk. He waved for her to sit on it.

"What?" She sat and tucked her feet on the rail, hands in her lap.

"I don't know how to do this, Soph, so I'm just going to say it." He took off his sunglasses, revealing red, agonized eyes. He swallowed. "Art has passed away."

"What?" Another of those chilling sensations went through her. A cold wraith. Something that stole a big chunk of her soul on its way by.

"I found him in his chair. I don't think he suffered. I think he just… stopped living. I'm so sorry, Sophie. I'm so so sorry."

The pain in her hand was him squeezing it, she realized. She didn't say anything about it, didn't try to pull it away.

"But he was fine," she insisted. He hadn't been fine, though. He hadn't been feeling well for weeks. "I was going to take him to the doctor this Thursday."

"I know."

"No." She tried to stand up, but her legs were noodles. When he tried to catch her, to keep her from stumbling, her limbs stiffened in rejection. Not of him, but of this news. "You're wrong. I'll go—"

"Listen first," he said, gentle, but firm, still holding on to her. "I called the hospital in Bella Bella. They said the coroner will come as soon as they can. A couple of hours maybe. You can go and sit in the house with him if you want to, but we can't move him or anything. Okay? Do you understand?"

"You're *wrong*, Logan."

"I'm sorry, Sophie. I'm so sorry."

"Stop *saying* that." She shoved at his hands, forcing them off her, then she leaned weakly against the cash desk, realizing she was shaking so hard her bones were rattling.

She knew how to do this. She'd been through it before. *Get a grip.* But it hadn't been like this. The last time she had had time to prepare herself, even though she hadn't been prepared. Not really. She had known what to do, though, because she and her mother had talked about it. *Gramps had been there to help her...*

Oh God.

Tears formed behind her clenched eyelids, leaking onto her lashes. He wasn't here for her. The emptiness of that emptied her mind, making it impossible to form a clear thought. She couldn't move and only knew she was breathing because each inhale felt forged in fire, each exhale nothing but noxious smoke.

"I'll walk down with you," Logan said, voice sounding far away. "Or I can stay with Art if you would rather not, but I need you to tell me what you want to do with Biyen? Trys will keep him. Or Reid and Emma. You can wait to tell him later if you want to."

Clarity arrived. "No. I have to tell him. Oh my God, Logan." Now it was coming. The agony of loss was seeping past her shock. It was becoming real.

"I know." His arms came around her, holding her together as she shook and fell apart. "I know. I know."

He did know. That was the excruciating, consoling, unbearable truth as she clung to him and massive sobs convulsed her. Many would mourn her grandfather, but no one else would cry this hard with her. While she wet the shirt under her cheek with her tears, he clenched his fingers against her back and released choked noises against her hair. He moaned in anguish, same as her. For long minutes, they were captives racked in the shared cage of losing someone precious.

Eventually, her nose was in danger of running all over him so she broke away and grabbed a tissue.

He took a couple for himself and ran them across his cheeks, eyes bloodshot, face lined as if he'd aged ten years. She must look equally devastated.

"Will you get Biyen for me?" she asked, voice rusty and thin.

He nodded and picked up his sunglasses, putting them on as he walked outside.

This was the worst day of his life.

Logan felt as though he walked through glycerin. The air felt thick enough to make every movement an effort. He could hardly breathe it in. His lungs were clogged and his throat was tight.

"What's going on?" Reid asked as Logan strode down the wharf toward him.

Biyen was on the deck of the *Storm Ridge*, putting on the life preserver Trystan handed him.

"Trystan is going to take me to the fueling station," Biyen said. "Is Mom coming?"

"Bud, I'm sorry. Your Mom needs to talk to you. She's up at the hardware store. Can you go see her right now?"

"Aweh." He glumly handed back the jacket.

"I'll wait for you," Trystan promised.

"What's going on?" Reid asked.

Logan held up a hand as he watched Biyen walk up the wharf and ramp, then break into a run toward the hardware store when he reached solid ground.

"It's Art. Can you…" Fuck this was hard. He scrubbed across his stubbled jaw, trying to make his numb lips work. "The coroner is on the way."

"Oh fuck," Reid breathed.

"Sophie's at the hardware store? I'll go sit with her." Trystan tried to hand off the keys to the *Storm Ridge* to Logan.

"*I'll* stay with her," Logan snarled.

For a minute, they held a staring contest through the lenses of their reflective sunglasses.

"I lost him, too." It felt almost childish to say it, but Logan's grief was too colossal to downplay. This wasn't like losing their father, where they all held a certain ambivalence about the man who had raised them. Art had been his teacher. He had patiently answered Logan's questions and helped him understand this world—the one filled with the smell of salt and the creak of wood and the endless rhythm of tides. When he was here, he was never lost.

There was nothing Logan could do about Art being gone, but he needed to be with Sophie, to look after her while she went through this. He needed to go through it with her.

Trystan gave a jerky nod. Then he abruptly clasped his shoulder and pulled him into a brief, hard hug, smacking his back once.

"I'm sorry, man. We all feel this one. I'll go ask her if she wants me to take Biyen for a while."

"Thanks." Logan swayed after Trystan released him.

Reid's hand on his shoulder steadied him.

"Have you called your mom?" Reid asked.

"Not yet." So many people would have to be told, not just here in Raven's Cove. Art was well known up and down the coast. They had just done this for Wilf, yet Logan couldn't pick apart the steps to figure out what needed to be done first. All he knew was that he had to do it so Sophie wouldn't be burdened by it.

"I'll call Glenda. Go see what you can do for Soph."

Reid squeezed his shoulder. "I'm sorry, Logan."

"Thanks." With boots made of lead, he started back to the hardware store.

THE LOCAL SEARCH and rescue crew arrived shortly after the coroner. They assisted in taking Gramps to the coroner's boat. Given his many health problems, his death was attributed to age and natural causes. Sophie would have to go across to sign paperwork, then he would be cremated and his ashes scattered on the same beach where he had scattered Sophie's grandmother's ashes.

She sat down on the steps of the porch next to his empty lawn chair. She wanted to cry again, but her taps had run dry for the moment. Her eyes were sandpaper, her throat a desert.

Logan sat down beside her. He'd been here the whole time as they waited, neither of them saying much. He'd made coffee and answered a few texts and looked over the copy of the will she had pulled from the freezer.

He had answered the phone a couple of times. Word was getting out. People would start arriving soon. Sophie knew how this went and it was a necessary purge of the collective sadness, but she dreaded it. It made it all the more real.

"We should have given him a last ride in his Gator," she murmured as her gaze fell on the shed and the rickety old machine he had kept running for so long. "To take him to the boat."

"Oh Christ, Sophie." Logan choked out a ragged laugh.

"Gramps would have thought that was funny."

"He really would." His chuckle became a near sob. "I feel like I wasted years when I should have seen more of him."

"Don't do that to yourself."

"I can't help it. I've done a lot of stupid, selfish things."

"Have you? Gosh," she said with mock horror. "Are you human like the rest of us? How sad for you to find out like this."

"Oh shut up." There was no heat in his words. He slid closer and looped his arm around her back, tilting her into him. His hand touched the side of her head, urging her to rest it against him so he could set his chin on her hair. "As much as I told myself I hated this place, I always expected it to stay the same. Everything would be here exactly as I left it if I ever came back."

Her included? Was that what he meant?

She didn't ask, just closed her eyes, allowing herself to lean into his warmth and strength, absorbing the comfort and closeness as they sat in this moment of quiet grief.

"I'm going to move back in here, if that's okay. I can't sleep in that shitty little bed at the house, wondering what you're dealing with over here."

"You'd rather the shitty bed upstairs?" She straightened. "You know Glenda will show up as soon as she hears? I should call her," she realized.

"Reid already did. Between me and Randy, we'll cover

everything at work for the next week or so, but…" His brow furrowed. "I need to be here as much as I can, making sure you and Biyen have everything you need."

This was what she needed, she secretly acknowledged to herself. This feeling that he cared about her. About them.

A movement on the hill caught her attention.

"Here comes Emma." She was glad, but also immediately tired. *And so it starts.* "Will you text Trystan? Let him know he can bring Biyen home?"

"Sure." He patted for his phone.

Biyen had been devastated when she told him. They had talked briefly about whether he should see Gramps a final time and Biyen had decided he preferred to remember his grandfather alive and joking over jelly beans, asking him to fetch his glasses, and admiring a near-perfect score on a spelling quiz.

Biyen would want to be home now, though. And she needed him. He had got her through the loss of her mother, not that she wanted to put emotional labor on him, but she knew his spirit would bounce back quicker than her own. He would help her do the same just by being himself.

She glanced at Logan's haggard profile. Maybe Biyen would help him, too.

"Yes," she said. "Move back in."

THE DAYS PASSED in a blur. Sophie didn't leave the house,

but she was kept busy and rarely alone. Logan moved in. Glenda arrived and took Biyen's bed while Biyen came into Sophie's bed with her. Aside from doing Gramps's laundry and making his bed, Sophie left his room alone. He had always kept it tidy and free of clutter anyway.

Emma spent a lot of time with them, sometimes bringing Storm, often taking home casseroles and other food to store in their freezer since Sophie's was overflowing after the first day.

People came and went in intermittent bursts. They were kind and sorrowful and they all asked her, "What are you going to do now?"

"I haven't thought about it. I just want to get through this week," she kept saying.

It was a lie. She thought constantly about what she would do next. There was no pressing reason to leave, but she didn't have to stay. That was the stunning reality she kept crashing into, each time she walked out of her bedroom and looked through the open door into Gramps's empty room. Each time she reached into the cupboard to check his meds. Each time she saw someone else sitting in his chair instead of him.

Biyen liked it here, but he was a resilient kid who easily made friends. He would fit in anywhere. She was very employable and didn't even have to sell this house. She could rent it out and have a nice little income to supplement whatever life she chose beyond Raven's Cove.

There was no hurry to make a big decision, but she had spent years feeling trapped here. *Left* here. Suddenly, the dam had broken open and she had options. Her thoughts couldn't help but flow outward, exploring all of them.

Why stay when she could go?

"Dude." Logan's deeply ironic voice broke into her weighty contemplations. "I cannot express strongly enough how much that isn't going to happen."

Sophie had come onto the porch with a casserole dish she had just washed.

It was drizzling and Biyen was on a playdate, taking a much-needed respite from people who wanted to hug him and tell him he had to be strong for his mom. He needed to be what he was—snuggly and kind and entertained by the silliest things so she could be, too.

"My son lost his grandpa," Nolan said. "I'm here to see if he's okay."

Sophie set the borrowed dish with the rest of them in the box on the lawn chair and moved to the end of the porch where she saw the two men standing in the spitting rain, Nolan with his backpack on his shoulder and an overstuffed duffel at his feet.

"Biyen is out right now. I'll text you when he's back. Meanwhile, your shit is not coming into that house. It stays on the lawn."

"Is this your house now? You live here?" Nolan scoffed.

"I'm renting a room. And pro tip? If you want to ask Sophie if you can move in, you fucking *ask*. You don't show up expecting it. Especially not before her grandfather is put to rest. Give your head a shake."

"Nolan," Sophie called. "You can pitch your tent by

the shed until after the service." That was tomorrow so it would only be two nights. "If you want to take Biyen camping after that, he'd probably like that."

"I'm staying here," Nolan told her. "Like, I'm going to find a place here so I can *be* here and see Biyen more."

"You and Karma broke up?"

"Yeah."

"Well, you do you, but don't make any big changes on our account. I don't know what I'm doing. We might not stay. I haven't decided."

"What the hell does that mean?" Logan snapped his head around. His face was sprinkled with rain, his hair beginning to flatten.

"Exactly what I said. I don't know what I'm doing. I won't leave you in the lurch at work, but…" She heard the phone ring inside and thought, *Gramps will get it.*

God, grief was so horrible, constantly hitting you out of the blue.

Glenda picked it up, but Sophie moved inside, expecting it was for her anyway.

Chapter Sixteen

"I'll expect you at Christmas unless you call to say you have a better offer," Glenda said when Sophie hugged her on the wharf Monday morning.

Glenda was sailing south with friends; otherwise she would have to spend another three days here, waiting for the ferry.

"Thanks so much for coming. I couldn't have got through this without you." Sophie meant it. In every way possible, Glenda had always tried to fill the void that had been left after Sophie had lost her mom. She loved her endlessly for it.

"Anytime. I mean that." Glenda gave her hair a smooth, exactly as Sophie did to Biyen. "Give Biyen my love."

"I will."

The whole Fraser crew had turned up so Glenda went down the line, hugging Logan and Trystan, then Reid and finally Emma, ending with a kiss on Storm's cheek.

"You all be good now," she said with a wave as they cast off.

"Has she met us?" Logan mused. "That's a pretty tall order."

"Are you sure you're ready to go back to work, Soph?" Trystan asked her as they filed up from the wharf and paused on the grassy overlook. "I'm here until tomorrow morning. I can cover for you today, if you want."

"It's your only day off and your only time with Storm. I'd rather stay busy anyway." And out of that too-quiet house. She was dreading going back to it tonight, even though Logan would be there with her.

He had slept with her last night, asking first if she wanted to talk. She'd said no, she just wanted to sleep so that's what they had done, but she sensed something heavy building between them that she wasn't ready to study too closely.

"But thanks, big guy." She nudged Trystan's arm with her shoulder. "I'm more concerned with what I'm going to do with Biyen once he's back from camping." He was at the awkward age of being too old for a sitter, but not old enough to be left alone for a full day.

"I'll take him," Emma said promptly.

"I know." Sophie smiled at her. "And I won't hesitate to ask you to take him if something comes up, but unless you're starting an out-of-school program, I couldn't impose. Not every day for the rest of the summer." Unless she left. If she left, everything would change.

The marina needed her, though. In a month, by mid-August, the traffic would begin to taper off. At that point, she could consider leaving without causing too much disruption.

She noticed that Logan was looking at her. Did his gaze

briefly measure the distance between her elbow and Trystan's? He was being very circumspect and hard to read.

"Running an after-school program sounds like fun," Emma was saying with a bright smile to Reid. "Technically, I'm not allowed to work until my residency is sorted, but I'm going to look into what's involved. What do you think?"

"I think that would be a great program for you to run at the community hall, not in our basement," Reid drawled.

"There's a day camp in Bella Bella," Trystan reminded Sophie. "My cousin runs it. I'll get a number for you."

"I forgot about that." Some of Biyen's school friends went, but she'd always had Gramps here so she had never looked into it. "Thanks."

"Okay, if I'm not covering for Sophie, how about you and me go for a walk?" Trystan held out his hands to Storm.

She tipped herself from Emma's arms toward him.

"I see who the favorite is today. I'll go to the garden and eat worms, then," Emma said.

"Or we could talk more about this after-school idea of yours." Reid snagged Emma's hand and turned her toward the house. "That sounds like resort business that needs further discussion at home."

"Everything's in the pram," Emma said over her shoulder as she let Reid tug her toward their empty house.

"Spoiler alert," Logan said dryly. "They are not going to discuss business. You know what else is going to happen?" he added with annoyance as he pointed to the office window into Reid's office. "Everyone up there is going to use the new door into my new office to ask me where Reid is."

"You better get to work then," Trystan said as he strapped Storm into her fancy all-weather, all-terrain three-wheeled buggy.

"Does that thing have a seat warmer?" Sophie asked facetiously.

"And heated handlebars."

"Are you serious? The company truck doesn't even have a heated steering wheel!"

"Tiffany ordered it, but I gotta say, I don't hate it." He zipped the bug screen around Storm and straightened. "We're going to see what the trail is like to the upper falls."

"Home before dark or we'll send a posse," Logan said.

"Copy that." Trystan steered the stroller toward the boatyard where a backroad would take them to the trailhead.

"And then there were two," Logan said as they fell into step toward the marina office.

An air of expectation seemed to condense between them. When they came in the door at the bottom of the stairs, they could hear Randy machining something in the shop.

They climbed the stairs. At the top, Sophie stepped out of her Skechers and into her coveralls and boots. She tied the sleeves around her waist and walked in to sit at her desk while she tied her boots.

"Oh, look at your desk." She craned to see through the window. "That looks good."

"Thanks." He hovered in the new doorway between her space and his.

She tensed, really not ready for the conversation he seemed to want.

Whatever he was about to say was interrupted by a knock on the door into the main office. Umi poked her head in.

"Is Reid coming in? I thought I saw him down at the wharf."

"He had to run home for something. He'll be in later."

"Do you want to sign these?" She held up a folder.

"Sure." He nodded at his desk and she left it there, then closed the door behind herself.

"We should talk," Logan said.

"I don't know what to say, Logan." She bent to double-knot her second boot. "I know that if you guys need to sell, it would go a lot more smoothly if you had an experienced manager-slash-marine mechanic in place here. I can't give you that commitment right now."

"That—I mean, you're right, yes. But selling is our problem, not yours. We need to talk about *us*."

Her heart tipped over in her chest. She scratched her forehead.

"I don't know what to say about that, either," she admitted. "Stay with us at the house if you prefer to give the honeymooners their space, but once Biyen's back, I don't want him seeing anything that might create expectations in him."

"Expectations." His blink was a small flinch. "Biyen's not the only one who might have some of those. You realize that?" His mouth was tense, his voice tight.

"What do you want me to say? That I think you and I have a future? Do you see one?" she challenged gently. "Are you going to stay here forever? Here." She pointed at the floor. "Or even in Canada?"

He was leaning on the other side of the doorway, scowling toward the dirty window behind her.

"Even if you said you did want to stay here, I don't know that I do," she said, quiet, but fervent.

"*I* have to stay here right now. You know that, right?" He snapped his gaze down to hers. "But we want to sell. Once that happens, I would go anywhere with you." His cheek ticked. "If you asked me to. I want to see where this goes." He motioned between them.

An urge to weep rose in her. Not hard tears, but quiet wistful ones because this was the thing she had longed for back when she'd been mooning after him as a teen. She swallowed past the ache in her throat.

"But you don't," he said with understated devastation.

"It's not just me," she said in an equally soft voice. "This isn't some sort of retaliation for what happened in the past. If I was making decisions just for me, I could take all sorts of risks. I could let you break my heart again. I already know I can survive it, but I can't do that to Biyen."

That hurt him. She saw him wince again. She read the tightness in his nod of acknowledgment and bit back saying she was sorry. She was only telling him the truth.

He opened his mouth, but there was another knock on the inner door. This time it was Tamara, the receptionist from the lodge.

"Is Reid coming in?" she asked.

"He'll be late," Logan said, leaving the doorway and stepping fully into his office. "What do you need?"

LOGAN OUGHT TO have finalized the redesign of the *Missionary II* by now. He'd fallen behind because of the reno and covering for Sophie and attending the service. Now he'd blown off his first day back at his desk by brooding.

I could let you break my heart again.

He didn't want to break her heart again. Did she get that? He didn't want to break Biyen's heart, either, and it stung really fucking deep that she thought he would.

Did she not have faith in his ability to be a father? Or his willingness to try?

Sophie had come in and out a few times, but had mostly been out, so they hadn't talked again after she had said that.

He couldn't blame her for being so ambivalent about their potential, but it ate at him that she was holding him off. His own feelings toward her were... *Ah, hell.* The word that leapt to mind was *necessary*. He needed her in his life. It wasn't just want, and it wasn't just sex. Everything he did with her felt right. When he thought of her leaving, the world fell away beneath him. He didn't see a future where she wasn't in it.

That was sobering. It was like sailing into mist without radar or charts. He didn't know where he was or where he was going, only that he needed to find *her*.

The door at the top of the stairs opened. He leaned back to see through the window, expecting Sophie, but it was Biyen.

"Hey, bud," he said with surprise. "I thought you were camping. Everything okay?"

"I wanted to see Mom," he said glumly. "Is she here?"

"She's down at the wharf, working on one of the boats. You can wait here if you want to."

Biyen looked around with discontent, then with more interest.

"I forgot you guys did this. It looks weird." He poked his nose into the painted bathroom, then studied the walls in Logan's new office.

"You know what the best thing is? Now we can go steal cookies from the breakroom. Umi brought chocolate chip. You want to get us a couple?"

"Okay. But if I get in trouble, I'm going to throw you straight under the bus."

"As you should," Logan said with amusement, watching him cross in front of his desk.

Biyen came back a minute later with three cookies wrapped in a paper napkin balanced atop a coffee mug full of milk.

"Umi said I could have two, but this is your last one." He held on to the cookie an extra minute until Logan met his gaze and understood he was serious.

"Got it. Pull up a chair, partner." Logan nodded at the chair he'd stolen from the breakroom so he could have a meeting in here if needed.

Biyen scraped it closer to the front of Logan's desk and set his milk on the edge so he could dip his cookie. He sucked the milk out of it and dipped again.

"How come you're home early? Did you get another wasp sting or something?"

"No. I just wanted to see Mom." Biyen's shoulders were slumped, his voice heavy.

"Are you missing your grandpa?" Logan got up to close the door into the hall, instinctively wanting to protect the boy's privacy if he was hurting and needed a cry.

"Yeah, but..." Biyen's dark brows were low and disgruntled as he watched Logan retake his seat. "Are you, like, my mom's boyfriend now?"

"Oh." *Shit.* This was what walking the plank felt like. No way to go backward, nothing good if he went forward. "What makes you think that? Because I've been staying with you guys?" He'd been planning to continue staying there after Sophie's half-hearted invitation. Now he wondered if he should.

"Dad said you were." Biyen looked at the cookie going into the milk.

"Ah." *Be very careful*, Logan reminded himself. He scratched the tip of his itchy nose. "You've done the right thing by asking me directly. I can see where your dad might have got that impression, but that's not what I am." He should be so lucky.

Biyen nibbled off the damp side of his cookie and turned the half-moon shape into his milk. His gaze came up again, wordless. Patient.

Logan tried like hell to remember if he'd left his underwear on Sophie's bedroom floor. He swallowed his dry bite of cookie and set it aside.

"Did you know that your mom was kind of my girlfriend a long time ago? It was before she met your dad. We all grew up here together here, me and her and my brothers."

"I know. But I didn't know she was your girlfriend."

"It was only for a short time. To be honest, I didn't deserve for her to be my girlfriend at all. I was kind of a jerk to her. I was actually a really big jerk. When we all came back here in April, she was still mad at me, but we've talked it out and I've apologized. The good thing is, she forgave me. Now we're friends again." Maybe that wasn't the whole truth, but it was pretty close.

"Your grandpa was also a really, really good friend to me." Good thing he had closed that door. His throat was closing and his chest felt like it was being sandblasted from the inside. "He felt more like an uncle. He was always really patient with me when I wanted to learn more about boats. You know how you feel about dinosaurs? That's how I feel about boats. I've always been crazy about them."

Biyen released a noise of amusement around his soggy

cookie. "I wish someone here knew more about dinosaurs than I do. Then I could just *ask*."

"Yeah, it's pretty cool when someone can help you with your interest. That made Art really special to me. If there is anyone here who feels as sad about him passing away as you and your mom do, it's me. When you're feeling this bummed, it's kind of nice to be around people who feel the same way. In fact, when I'm with you guys, I don't miss him quite as hard." Very true, even if it did make him feel bloody vulnerable to admit it. "And I feel like your grandpa would expect me to do my best to look after you and your mom, now that he can't."

"Dad said you won't let him live with us even though he wants to."

Logan's mouth fell open. He clapped it shut, making himself take a calming breath and think this through before he answered. Sophie had warned him to never get between her and Biyen. She might think Nolan was king of the shitknots, but she never deliberately wedged distance between him and her son, only held her own firm boundaries.

This wasn't about Sophie's relationship with Nolan anyway. It was about what kind of relationship Logan wanted to form with Biyen.

"I did say something like that to your dad," Logan admitted. "I shouldn't have. It's not my decision to make. We all get emotional when someone close to us dies. I felt cranky that day so I was rude to him. He's your dad, though. I like you so I should show your father respect. I will in future."

He was starting to think parenting was one long exercise in self-control and personal accountability with a side of humble pie. It kind of sucked, but as he watched Biyen kicking his feet and frowning thoughtfully, he honestly didn't care what it cost him so long as he protected this kid from life's worst knocks.

"Dad said Mom might move away from Raven's Cove. He said I could live with him if she wants to go live with you." Biyen's eyes were huge now. Worried. His cookie was forgotten.

Logan was instantly livid, not that he showed it. He took another slow breath in and out, even though he could hardly see through a haze of red. What kind of asshole laid something that heavy on an eight-year-old?

"I can see why you wanted to come home and talk to her. That would be a huge decision, but you know what? I am very confident she would never make a decision like that without discussing it with you first. Your mom is the only one who can say for sure what she wants, but I do know she loves the heck out of you. She would never move *anywhere* without you."

"That's kind of what I thought." Biyen relaxed a little and dipped the last piece of cookie into his cup.

Logan could have left it there, but he wanted to be as truthful as possible.

"Look. I want you to know that I care about your mom a lot. If she did want to be my girlfriend, I would like that, but it's a complicated time for both of us. The important thing for you to know is that I'm not a dickhead. If she wanted to become a big part of my life, I would want and expect you to be a big part of my life, too."

Biyen's teeth flashed as he stuffed the final bite of cookie into his mouth. "I don't think you should let Mom hear you say that word."

"Which one?" Logan played dumb. "*Girlfriend?*"

Biyen tucked his chin, looking so much like Sophie at her sternest, Logan had to chuckle.

"Gramps let me swear sometimes." Biyen's chin came up with pride as he gathered his mug in two hands.

"Yeah?"

"Uh-huh." He took several gulps to drain it, then swiped his wrist over his lips. "The d-word. The one like the beaver builds."

"I know that one." Logan nodded.

"The f-word. Fart," he mouthed. "Not the other one." His eyes widened.

Logan would have wondered what sort of fairyland they occupied if Biyen hadn't at least heard the other one.

"And the s-word," Biyen said. "The poop one. Except that was because I dropped my whole tub of LEGO."

"What else do you say when that happens?"

"That's what Gramps said!"

They shared a solid laugh of enjoyment over that one.

Chapter Seventeen

For a kid who'd only been away from her for one night, Biyen sure had a lot to say.

"Logan couldn't decide if the pilot house should be a dining room or a reading lounge and I said why don't you let it be a playroom for kids who want to pretend they're steering the boat? He said that's a great idea and tomorrow I can go inside with him so we can talk more about it if that's okay with you."

"Is this what your job is?" Sophie accused Logan playfully. He was walking alongside them as they made their way home. "You plagiarize other people's great ideas and take all the credit?"

"And all the money." He nodded. "In this case, I will not be compensated, so you're welcome to fifty percent of a big, fat zero."

"Sounds about right."

Biyen started to break into a run, then halted.

"Oh." His shoulders fell. "I was going to go tell Gramps. I forgot he's not there."

"Yeah." A bolt of loss went through her chest, leaving an ache. She hugged him into her side and gave his hair a brief stroke and kissed his crown. "It's okay to forget for a minute. It's something we don't really want to remember."

He nodded. "I'll go tell Dad."

"Go for it."

He ran head, veering toward the tent on the lawn.

"Hey, you should know he didn't just come home because he missed you." Logan lowered his voice and touched her arm, slowing her step. "He asked if I was your boyfriend. Nolan told him you were thinking of leaving and said Biyen could live with him if you decide to live with me."

"Fuck me," she said under her breath, halting in the middle of the driveway. "What did you say?"

"That we weren't together, but if you wanted to be, I would expect he would be as much a part of my life as you are. I mean that, Soph. Take as much time as you need to figure things out, but know that I want you both in my life. I'm late to the party, but whatever this is?" He pointed between them. "It's not going away. Not for me."

She had tried. God knows, she had tried to get over him. To hate him. To exile him from her life. It hadn't worked. Nothing worked.

Biyen laughed and Logan turned his head to look that direction.

"I know this package includes Biyen's father, too. I don't love that part, but I accept it. I won't interfere in how you manage him, but I will hold the line on whatever boundaries you set so tell me what they are and that's where I'll stand."

Was it the romantic declaration she had always yearned

for him to make? No. But it was one of the most meaningful promises he could make to her. He was telling her he accepted how flawed and messy she was. That he understood her.

She wanted to hug him. She wanted him to hold her while she leaned on him and let him give her the sense that, just for a minute, she wasn't alone in this battle called life.

She wanted to tell him she loved him. Because she did. And yeah, he was right. It wasn't going away.

"Thanks." She gave his arm a squeeze and cleared her throat before calling out, "Hey, bud? Can you help Logan start making supper? Your dad and I need to talk."

"What are we having?"

"I don't know," Logan called. "But there is a metric ton of casseroles in the freezer up at the house. You want to walk up with me and see what looks good?"

"Sure. Maybe Emma would let me Facetime Immy and Coop."

"Let's go ask."

Sophie watched them head up the path before turning her attention to Nolan and the latest boundaries she needed to set.

THEY FOUND A vegetarian lasagna and left it on the washer while Biyen used Emma's tablet to chat with the Kiwi kids. The timing had worked out perfectly since they'd just arrived home from their day at school.

Logan was trying to feed Storm while Emma prepared their own dinner, but Storm kept turning her head to where the kids were giggling.

"You got a bad case of fomo, don't you?" Logan scraped the pureed yam from her cheek and pushed it toward her mouth again.

She made a face of disgust and turned her face away, then held out her hand toward the counter. "Ta? Ta?"

"Oh, that's my bad, leaving those where you can see them." Emma noticed the clear box of blueberries she had removed from the fridge in her search for something else. "All right. A few of these, then you eat your dinner."

She washed a small handful and brought them to Storm's tray.

"How's Sophie?" she asked while she was close enough to speak softly.

"It's going to be a constant adjustment." Logan shrugged philosophically. "She"—He glanced at the back of Biyen's head—"She's thinking about leaving," he whispered.

Emma's eyes almost fell out of her head.

"Don't…" He motioned toward Biyen.

"No, I know." She chewed the corner of her mouth, as filled with consternation as he was. "What about…" She searched his eyes, still speaking under her breath. "Are you two…?"

"I'm not sure." It said a lot about how much Emma had become like a sister to him, when he found himself saying, "I don't want to push her because…" He shrugged to indicate his past mistakes. "But I really want to push her."

Em's mouth quirked with sympathy.

"Ta?" Storm's blue hand opened and closed while she looked to the fridge.

"You're not going to eat anything else, are you?" Emma stroked Storm's hair and started to lean down to kiss it, but stopped to look at the smear of orange in her palm. She made a face, then said wryly, "I've picked up worse off you, though, haven't I?"

She went to wash more blueberries.

SOPHIE HAD THE oven preheated when Logan and Biyen got back. Nolan had gone to have a beer with friends so she left Logan making a salad and said to Biyen, "Let's go for a walk."

"Am I in trouble?" Biyen asked as they started toward the beach.

"No. Am I?"

He giggled. "No. But I thought you might be mad that I keep coming home from camping."

"You can always come home to me. I'll never be mad about that."

"Is this our home, though?" he asked with a worried pull of his brow. "Isn't it Gramps's house? Like, what happens now?"

"Oh, bud. I didn't realize you were worried about that.

I should have explained." She was starting to think Nolan had actually thought he was reassuring Biyen when he told him he could live with him. Nolan wasn't canny enough to be passive-aggressive or tough enough to be aggressive-aggressive. He was water, always looking for the path of least resistance.

"Gramps and I made wills after you and I came to live with him. He made sure the house will become mine. There's a bunch of government stuff like probate and taxes and title transfer that I will complain about for ages, but this is definitely our home unless we decide to live somewhere else."

"Do you want to?" His anxious gaze came up to hers.

"I don't know." They reached the beach and stepped down from the grass. Sophie moved to sit on a weathered log. "What do you think of that idea?"

"I don't know." He dropped to his knees and began pushing his hands around in the dry, coarse sand. "Would we live with Logan?"

"Logan doesn't have a house at the moment, so that would be tricky. Also, Logan and I have a lot of things to work out before I would want to live with him."

"He told me that you used to be mad at him and then he apologized." He drew a circle all the way around himself. "Couldn't Dad apologize, then you not be mad at him?"

"He could." He fucking well could and good luck waiting for that particular corner of hell to freeze over. The man had seen absolutely nothing wrong with telling Biyen he wanted to live here with them and putting it on her to tell Biyen that it was never going to happen. "I'm not really mad at your dad. We think differently and that makes it hard to spend a lot of time together. It's like how you and Immy and Cooper got along really well, right away, but you don't always want to play with JayJay, even though he's right here and wants to play anytime."

"JayJay only wants to play video games. I like to go outside."

"Exactly. You guys are different and seeing each other at school feels like enough."

"But you and Logan are more the same?"

"We have a lot in common, yeah. We have similar values." Logan would always pay a bill and pull his own weight. She knew that. He treated her as an equal, whereas Nolan treated her like a convenience store.

"Would you marry him?" Biyen asked.

"Honestly? When I was growing up, I was sure that I would marry him someday. Then he went away and I had you and I stopped imagining that." She wasn't ready to go there again. The ground was still too soft, the bruises still tender. "For me to marry anyone would be a huge decision that would affect you so I would want your opinion before I did anything like that."

"I like Logan." He shrugged. "He's funny sometimes."

Sometimes. Sophie would be sure to let him know it was only *sometimes*.

"Would you guys have a baby?"

"Whoa. Buddy. We are a long way from talking about

babies. Why?" She caught the slump in his shoulders. "Do you want a little brother or sister? Babies are a lot of work, you know. They cry and make a mess."

"I know. Storm cried *so much* in Vancouver. But she was happy to see me when we went over for the lasagna. She tried to crawl to me, and when I sat on the floor by her, she put her head on me." His shoulders came up to his ears and he grinned with goofy pleasure.

"She's a cutie-pie, isn't she?" Maybe it was time to seriously consider a dog.

"I'm old enough to help you with a baby," he pointed out. "I don't want to change one. Not a poopy diaper," he said firmly. "But I could read to them and play with them. I think you should think about it."

"Oh, do you?"

"Uh-huh. Then when I go away to college, you would still have someone here. Unless you were married to Logan. I guess that would be okay, too."

He was such an innocent sometimes, then he turned into Gramps, carrying the wisdom of a lifetime.

"What about Dad?" he asked.

"What about him?" She tensed.

"He doesn't know where to live because you said we might not stay here."

"I know, but he is a grown adult who can make his own decisions. It's okay that he's talking to you about it. I'm doing the same thing, asking your opinion because it affects you, but you don't have to fix anything for your dad. I already told him that if he needs some money for rent, I'll do what I can to help him with that."

"Okay, but like, I like to see him and usually I like camping, but right now I feel like I need to be at home with you. This is a really sad time for us."

God, she loved him. Tears welled in her eyes and her lips started quivering, making it hard to speak.

"It really is," she agreed, mouth wobbling.

"If Logan wants to stay with us, we should let him. He's really sad, too. But Dad keeps trying to cheer me up. I feel like I have to be happy when I'm with him, even though I'm not."

"Not everyone knows how to act with someone who is grieving. It's never easy for anyone. It's okay to tell your dad you want to have some quiet time in your room, if that's how you feel, but we do have to talk about one other thing. Now that Gramps is gone, I can't leave you home all by yourself while I'm at work."

"Logan said I could help him tomorrow."

"I know. That's fine, but if your dad is here, you could spend time with him. Otherwise, what would you think of going to the day camp in Bella Bella?"

"Really? And go on the seabus all by myself?" He perked up with excitement.

"With the other kids who are going, yeah." Apparently, there was a teenaged chaperone who took them across and made sure they got in the van. "They said you could try it for one or two days to see if you like it."

"The one with the nature walks and crafts? Yeah, I want to do that." He nodded.

"Okay. I'll call tomorrow and set it up."

"Can we go home now?" He stood and brushed his knees. "I'm starving."

"Me, too. Let's go."

It was Sunday. Nolan had caught the ferry north this morning, planning to visit friends in Prince Rupert. Biyen had just left for a playdate. Randy was on call at the marina.

Logan was about to start the dishes but caught Sophie looking at him. Heat rolled straight into his groin.

He ran his tongue over his teeth. "You don't need to ask. I'll race you there."

"We can walk." She deliberately brushed up against him on the way to her bedroom. "I don't want any stubbed toes slowing us down."

He mostly slept upstairs, in the room next to Biyen's. They had only managed a couple of quickies in the last week and hadn't talked again about what it meant that they were messing around like this.

It meant a lot to him, not that he was sure how to say so. Or whether he should. He didn't want to pressure her, but he did want her to know this wasn't casual for him. In his mind, she was setting the pace, but they were definitely moving toward a life together.

His heart took a swerve as he fully accepted that. Sophie. Marriage. More kids, maybe? He had never imagined it for himself, but now it was something he saw very clearly. Thinking of it only made him want it more.

He watched her peel out of her T-shirt and drop the cutoff shorts she was wearing, then slip free of her bra and drop her plain, white undies.

"What's wrong?" she asked as she pulled the scrunchie from her kinky hair so the tresses fell around her freckled shoulders.

"Not a damned thing. I'm enjoying the show."

"I don't need to get a tape measure or my laser stud finder?"

"Hello. You got a stud right here." He stripped off his own clothes, catching her eye-roll.

We should talk, he wanted to say, but she sauntered up to him and took hold of his hardening cock. His brain turned to lava and all he could think at that point was that he wanted to be inside her.

He gathered her up, always loving the soft warmth of her over the sturdy resilience of muscle and pure grit. He dropped his mouth to hers, gently feasting, enjoying the chance to take it slower this time.

Or not. She rolled her thumb over the weeping eye of his cock and a sharp sting of pleasure shivered down into his balls. He groaned into her mouth, combing his fingers into her hair to hold her for a long, deep kiss, trying to tell her how important she was to him.

She paused briefly, opening her eyes. She looked very young in that moment. Uncertain.

"Okay?" he murmured.

"I get scared sometimes," she whispered.

Scared that he would hurt her? That he would leave her again?

"Me, too," he admitted, not realizing what he was going to say until it came out. "Because I love you with everything in me and I don't know how to make you believe that."

She bit her lips together, then, "I love you, too."

He hadn't expected such simple words to rock him to his core. He was naked, so fucking naked, but she was right here, naked against him.

She touched the back of his head, urging him to kiss her again and he did, even more reverently than before. He wanted to pour himself into her. This was raw and new and far, far more profound than he could have imagined, but it was good. So good to hold her and touch her and kiss her. To make her twitch and writhe at the lightest touch against her lower spine and to hear her breath catch when his fingers grazed the side of her breast.

They stood there a long time, kissing and touching, maybe using this time to deliberately let the old hurts flow away because guilt and pain and shame were all there, imbuing each caress as he tried to heal up each scar he had left on her, then it slowly became only her. Sophie and heat and need.

She was wet against his fingers as he caressed between her thighs. He was so hard he thought he'd burst when she rolled the condom on him.

They went onto the bed together, moving in unspoken

tandem. She parted her legs and he guided his tip against her hot, slippery flesh. Then he was sinking into her heat in one slow thrust.

Her legs came around him and he leaned on his elbow while he tucked her securely beneath him. He loved sex with her. He wanted to do all the filthy things, but those could wait. Right now, this was all he needed or would ever need. Just this quiet, perfect connection with her.

They moved a little here and there. Her inner thigh stroked his waist and her foot rubbed his leg. She sifted her fingers through his hair and sucked on his tongue until he could have come from that alone.

He nibbled her bottom lip and her earlobe and circled her turgid nipple with his thumb. He loved how plump and swollen her nipples got when she was this aroused. They were so sensitive that his lightest touch made her breath hitch and her pussy clench around him.

"I need to come," she gasped.

It only took a few strokes for both of them. Not even hard ones. He ground his hips into her pelvis and they were tossed into the throes of a long, incredible, simultaneous orgasm.

Chapter Eighteen

LOGAN WENT TO the bathroom. When he came back and stretched out beside her, he exhaled pure satisfaction and reached for her.

Sophie snuggled into his warmth. It was a cool morning and the sex heat was dissipating from her bloodstream. She wanted the closeness, too, but as perfect as this felt, she was troubled. Unsure.

Did she believe Logan loved her? She didn't disbelieve him, but she wasn't ready to take on faith that they would last a lifetime. She couldn't tie her whole future—and her son's—to his. Not on one albeit wish-fulfilling declaration.

"I think…" She came up on an elbow and set her hand on his chest, kind of bracing him for what she needed to say. "I think I need to at least try some time on my own, the way you did when you left here."

His mouth tightened with dismay.

"I know that's not what you want to hear." She set her lips against his shoulder. "But I came back for Gramps and I don't regret that, but that hobbled me from exploring other opportunities or my own potential. I'll still have Biyen, obviously, but I think it would be good for him to see a broader world than this one, too. Please don't be mad."

"This is one of those no-win situations, Soph." He picked up her hand and wove his fingers through hers, bringing their joined hands to his mouth so he could kiss her knuckle. "I hear what you're saying. I get it. I'm not going to lay a guilt trip on you or try to convince you differently, but don't you dare take my accepting what you're saying as me not caring. It fucking kills me that you would leave when I can't."

"Oh, Logan." She dipped her head against his shoulder.

"But listen." He cupped the back of her neck.

She lifted her face.

"I'll wait," he vowed.

The skewed sensation in her chest sharpened. "I can't ask you to do that. I won't."

"You're not. I'm telling you that's what I'll do. As long as it takes for you to come back to me."

"I didn't wait for you," she reminded with a cringe of anguish. She had gone straight out and got herself pregnant with Biyen, maybe not on purpose, but the sex had been pursued out of spite.

"You did wait, though." He shifted his touch so his thumb could trace her bottom lip. "You waited all through school, then gave me a chance and I blew it."

"This isn't a test, Logan."

"I know. It's not one for you, either. I'm telling you how it is for me now. I can't imagine anyone else in my life. Maybe if you marry some other guy and start having kids with him, I'll have to think about moving on, but I can't see myself with anyone else. If you need to try another job or give Biyen more options or visit foreign countries purely for the experience, do it. Make the life you want for yourself. When I'm able, I'll join you."

"Just like that?"

"Why not?"

Because no one had ever given her that much consideration. She didn't know how to accept it.

As she fought to swallow the lump in her throat, the sound of heavy footsteps landed on the porch, followed by an abrupt knock on the door.

"Soph? You home? It's me."

"Me" could have been anyone in Raven's Cove, but they both recognized Trystan's voice and shared a grimace. *Busted.*

SOPHIE THREW ON a robe, then gathered her clothes and slipped out the door and into the bathroom, calling out, "Gimme a sec."

Logan pulled on his boxers and shorts, then shrugged on his T-shirt as he walked out to the kitchen. He would take the hit broadside to spare Sophie whatever reaction Trystan was about to have.

As glowering went, Trystan was actually better at it than even Reid. It was the scarcity of his bitchiness. Reid had a resting scowl-face and overused it, diluting its power. Logan was too vain to risk the frown lines so he avoided frowning.

Trystan was more impassive than both of them, rarely riled by anything and even when he was, he didn't let it show. Thus, when he pulled out a sneer of profound disgust, you really felt it.

He underlined this one with a contemptuous, "What the fuck? We talked about this."

"Swear jar's on the counter." Logan nodded. "That one costs a dollar. Don't ask me to cover it. I'm tapped out." He held up his empty hands.

"No fucking doubt," Trystan muttered, glancing at Art's chair and wincing. When he looked back at Logan, his demeanor was all put back together into its tidy packsack. "We need a family meeting at the house. Why are you still staying here?"

"I'm paying rent."

"Is *that* what you were doing?"

"Oh fuck off. What's the meeting about?"

Sophie came out of the bathroom and said, "Don't give Logan a hard time. I'm a grown up and make my own choices."

Trystan flicked a look between them, maybe trying to decide whether to condone this affair or continue to give his brother grief about it. He decided to go back to glowering, this time at Sophie.

"What is this I hear about you leaving?"

"Is *that* why you're here? I thought you were the sex police doing random stop and frisk. Who told you?"

"Randy was on the dock. I asked him how you were

doing, and he told me you're leaving. That was news to me, and I wanted to know more before I chat with the Brothers Grimm about something else." He flicked another look at Logan.

"I'm *thinking* of leaving," she stressed, but sent Logan a fresh grimace of apology. "I didn't mean for it to get all over the island. Nolan has a big mouth and Biyen's been processing a lot of feelings about a lot of stuff. It's not something I'm doing tomorrow, but, you know, maybe before school starts? I realize that could make it harder when you sell the resort. Randy is a great mechanic, but he doesn't have the management skills. Logan will be here, though."

"*Will* Logan be here?" Trystan turned a cool look on him, one that judged him no matter which way he jumped. If he went with Sophie, he was abandoning his family. If he stayed, he was screwing with Sophie's heart all over again.

"I would love it if you minded your own business." Logan folded his arms. "Try it once. For me."

"Your business is my business when it's a fucking mess on the floor that I have to clean up," Trystan snapped.

"Wow. Since when—"

"Oh stop it." Sophie waved her arm between them to break their locked stare. "You're both big men who can pee really far. Do you want coffee, Trys? We have some leftover cabbage rolls from last night. Mrs. Sokal made them. They're really good."

"No, thanks. I texted Reid that we need a meeting. You might as well join us. Hear it from us instead of the grapevine."

"Something about Tiffany's sister?" Logan asked with concern.

"No, I caught up with Eli Schooner in Ocean Falls. His mother is on the tribal council here in Bella Bella. Things are moving forward with their Truth and Reconciliation settlement. He told me they want to make an offer for the resort."

"Holy shit." Sophie's eyes went big.

"We have to do that." Logan was equally stunned by the news, but he immediately knew there was no other option. They already leased the land from the Heiltsuk Nation, but the buildings and business had always been run by settlers.

"My thought exactly," Trystan said. "We need to talk with Reid about what that might look like."

"It looks like us being hobbled by bureaucracy," Logan said with anticipated frustration. "What if we need the money sooner than government wheels can turn?"

"That's a given," Trystan muttered while they put on their shoes to follow him up to the house.

"Biyen will turn up here soon," Sophie told Emma as she came into the kitchen with Logan and Trystan. "I texted Quinley to tell him I was here."

"Oh sure." Emma was sprinkling seasonings over a raw, plucked bird that was already in a roasting pan. "Do you want to stay for dinner? I expected Trystan to join us so I took out this chook and look at it. It's a monster. I'm starting to think it's a turkey. How do you tell?"

"You read the label when you buy it."

"The label said it came from a farmer's market in Port Hardy. Glenda must have brought it."

"Helpful." Sophie leaned closer to give the bird a sniff, but only caught a noseful of thyme and rosemary. "We'll find out when you cook it, won't we?"

"Soph?" Logan's hand squeezed her waist as he came up beside her. "You want something to drink? Beer? Wine?"

"Day drinking on a Sunday sounds like a nap before dinner, but sure. White, please."

"I could have sworn you two already had a nap," Trystan said under his breath, but not really, as he reached into a cupboard and handed a glass across to Logan.

"You got something to say, sailor?" Sophie challenged.

"Wouldn't dream of it. Em? Wine?"

Emma was swinging her head like she was watching a tennis match.

"Thanks." She nodded at Trystan.

He passed a second glass to Logan and closed the cupboard. "Where's Reid?"

"Getting up from his own nap, I imagine," Logan drawled.

"Getting Storm up from hers," Emma corrected indignantly. Then in an aside to Sophie confided, "But I have made the bed twice today." Her gaze flickered curiously between her and Logan.

"I only make it when I put clean sheets on it," Sophie said. "Otherwise, I'm wasting time I could spend sleeping in it."

"Ta." Emma smiled at Logan as he set her filled glass within reach.

"I'll get the beer then?" Logan said to Trystan. "Since you're going to stand around sulking because you didn't get your own nap today?" He turned and went down the stairs.

"Sometimes I feel so sorry for Glenda," Sophie said to Emma as she rolled the stem of her glass between her fingers and thumb. "Can you imagine eighteen years of these three locking horns?"

"She's a saint. Is the oven hot, Trys? Can you—Oh, thanks."

He opened the oven and took the roaster from her, sliding it onto the rack.

"Hopefully we'll eat by six. Who wants scalloped potatoes?" Emma asked.

"Who doesn't?" Sophie asked, eyeing Trystan, trying to tell if he was genuinely annoyed at her and Logan hooking up or using it as an excuse to needle his brother.

"I'll start those in a little bit, then." Emma washed her hands and was drying them on a tea towel when Reid walked in with a sleepy Storm.

"Oh, hello," Sophie said warmly.

Storm wasn't interested in a bunch of people, even the ones she loved. She turned her face away and sucked her fingers, head resting trustingly on Reid's shoulder.

"She hasn't had her coffee yet," Reid joked, rubbing her

back. "How are you, Soph?"

"Well enough." She kept to herself that she cried every morning when she woke and remembered all over again that Gramps was gone.

He nodded and asked Trys, "So what's up?"

"Let's sit down."

Logan returned with cans of beer and handed them out as they all took seats in the living room. Logan sat on the floor in front of Sophie, resting his back against the front of the sofa, something that Reid noted with a glance toward Emma.

There was a round of pop-hisses as they opened their cans, then Trystan caught them up on what he'd learned. "I'm confident they'll pay market value," Trystan wrapped up, speaking to Reid. "I know you were hoping we'd be turning a profit by end of season, and that competing bids would drive up the price once we put it up for sale."

"I was, but there's no other option now. We have to sell to them. It's the right thing to do," Reid said matter-of-factly.

"I agree." Logan nodded. "Let's set up a meeting with the council to tell them we agree in principle. Do you want one of us to make that call?"

"I can do it," Trystan said.

They all sat in silence for a minute, absorbing this sudden new direction.

It made sense that the Heiltsuk Nation take over the resort, which was smack-dab in the middle of their traditional territory, and provide opportunities for their own people to run it. Sophie would happily provide any support they needed through the transition. This development also relieved her of any sense of disloyalty toward Wilf and the marina, but did it also spell freedom for Logan sooner than either of them would have expected?

A bubble of pressure began to form inside her, one filled with expectations she wasn't sure she could meet. He had promised to wait for her, but she was still really, really fearful of trusting him.

The silence had Storm picking up her head with curiosity. She held out one arm toward Trystan.

"Tst."

"Show him what you can do." Reid sat her on the floor.

Instead of crawling to Trystan, she grinned at Logan and clambered against his leg, clumsily trying to crawl up him until he gathered her to stand on his thigh. His big hands caged her stiff body, supporting her as she practiced her wobbly balance.

"Where would we go?" Emma asked Reid with a worried look.

"This does shake things up, doesn't it? We have to stay in BC until…" He nodded at Storm. The gesture encompassed the finalizing of Emma's residency so she could adopt Storm with him. "Then… I don't know."

"Do you have any sense of timing?" Logan asked Trystan.

"It's the government. Took twenty years for them to get this far," Trystan said with a twist of his lips. "Two hundred and twenty, if we're being honest."

No kidding. Sophie experienced a pang of white guilt and hurt on Trystan's behalf. He had never talked much about how the residential school system had affected him and his mother's family, but she knew his grandmother had been taken in the Sixties Scoop. As a mother herself, Sophie couldn't fathom having her child snatched from her home or what it would do to Biyen to be wrenched from all he knew.

The Truth and Reconciliation process with the federal government was intended to repair some of the damage done by colonial settlers to the many Indigenous nations across Canada, but it was a slow, painful process.

Sophie was glad the Fraser boys were willing to make a deal so unhesitatingly, though. No amount of money could erase the history and damage done, but it was a step in the right direction.

Logan lifted Storm to growl into her stomach, making her release a baby giggle that was highly infectious, putting smiles on all their faces.

Poignant ones, though.

These siblings had finally come together into something like a family. Now they were talking about leaving the place that had been their childhood home and fragmenting again.

The front door suddenly flung open. Biyen burst in, panting as though he'd run across the entire island. "Is my mom—Oh. Hi, Mom."

"Hi, bud. Knock first when you come in here, okay? Close the door and take off your shoes. Did you have fun with JayJay?"

"Yup." He toed off his shoes and came around the sofa to drop on his knees beside Logan, ignoring all the adults to say, "Hi Stormin' Norman McDoorman." He touched Storm's hand, inviting her to grab his finger.

Storm toppled herself straight at him, steadied only by Logan's firm grip on her.

"Oh no, I'm being attacked. Help, help!" Biyen folded himself to the floor and pulled Storm onto his chest, hugging her there while he rolled his head as though helpless. "She's going to eat me and kill me. Logan," he gasped. "Save me."

"I'm paralyzed by baby spit, bud. You're on your own." He kept a hand outstretched, though, ready to protect Storm's head if she rolled off Biyen and into the edge of the couch.

"Mom. I'm your *only* son."

"That we know of."

Biyen giggled and Logan sent her a pithy look over his shoulder.

She thought, *This is what I want.* It was simple and maybe even clichéd, but she wanted that man and that boy and a baby who would turn into another child who played silly games with all of them. She wanted these people around her, maybe not keeping her safe from the hardships of life but buffering her from the worst of them. Supporting her through them. She wanted all of this so badly, she could hardly see straight.

"Ack!" Biyen turned his face and stuck out his tongue.

"Why does she always put her fingers in my mouth? And why are they always *wet*?"

"She's looking for food," Logan teased. "Don't you have some old gum in there she could have?"

"That is so gross. I changed my mind. I don't want a baby brother or sister."

There was another potent silence.

"I'm just kidding," Biyen said, misinterpreting the reaction around him. He snuggled Storm more closely. "I wish Storm could be my sister."

"Then I would have to marry Reid and I think Emma would have something to say about that," Sophie said lightly. "Biyen and I have been talking about a lot of different things lately, while we consider our next steps, haven't we?" She spoke to Biyen, but she was addressing the high interest that was charging the air around them.

"Yeah. I kind of want everything to stay the same, but I guess it can't," Biyen said.

"Mouths of babes," Emma murmured.

"What do you mean?" Biyen gave her his quizzical look, then looked at Storm's mouth.

"It's just a saying." Emma smiled. "But Storm is probably hungry." She rose to lift her off Biyen. "Would you like a snack, too? Dinner won't be ready for a few hours."

"Yes, please. Can I feed her?" Biyen stood up to follow Emma into the kitchen.

"You can try. She thinks she can feed herself so it gets pretty messy."

"That's okay. We're all bad at stuff until we learn. We

still need to try."

"That kid is a walking fortune cookie," Reid said, watching him go.

"Right? He's smarter than the three of us put together," Logan said.

"I would love to argue with you," Trystan said. "It's kind of my favorite pastime, but I gotta agree with you on that one. You've done good, Soph. You know that, right?"

"Oh, don't," she said, starting to choke up. She snatched up her wine and shuffled her legs past Logan so she could rise and follow Emma to the kitchen.

"No, listen." Logan caught her hand, keeping her from walking away. "We're serious. He's got Nolan, we know that, but we're here. Anytime. No matter what."

No matter whether she was involved with him or not, that's what Logan was saying, and it really meant so much to her, she could hardly bear it.

"Seriously, my emotions are *right here* these days." She pulled her hand free and set it in front of her nose. "Please don't do this to me right now." She took a step, then made herself say, "But also thank you." She hurried away.

Chapter Nineteen

THE MEN WENT over to Bella Bella the next day, borrowing a bowrider so they didn't have to wait for the seabus. Biyen was at day camp and Randy had taken a few days off to visit his girlfriend in Nanaimo, promising to cover the weekend when he returned. That meant Sophie was on her own.

She was making her way to the office after a quick tape of a leaking pipe on a pleasure yacht when Quinley called down from the patio of the pub.

"Hey, Soph."

"Hi, Quin." Sophie paused. "What's the soup today?"

"Corn chowder. Are you still renting a room to Logan?"

"Yes. Why?" She narrowed her eyes. *Say something, Quinley. I dare you.*

"Someone looking for work." She tilted her head toward a woman in her early twenties who was seated near the rail. The woman offered a friendly, hopeful smile.

"I was telling her we can always use another server, especially in the summer, but finding a place to stay is tough. I wasn't sure if you were taking other renters or…" Quinley tucked her tray under her arm.

"No. Sorry." Sophie wrinkled her nose in apology.

A brief moment of déjà vu struck as she met the stranger's gaze. She seemed familiar, but Sophie knew all the locals along with the regular boaters and fishermen. By this point in the season, she also recognized the faces of temporary workers in the area like nurses from Bella Bella who might come into Raven's Cove on a day trip for a change of scenery.

This woman, with her brown pixie cut and pointy chin and possibly mixed-race skin tone, didn't immediately tweak as someone she'd seen recently. Maybe she had come through last year. Students and backpackers sometimes traveled up the coast on working holidays, only staying long enough to make ferry fare before they carried on to their next destination. Maybe she had done something like that and came back because she liked it here.

"Logan is a family friend," Sophie explained. "That's the only reason I'm giving him a room."

"Is that the reason?" Quinley said pithily.

"Are you seriously going to start up with me again? After we can finally have a civilized conversation?"

"Are you seriously going to get another stick up your ass over a *joke*? Lighten *up*, Sophie." Quinley stalked away.

"I'll take my chowder to go," Sophie shouted after her. *Cow.* "Sorry about that," Sophie muttered, embarrassed by her outburst. "We're old friends. Maybe look on the board at the grocery store. Sometimes locals advertise a room there." She started back to the office.

"Wait. Excuse me!"

Sophie halted and turned back to see the customer had come to stand at the rail.

"Is your renter Logan *Fraser*?" she asked.

"Yes. Why?"

"I was hoping to meet with him." She bit the edge of her lip. "Is he around?"

A sticky, suspicious nausea settled into the pit of Sophie's stomach. Her thoughts leapt to Florida and all the types of history Logan might have there. It was a long way to chase a man, but that only made this woman turning up here all the more threatening.

"He's over in Bella Bella for the day. He'll be back later."

"Oh. Figures. I came from there this morning." She shook her head at her bad luck. "Are both his brothers with him?"

"Yes. Why?"

Her expression became conflicted. She looked as though she wasn't sure what to say or how to say it.

Sophie searched her expression, growing ever more prickly, but Quinley came back outside with the coffee carafe to refill the woman's cup.

"Moody is putting your chowder on the bar," Quinley told Sophie sullenly.

"Thanks." She'd have to pad her tip so Quinley didn't tell the whole island she was on her period.

"Can I get you anything else?" Quinley asked the customer with more warmth, drawing her back to her table.

"No, this is perfect. Thank you."

Sophie glanced back once as she went around to the pub entrance, not sure why she was disturbed by the unfinished conversation. She had work to get back to, though, so she paid Moody for her chowder and took it to her desk. Kenneth had left a pile of receiving documents that needed checking and entering so she sat down to do that while she ate.

She was finishing up both when she thought she heard Emma's voice in the main office. She leaned to glance through the window into Logan's empty office just as a rapid knock sounded on his internal door.

"Come in," Sophie called.

Emma pushed in, clutching Storm. She was crying. Not Storm. Emma.

"Em. What's wrong?" Sophie rose and moved into Logan's office.

"She's here." Emma pressed the door closed with her backside, hugging Storm with two arms, tears still streaming down her cheeks.

Storm was cheerfully oblivious, smiling at Sophie and showing off her teething ring.

Sophie spared her a quick smile and caught Storm's batting hand, but asked Emma with concern, "Who?"

"Tiffany's sister! Cloe. She came to the house and said, 'You must be the nanny.' She wanted to see Storm."

"Oh my God. Okay. Sit down." Sophie guided her into Logan's fancy office chair and fetched the box of tissues from her own desk. "What did you do?" she asked as she brought them back.

"I said she could wait on the deck and that Reid would be home soon. Then I got Storm up from her nap and snuck her out the basement door. Reid's not back yet. I don't know what to do, Sophie! What do I do?"

OUT OF RESPECT for their meeting, Logan and his brothers turned off their phones when they sat down with the tribal council.

There was a strong representation of women on the council including the chief councillor, Hazel. She was a cousin by marriage to Trystan's mother and welcomed him warmly before introducing the rest of the councillors.

Only nine of the twelve had been able to make it on short notice, but Trystan had assured them they only wanted to impart information today.

"You know my brothers," Trystan said, introducing them.

The conversation was social for a few minutes as everyone used this opportunity to catch up on family news, especially contemporaries from their school days, learning who had settled where as they married and started families.

Logan kept wondering what selling to the Heiltsuk Nation could mean for his own future with Sophie. Would knowing the sale was a sure thing make it easier for her to leave? What about him?

He wasn't sorry he had told her he would wait for her. It was the raw truth, but he didn't *want* to, especially after last night. They'd all ribbed each other over dinner and he had realized he liked being together with everyone, especially with Sophie and Biyen at his side. It made him feel calm and centered in a way he couldn't recall experiencing, at least not since he was a very young child.

That was the life he wanted to start right now, with both of them, but he couldn't. Not while he had commitments here. Selling to the Heiltsuk Nation was the right thing to do, but it could drag on for years. That worried him.

Nevertheless, as the chitchat wrapped up, he was in complete agreement when Trystan stated their support for the Hieltsuk Nation to purchase the resort buildings along with taking over the running of the business.

"We'll need time, though," Tracy, one of the councillors, said. "Not just for working out the fine points, but for the actual transition."

"Of course," Reid agreed.

Raven's Cove already employed a number of people from the Heiltsuk community, but Umi held the most senior position as their head of accounting. Finding the right people for other skilled positions like marine mechanic and hotel management could require a couple of years of training before they were ready.

"For the moment, we'll focus on finishing our existing projects, so an appraisal can be done at the end of October," Reid said.

That was a deadline the three of them had agreed on when they had decided to stay and work out the season, but now there would be added pressure to ensure everything was turning a profit by then. Otherwise, they'd risk being valued too low to recoup what they had invested in the resort to keep it going through this summer.

It meant Logan was definitely not going anywhere until that happened and also made the pending departure of Sophie more impactful.

He put a brave face on it, though, smiling with everyone else as they rose to shake hands.

Moments later, they all turned on their phones. Logan's heart stopped as he picked up Sophie's message.

Tiffany's sister is here. She's at the house. Emma and Storm are in Reid's office.

Reid must have had a similar message from Emma because he barely bit back a curse.

"I'm so sorry. We have a family emergency," Logan explained to the concerned councillors as he showed Sophie's text to Trystan.

"No one is hurt," Trystan assured them grimly after reading it. "But we have to hurry back. Please excuse us."

Reid was already pressing his phone to his ear as he headed for the exit, asking Emma, "Are you okay? What exactly happened?"

They hurried back to their borrowed bowrider, an agile vessel that Logan leapt in to helm, pushing it fast and flawlessly across the passage. None of them spoke. Reid was so far into himself, he looked like one of those black holes that swallowed themselves. Logan felt exactly the same. He knew what they were all thinking: They had royally fucked themselves with the promise they had just made.

All of their capital was now tied up in the resort until such time as the wheels of bureaucracy released it. How the hell would they fight a custody battle if they were drawn into one?

By the same token, they'd had a good case for keeping Storm when Reid and Emma had planned to keep Storm here, in her own home. With this agreement today, Storm's eventual home was in the air with the rest of them. If they were prepared to move Storm elsewhere, why couldn't she go with Tiffany's sister to California or Chicago or wherever the hell she'd come from?

This was an added blow to his already painful sense that his life was fragmenting in all directions. Logan had never suffered mal de mer, but he nearly threw up off the side of the boat during that short journey. His protective instincts were jangling so hard in his ears, he couldn't hear the high-pitched roar of the boat's engine.

She can't have her, was all he could think. *She can't.* Storm belonged with Emma and Reid.

She belongs with *us*.

Chapter Twenty

SOPHIE ASKED UMI to open Reid's office so Emma could wait there. Reid kept it stocked with snacks and diapers along with Storm's saucer and playpen. Also, it allowed Emma to see the wharf so she could watch for the men to return.

Sophie made Emma some tea, texted Logan that they should come home ASAP, then walked up to the house. She didn't know what she would say or do, but she didn't think leaving a stranger alone there was a good idea.

What she did know, deep down, was that it would be the woman from the patio of the pub. And, even though she was expecting to find her there, it still took her aback to see her asleep on one of the loungers on the deck.

Sophie didn't like to leap straight into wondering if someone had a drug problem, and tried not to judge them if they did, but Tiffany's sister had had some kind of trouble with the law. That's why lawyers hadn't been able to reach her to tell her that her sister had died.

Her sister had died. It had happened only a few short months ago. Sophie swallowed the burn of her own very fresh grief and reminded herself to tread carefully.

She knocked on the glass door, then slid it open. "Hi,

again."

Cloe sat up, startled and disoriented.

"Um." She frowned with confusion, looking back into the house before trying to make sense of Sophie not being Em.

"I'm Sophie, Emma's friend. You're Cloe? Tiffany's sister?" She moved close enough to offer her hand.

"Oh, um, hi. Yes, I am." She rose and shook Sophie's hand. "Tiff and I had different dads." She said it in a rueful, philosophical way that suggested it was something she had had to say often so she just pushed it right out there. "That's why she was so much taller than me. Older. Blonder." She waved at her hair. "I cut all my blonde off, actually." She seemed really nervous.

Sophie could have told her that blended roots were kind of a theme in this family, but only said, "I can see your resemblance to her."

Tiffany had had the same gray-blue eyes and the slight overbite that made her smile very cute and engaging.

Cloe was still trying to catch her bearings after waking up so abruptly, hugging herself and blinking dazed eyes, brow creased with anxiety.

Now that Sophie got a better look at her, she saw Cloe's blue jeans and striped T-shirt were a little too big on her and well worn. So was her small backpack. She looked tired. Not from one lost night of sleep, but months of them. Weary tired. Sad. And vulnerable.

Since the men had arrived to look after Storm, Tiffany's sister had loomed as a huge threat, distressing Emma and the Fraser men with what could happen if she decided she wanted custody of her niece.

It was still a mystery what she might expect or why she had shown up here unannounced like this, but Sophie instinctively felt for her. She seemed at a loss and Sophie kind of wanted to hug her.

"Do you live here?" Cloe asked with sudden shock. Her expression grew appalled as she seemed to realize Sophie was the woman she'd seen in coveralls earlier. "The server at the pub told me this was where Reid Fraser lives. Was she messing with me to mess with you?"

"No." Sophie had to chuckle at that. "I mean, she *would*. We behave worse than our children, as you witnessed. I do, anyway." She hitched her shoulder in self-deprecation.

"Been there," Cloe said wryly and they shared a smirk.

"No, this is the Fraser house," Sophie assured her. "They should be back soon. They won't mind that we're here, waiting for them."

She checked her phone and saw Logan had texted, *Leaving now.*

"Do you want water? Coffee?" Sophie waved toward the kitchen.

"I have a glass of water." Cloe picked it up from the table next to her lounger. "The nanny gave it to me then… I don't know where she went." She craned her neck to peer with puzzlement toward the glass doors. She grimaced as she caught her reflection and smoothed her shirt. A sigh of defeat followed. "I didn't mean to fall asleep. The ferry dropped me off really late last night. I knew I had to get into town to catch the water taxi, but I didn't realize how far I'd have to walk."

"You walked?" It was three kilometers.

"I waited until it started to get light. I thought I'd see traffic by then, but nope. It was just me and whatever those noises were in the bushes. I'm a city girl." She pulled her bottom lip wide in a grimace. "I was thinking the whole time, *So this is how I die.*"

"At least it wasn't raining," Sophie said with amused sympathy, thinking, *Help. I like her.*

"It was actually kind of peaceful, once I got to the wharf." She looked out at the water. "Listening to the waves and watching the sun hit the other side of the bay."

Passage, but Sophie didn't correct her.

"I should have called first, instead of showing up like this." Her brows crinkled with consternation. She picked at a hangnail. "I don't actually have a phone. It's a whole thing. My life has been really complicated since before Tiff passed. Now that I'm out of that vortex, I wanted to get away and"—she sent a wistful look toward the upper level of the house, then down toward the marina and village—"I wanted to see where she was."

Storm? Or Tiffany?

"I'm really sorry about Tiffany." Sophie waved at the lounger where Cloe had been sleeping, inviting her to retake her seat while she lowered onto the one beside it, facing her. "You probably have questions. Is that why you're here? To find out more about what happened? I'll tell you anything I can."

"I know what was on the news, that it was a plane crash." Cloe sat and looked into her half-empty glass. It wobbled as her hand began to shake. "Wilf was the pilot. He was flying them to Vegas to get married. Tiff asked me to meet them there and come back with them, but I couldn't. Was he nice, though?" Her worried gaze came up. "I know he was a lot older than her. I was surprised when she told me she was pregnant, but she was really happy about it."

"She was," Sophie agreed, even though it had been in the way of certain women who went into a blissful state of denial when they got pregnant. *This baby won't change my life. I can do it all.* Then the baby arrived and everything changed and it nearly broke them in half, they were so unprepared.

But Sophie was trying to be kind so she didn't get into how Tiffany had seemed at the end of her rope from the jump. Looking back, maybe her underlying tension had had something to do with her sister's legal troubles? Sophie didn't think it was appropriate to ask what kind of "vortex" Cloe had been spinning in all this time.

"I knew Wilf my whole life," Sophie volunteered, smiling with genuine affection. "My granddad worked for him and so did my mom. He gave me my first job, then hired me again four years ago when I came back here. He was colorful." Understatement. "Not the most sentimental person. He definitely fancied himself both a man's man and a ladies' man, but he was funny. Generous. Definitely too old for Tiffany, but he really cared about her."

For all the talk among the locals that Tiffany had been his nurse and Wilf her purse, they had seemed to have more between them than that.

"Wilf had always had a vision for this place that he never quite got off the ground. Before Tiffany came along, it was falling into disrepair. She saw its potential, though. She was willing to do the work to make it happen. That put a fresh sparkle in his eye. I think, in some ways, he saw their marriage as a do-over." Sophie hadn't completely put that together until she said it, but it rang true. "He had a couple of failed marriages behind him. His sons were grown and gone. He had regrets about his relationships with them." Estranged. Strained. "When Storm came along, he wanted to get it right. He was definitely happier with Tiffany than he'd been in a long time."

"And Tiff? She was about to marry him so she must have been in love? Did she really want to stay here with him forever?" She sent another uncertain look toward the marina and its desolate location.

"Honestly? I wish I'd made more of an effort to get to know her." It was true. Sophie regretted now that she'd remained so aloof, but she'd only been back a couple of years when Tiffany had arrived and started changing things. Her defenses had been pretty high.

"Tiffany was the boss's wife and was pushing to make all these changes," Sophie noted with a quirk of her mouth. "I don't know why we all felt so threatened by that. Small town, small minds, I guess." Also, Tiffany had skimmed all the working capital from the marina, making Sophie's job infinitely harder, but Tiffany hadn't been trying to line her own pockets with it.

"She seemed to want to make an impact. I could see that she was excited to do something big and meaningful. There's nothing wrong with that."

"That sounds like her." Cloe was smiling, but her eyes were wet, her voice husky with emotion. "She always had goals. She always wanted to be taken seriously and prove herself. I miss her so much." She wiped under her eye. "I should have come when she first told me she was pregnant. She wanted me to, to help when the baby came." Anguish flashed across her expression. "Is she here? Storm?" She looked longingly toward the upper floors again.

"Emma took her to Reid's office." Sophie pointed vaguely toward the village. "They're married now. Did you know that?" she asked tentatively. "They want to adopt Storm."

"Oh. No, I didn't know." Cloe's voice went hollow. She seemed rocked by that news, gaze turning inward. "That's why I'm here. I mean, not to adopt her. To see her. To make sure she's okay."

"She is. Emma really loves her. So did Tiffany. She absolutely loved Storm to bits. It was just a lot for her to help Wilf and keep house and have a new baby. This place is very isolating. That was hard on her. That's why she hired Emma. Then, when the plane crashed, Emma spent so much time with Storm, she bonded with her."

She's her mother. Sophie wanted to hammer that home, but made herself keep the kid gloves on.

"If only"—Cloe fisted her hands against her brow, elbows on her knees—"I wanted to come. I just *couldn't*."

It almost sounded as though Cloe wished she had been here so her niece would have come to her after the crash, instead of Emma. Sophie felt a tug of empathy for her, but her loyalty was to Emma and Reid all the way.

"Here come the men," Sophie noted with relief.

Down at the marina, the Fraser brothers were tying off the bowrider and striding purposefully up the wharf.

LOGAN MOVED WITH grim purpose alongside Reid and Trystan, crossing the village grounds and climbing their drive.

Fear nipped at Logan's heels. Fear that he was losing everything that meant anything to him. He could stand to sell Raven's Cove, even though it had come to feel more like home in the last months than it had during any other time in in his life.

He was losing Sophie, too. He had no right to hold her back so he had to let her go.

But Storm? If Tiffany's sister was thinking she could take her, if she somehow managed to, what would he have? His brothers both had lives to go back to. Even his mother had built a new life without him.

He would wind up alone in some far-off place, trying to convince himself he was happy when he knew damned well he was faking it. As they pushed into the house,

Sophie opened the door to the deck off the kitchen.

"We're out here," she said cheerfully.

Cheerfully? Didn't she realize his entire fucking world was ending?

They filed out to see a woman in jeans and a white-and-yellow striped T-shirt rise from a lounger and wipe her palms nervously on her hips. She offered a tentative smile.

"Hi. I'm Cloe, Tiffany's sister." She sounded sheepish as she offered her hand.

"Logan." He was closest so he shook first.

She didn't look much like the blonde, very white bombshell that Tiffany had been. She was pretty, but shorter. The shape of her eyes were Storm's all the way, but there wasn't much else that resembled his little sister. Logan wasn't about to ask her to prove her identity, though. Not when he'd been asked in the past if Trystan was his "real" brother.

He was. And, lately, Logan had started to *feel* like he had brothers.

The tension in his chest cranked up another notch.

"Reid." He stepped forward and gave her hand one firm pump.

"Trystan."

"Hi." Cloe's intimidated expression became more starstruck. Color blossomed in her cheeks. "I, um, recognized you as I was getting off the water taxi this morning. I didn't mean to stare. I should have said something, but… I was nervous. This is a lot." She withdrew her hand and swallowed, flicking her gaze between all three of them.

Logan had noticed Trystan's distraction this morning, but any sign of male interest was gone from Trystan's expression now. Good. They needed to find out what the hell this woman wanted, then get her on her way. "Should I call Em?" Sophie asked in a helpful tone.

"No," they said together.

Logan glared at her. Did she not understand the stakes. Em had been *scared*. *He* was.

Sophie rocked back on her heels, seeming shocked by their collective hostility.

"What are you doing here?" Reid asked Cloe gruffly.

"I'd like to see Storm if that's okay." Her blue-gray gaze shifted from man to man to man. She tried to stand tall and lift her chin, but she was too petite to pull off looking tough.

"Why?" Reid folded his arms.

Logan couldn't help mirroring that and so did Trys.

"Because she's her *aunt*," Sophie said with admonishment in her tone. "Can you guys all take one big, collective breath? You're coming on *really* strong."

"Sophie," Logan warned in a lethal voice. "Do you remember telling me never to get between you and Biyen? This is like that." He would do *anything* to keep his sister. She must understand that.

"I'm not telling you what to do with Storm. I'm telling you to bleed off some of that testosterone you're all gassed up on. You're being scary when Cloe is a perfectly normal person who does not have a gun to your head. Everything is fine."

"No, it's not!" Logan said and, damn. That had come out really fucking loud.

He knotted his fists and looked to the water, instantly embarrassed. He tried to get a grip on himself, but it wasn't easy.

"Logan," Sophie said gently as she came to stand in front of him.

He could feel everyone staring at him. Her hand settled lightly on his chest where his heart was slamming with fear. Real fear.

"It's going to be okay, Logan."

"No, it's not," he insisted, reaching for her upper arms. Her firm biceps were so *her*. Everything about her was so fucking precious and so fucking *not* his. His eyes were hot, his throat aching all the way down into his chest. "Art is gone, you and Biyen are leaving, we're selling this place, and now *Storm*? These two will fuck off." The way they always had. "There won't be anyone left."

He felt like such a tool, standing here already lonely, but he was. His nose was stinging and his throat was aching and he couldn't stand it.

And there was Sophie looking up at him with her fall-into-me eyes.

Into the resounding silence, he heard the front door open.

"Reid?" Emma called from inside the house. "I saw you all come back."

"I'd really like to see her," Cloe pleaded in a soft tone. "She's all the family I have left."

Logan's heart lurched. He knew exactly how that felt.

He couldn't deny her. When Reid glanced at him and Trys, Logan nodded jerkily to allow it.

"WE'RE OUT HERE, Em," Reid called over his shoulder.

Sophie could feel the tension in Logan, as though he was braced for a body blow. She hadn't appreciated how threatened these men were by Cloe. How threatened Logan was by her own talk of leaving.

She pressed herself to his side and looped her arms around his waist, trying to reassure him with her closeness. His arm curled firmly around her, but she thought she detected a tremor in him. He watched closely as Emma came warily out the door onto the deck, Storm in her arms.

Reid lifted his arm in invitation, and Emma tucked herself against his side.

Cloe's gaze was fixed on Storm. Her voice shook as she said to Emma, "I should have called first, so you weren't blindsided when I showed up on the doorstep. Sophie told me you two are married and want to adopt her?"

"Yes," Reid confirmed with a nod.

"I'm not here to get in the way of that," Cloe's brow tilted in anguish. "I'm not actually in a position to take her. I came to make sure she was in good hands, that's all. It looks like she is." She was eating up Storm's fine hair and big blue eyes and teething-rashed cheeks with a poignant smile.

"I shouldn't have run out like that. I panicked." Emma's face was still splotchy with tears, but she offered an uncertain smile to Cloe.

"It's okay. I…" Cloe trailed off and tilted her head down, trying to catch Storm's eye. "Hi, baby."

Storm smiled, watching this new face curiously.

"Will you go see your Auntie Cloe?" Emma asked Storm, starting to offer the baby to her.

Cloe held out her hands in invitation and Storm wavered. One little hand clutched onto Emma's shirt before she changed her mind and decided she would meet this new person.

"Oh, hello." Happy tears came into Cloe's eyes as she drew Storm into her chest and lowered onto the lounger, holding her in her lap. "It's very nice to meet you." She took one of Storm's hands and tucked her thumb into Storm's curled fist.

Sophie's heart was going to break wide open. She looked up at Logan and saw his nostrils were flared with his effort to hold on to his emotions.

"Let's get everyone some drinks," she murmured, nudging him.

He nodded jerkily and guided her ahead of him through the door. When she would have paused in the kitchen, he snagged her hand and drew her all the way down the stairs into the cool basement.

"I don't think anyone wants a beer this ear—"

He stopped at the bottom of the stairs and his arms came around her. Hard. So hard her breath was squeezed out of her. Her nose was mashed against his chest.

She turned her head so she could hear his heart thumping and feel it against her cheek. She wrapped her arms around his waist, holding on to him just as tightly.

"It's okay, Logan. She's not going anywhere." Had he not heard Cloe say she wasn't in a position to take her?

"It's not her I'm worried about. I mean, I am, but—Christ, Sophie. Why is everything so hard?"

She brought one hand up to cup his jaw. "I don't know, but we'll figure it out and get through it."

"How? How am I supposed to do it without you?" He closed his eyes in remorse. "I can't ask you to stay. You *know* that. But I already miss you. It's eating me up." His anguished profile looked out the window to the lawn.

And she thought, *Why?* Why would she put him and herself through a separation when being together was what they both wanted?

Was she trying to prove she could live without him? She could. She had already done it. And, as painful as his coming back into her life had been, it had also been the most alive she had felt since he'd left it eight years ago.

As for Biyen, she trusted Logan to be a good surrogate father to him. He was already knocking it out of the park with his kid sister. *He* might not have much faith in himself in that role, but she did.

"You don't have to ask," she said gently. "I make up my own mind, and I've decided that I love you. I've always loved you." Her heart was swelling too big for her chest, constricting her throat so her voice grew thin and strained.

"I'm going to stay with you. *We* will. When things change, we'll make a decision together to do something else."

"Sophie—" He was holding her arm too hard. Her muscles were twitching in protest, but she understood he was hanging on tight because he was scared. Terrified. "What if love isn't enough? It wasn't enough for Mom. It sure as hell didn't fix Dad."

"You're right," she said with a little laugh. "Love isn't a magic potion that fixes everything. If only! All it does is cushion you against the hard reality of life. Did Glenda loving the shit out of you and your brothers fix you guys? Heck, no. You're all a walking disaster, but imagine how you would have turned out if you hadn't had her."

"And you." He finally released her arm and brought his hands up to cradle her face. "Your love shaped me. I know that because when I lost it, nothing felt right. And when I had you back, really back in my life and my heart, the world made sense again. I will do anything for you, Sophie. Anything. I thought if I let you go, it would give me time to get my shit together. To become the man who deserves your love, but… I don't think I care who or what I am if you're not here for me to *want* to be better."

"Why don't you think you're enough as you are?" She cocked her head, genuinely baffled by this. "Look at all you've accomplished, Logan. You're ready to go to war for a baby you didn't know a few months ago. You were right there for me, every minute, when Gramps died."

"I should have been with you when you lost your mom. I should have been better sooner."

"Me, too," she assured him. "Do you want me to start wondering if I'm good enough for *you*?"

"No." He scowled and folded his arms around her shoulders, pulling her closer. His lips touched her brow. "You're perfect."

"See, that's how I know you really love me." She smiled shakily into his collar. "You have become oblivious to the fact I'm actually very catty with messy hair and I smell like diesel most of the time."

"I love the smell of diesel on you." He drew back a little, expression shifting between tender and grave. "Do you really think we have a shot at forever, Soph? Because that's what I want. You. Forever."

"Oh God, you idiot." Tears rose in her eyes. "It's what I've *always* wanted."

"Still?" he asked very, very softly while his thumbs grazed her cheeks and his mouth lowered to hover against her lips.

"Always," she repeated.

His mouth settled across hers and something cleaved open in her chest. Not breaking. Blossoming. Opening and offering herself to him even as she felt something huge emanating from him. His chest swelled against hers. His breath hissed as though he was enduring something equally cataclysmic.

He slid his hands low in her back, arching her into him as he feasted on her mouth, but he gave, too. It was back and forth, greed and generosity, lust and love. Rough hunger that turned fond and soft as he stole a few last kisses before lifting his head.

"We have more to talk about, but I should…" He cocked his head toward the stairs.

"Yeah, I should get back to work before my boss docks my pay."

"Your boss is too scared of losing you to do any such thing. You've kind of got him over a barrel, actually."

"Oh? Good time to ask for a raise, then."

"You realize you take home more than I do, don't you?"

Because of all the overtime, she presumed. "That's nice to know, but I still want a raise."

He rolled his eyes. "We'll talk about that later, too."

Chapter Twenty-One

THEY CAME UPSTAIRS to find everyone had moved into the kitchen. Storm was in her high chair. Emma was sneaking spoonfuls of orange mush into Storm's mouth around the plastic spoon she was clutching and sucking.

Trystan and Cloe were sitting at the small kitchen table, each with a cup of coffee before them, each wearing an air of tension like a pair of cats that were pretending the other didn't exist and wanted them to know it.

Logan recalled again that Trystan had been checking her out this morning, which actually wasn't like him. He could have the sex life of the average rock star if he wanted it, but he never had. So what was going on here? *Hmm.*

"We thought you two left." Reid was leaning his hips on the counter by the coffeemaker, holding his own cup of coffee.

"I am leaving," Sophie said. "My boots are up here." She motioned to the door.

"You'll come back for dinner?" Emma's voice edged toward shrill. "I've invited Cloe. Trystan will be here, too."

"Sure. Thanks. Why don't you see what's left of those casseroles in your freezer. Keep things simple." Sophie glanced around the stiff tableau.

Cloe was looking at her as though she was losing her only friend.

"Let me know if you need anything from the store," Sophie added.

"Will do. And you'll bring Biyen," Emma said.

"Sure will. See you later." Sophie lifted her hand in a wave. Logan made a grab for her before she walked away.

"What?" she asked with surprise.

He stepped closer and dropped a kiss on her lips. "I'll see you later."

"We do that now?" she asked, trying to sound amused, but her cheeks went pink with pleasure.

"We do. What time is Biyen back?"

"Usually around four."

"I'll meet him."

"Thanks. I love you." She threw that at him in a dare, laughter glinting in her eyes.

"I love you, too," he said unhesitatingly, clear and firm and loud enough to be heard in the other room. *Take that. I'm not a coward.*

She bit back a smile and didn't look back as she closed the door behind her.

When he returned to the kitchen, every pair of eyes was on him.

"You're all going to pretend you were the last to know?" he asked blithely.

"I'm guessing I was," Cloe said under her breath in what would have been a solid joke in this crowd, but they were all still trying to figure her out.

She wasn't in a position to adopt Storm. That was good. Right?

She dropped her gaze from looking at Logan and stared into her cup.

Logan helped himself to a coffee mug and Reid moved out of his way so he could pour. "What did I miss?" Logan asked.

"Not much," Reid said. "Cloe was going to explain why she couldn't come sooner, but Storm got hungry. We decided we all wanted coffee, then you and Sophie came up to neck in the living room."

"If he thinks that was necking, then I'm sorry, Em," Logan said with mock concern. "I'll have The Talk with him later and explain special hugs."

"No need," Em said firmly. "Reid has all the bases covered. *All* of them," she added in a deliberately throaty voice.

"Thanks, babe. You too," Reid said with a slow wink at his wife.

"Ugh. Okay, you win," Logan groused. "It's like thinking about my parents having sex."

There was another snort of amusement from Cloe. A wistful smile played around her lips, but she kept her attention on her coffee.

"Seriously, Logan," Reid said more gravely. "I had to leave because of my mom. You know that, right? I could have handled things better back then. We all could have. And I definitely could have come back for a visit before you left, but I didn't have much choice about leaving when I did."

"I know. Don't worry about it." He would rather pull his own teeth than admit he had missed that lunkhead after he had left for university, but at least Reid wasn't mocking him for his outburst earlier.

"I kept trying to do an Everglades episode," Trystan said. "Producers never went for it, but I could have pushed harder."

"You guys have lives. It's fine," Logan insisted. "I wasn't suggesting you didn't care, just because you had other things to do."

"This has been a rough year," Reid said. "None of this has been easy on any of us, but we're not going back to the way it was. I don't intend to, at least. I can't speak for Trys. Remember Em reading us the riot act because we hadn't seen each other in years?" He smirked and glanced over at Trystan.

"Which lecture was that?" Trystan asked, eyeing Emma. "There've been so many, they all blend into one."

"You're about to hear another one," Emma warned tartly. "And you"—she pinned Logan with a stare—"can expect a thorough interrogation about your intentions before I sign off."

"I'll pass." He plucked one of the folded face cloths from where she left a stack on the counter and wet it. "I mean, I'll pass the test." He wrung it out and brought it to the high chair. "Is she done?"

"Yeah, she's lost interest. Thanks." Emma took the dirty dishes to the sink.

"Here it comes, kid." Logan started with her hand.

Storm was already turning her face away, squawking her displeasure.

He got the job done as quickly and gently as he could, but she was still mad at him, reaching for Trystan as soon as her bib was off and the dirty tray removed.

"How long are you staying, Cloe?" Logan asked as he wiped down the tray. "*Where* are you staying?"

"I was so intent on getting here, I haven't planned beyond this moment," she said with an unsteady smile. "I'd like to stay a few days and see a little more of Storm while I work some things out, but I wasn't able to find anything to book ahead. I was hoping one of you would know of something that isn't too expensive?"

They all looked at each other. The decent thing would be to offer to let her stay here. She was Storm's aunt, but Logan didn't expect Reid to put her up in this house. They didn't know yet how far they could trust her.

"She can stay aboard the *Storm Ridge* until I leave on Wednesday. It's my day with Storm tomorrow anyway. We can spend the day with her." He directed that at Cloe.

"Really?" Cloe lit up like a Christmas tree. "Thank you. I'd love that. Would it be possible to shower there before dinner? I've been traveling."

"Use the shower here. I'll show you." Trystan rose to lead her downstairs, handing Storm to Reid on his way, saying, "She needs a change."

"Of course she does." He wrinkled his nose at whatever perfume was coming off the kid.

"So," Emma said to Logan as footsteps traveled up and

down the different sets of stairs. "Let's talk about Sophie."

"Look at the time." He consulted his bare wrist. "I have to meet Biyen. I'll see you at dinner."

"Hey, Biyen."

"Hi, Logan"—Biyen halted as his feet hit the wharf—"where's Mom?"

Shit. It struck Logan that the last time he'd come to the wharf for Biyen, it had been because his grandfather had died.

"She's totally fine," he hurried to assure him. "She's in the office. We'll go see her in a sec. I wanted to talk to you about something, first. You got a minute?"

"It's summer vacation. I have nothing but time."

"Live it up, kid," Logan said with amusement. "You want to ruin your dinner with an ice cream?"

"What's for dinner?"

"I don't know. Emma's cooking."

"I'll risk it."

What a nut.

Biyen started to run, but remembered he was still on the wharf and held himself to a walk until they were at the ramp, then he grabbed both sides of the rail and ran up fast enough to make his backpack woggle.

They bought their ice cream, then walked to the picnic table to eat it, both sitting with their backs to the table so they could face the water.

"What's on your mind?" Biyen asked as he slid his tongue around his scoop of tiger stripe.

Only that every time this kid spoke, Logan was more certain he was making the best decision of his life.

"It's something we talked about once before. Your mom and I have decided we love each other. I wanted to ask you what you thought about my asking her to marry me."

He sat up taller. "Are you going to have a baby?"

"Are you asking me if I'm pregnant? No. And we'll circle back to that because I feel like you're missing some information."

Biyen giggled. "I mean *Mom*."

"Your mom is not pregnant, but if she wants to have a baby, I'd like that. What about you?"

"Mmm-hmm." He nodded. "Then Storm would have someone to play with who is her age. That will be really confusing, though," he said with a wide-eyed look of befuddlement. "If you're Storm's brother, but you married my mom, what would the baby be?"

Whatever it wants to be, was the correct answer, but they'd circle back on that another time, too.

"Storm would be the baby's aunt and she would be your step-aunt."

"But she's a *baby*." He was so tickled he couldn't seem to lift his cone to his lips. "Auntie Step Storm." He giggled through his orange-milky lips. "Like, Anti-Storm. What's that? A nice day?"

Logan chuckled, as amused by the boy's ability to entertain himself as he was with the things coming out of his mouth.

"What I'm hearing is, you don't mind if I ask your mom to marry me. Is that right?"

Biyen cocked his head to the side. "Would we still live here?"

"For a while, but I don't know about forever." Logan sobered. "My brothers and I have made some big decisions that will affect where we live eventually." It bothered him that that part wasn't settled, but he didn't feel as adrift now he knew Sophie would be with him no matter what. "I think for the time being your mom wants to stay here, so I'll move downstairs into her room. With her," he clarified as Biyen's brow quirked up.

"You guys should sleep in Gramps's room. It's bigger."

"Maybe we will. I'll let your mom decide that. She might want to keep it the way it is for a while."

"Yeah. That's okay." He nodded. "At least now I can have my playroom back. Yesss." He pumped a fist.

"You know, I was actually worried you might be upset about this. I thought you might be wishing your mom would marry your dad."

"Not really. Mom likes you better. When she talks to Dad, she sounds really annoyed. When she talks to you, you guys laugh." He shrugged, then sat up taller. "Hey. Am I ever going to get to see the *Storm Ridge*?"

"Have I got news for you, kid. We can get the key from Trys and take it for a spin right now if you want to."

Chapter Twenty-Two

Dinner was a meal of stilted tension broken by moments of free-flowing laughter.

Cloe said she was planning to head north at the end of the week, taking the ferry to Prince Rupert and onward to Alaska where she would look for work, so Logan was finally able to relax and quit worrying about her intentions.

When Trystan and Cloe left for the marina, he walked home with Sophie and Biyen.

"Straight into the shower, then bed, buddy," Sophie said as they entered the house. "It's already late and it's a work night."

"Day camp is like going to school." Biyen set his backpack on the chair and emptied it onto the table. "I wish Gramps was here so I could sleep in."

"I have to work, too, bud. Otherwise, I'd stay home and sleep in, too," Sophie said.

"Same," Logan said. "But let me know if there's a day you could spend with me on the *Missionary II*. Then you wouldn't have to get up so early."

"I wish I could," Biyen said in a very mature and resigned way. "There's a lot going on at day camp. They really need me."

Logan looked at Sophie.

"I know," she mouthed.

"What's keeping you so busy?" Logan was compelled to ask.

"We go for walks with the elders and we each learn our facts and tell them to the rest of the group when we get back. Did you know that the bears take the salmon into the forest and that's what helps the trees and berries and everything grow the next year?"

"I didn't know that, but it makes sense," Logan said.

"That bears are gardeners?" Sophie asked. "They don't have thumbs. How can they have green ones?"

"Oh, Mom." Biyen shook his head pityingly and went to shower.

"That kid should have his own stand-up special."

"I know. He—" She held up a finger as the shower came on, then hissed, "So what do you think of her?"

"Who? Cloe? I think she's broke." He moved Biyen's water bottle and lunch container closer to the sink, then hung his backpack on its hook. "It seems convenient that she can't talk about why she was in police custody. I'd like to know more."

"It's legal stuff."

"It's shifty. And she doesn't have a phone? Or a home to go back to?"

"She's trying for a fresh start. I think she's been through a lot. Don't forget she lost her sister."

"It sounds like she's on the run." Logan was concerned about that. "And Trystan wants to spend the day with her?

Since when does he invite anyone but Em to go along on his hikes?"

"He's got strong feelings about family," Sophie defended.

"Mmm." Or, more specifically, strong feelings against denying family the chance to know each other. Logan respected that, but he was counting the days until Cloe left.

Biyen came out a minute later, scrubbed shiny, hair every which way, wearing his jammie shorts with a short-sleeved shirt with the Spiderman logo on it.

"Teeth brushed?" Sophie asked.

"Uh-huh. Hah." He offered a breath for her to check.

"Minty fresh. Wonderful. Sleep tight. I love you." She hugged him.

"I love you, too."

He looked at Logan.

Until now, it had always been a cheerful, "Good night." Now Logan felt the significance of his decision sinking into him.

"What's your preference? Hug? Fist bump?" Logan crouched down on one knee.

Biyen held out his fist. They bumped and exploded it.

"Good night, bud."

"G'night." Biyen started to turn toward the stairs then spun back. "Wait. Are you—" He rushed up to Logan again.

Logan bent and listened while Biyen's hot breath tickled his ear.

"Yeah, I'm going to do that right now." His heart started hammering with nervous excitement. "I just have to go up to my room for a sec. Do you want to stay?"

Biyen looked between Logan and Sophie, then nodded shyly.

Logan went through the door. The stairs creaked under his weight as he climbed them, then thudded as he came back.

"What are you two up to?" Sophie asked as he reappeared.

"I wanted to do this right," Logan said.

He went down on one knee again.

"Oh my God." Sophie genuinely nearly fainted. She stacked her hands over her heart, but it was going to fall out anyway.

"Mom gave this to me before she left last time." Logan's hands were shaking along with his voice. "She said you were the only person she could imagine wearing it so if I ever wanted to give it to you, I could."

He showed her the ring. It was a simple gold band with a single, pretty round diamond set in four gold claws. She recognized it as one Glenda had worn for a solid twenty years. Wilf had given it to her.

"Will you marry me, Sophie?"

Every part of her was tingling as though swirling in a whirlwind of sparkling thrill. Skin, scalp, blood, bones, they were all filling with pure joy. Her throat was tight, her heart battering, her eyes growing hot and wet.

She looked to Biyen. He was watching closely, grinning ear to ear. He nodded enthusiastically and the tears in her eyes grew so thick, she couldn't see him.

Her chest expanded with happiness. Her breath was forgotten, her voice nonexistent, but somehow she conjured the words she had practiced every night for her entire childhood.

"Yes, Logan. I will marry you."

Epilogue

February, the following year…

THE HOWLER MONKEYS were greeting the day as Sophie came on deck with mugs of coffee for Logan and his crew—Tyrone, Emil, and Lionel, who had all signed on as line handlers, wanting the experience of traversing the Panama Canal before they brought their own vessels through.

They had slept aboard last night, everyone retiring early so they leapt on the coffee due to the dawn start, not because they were nursing hangovers. All three men were known to throw lavish parties on their luxury yachts, but they were keeping it tight, wanting to take good care of Logan's sailboat.

Two of them were previous clients of Logan, and Lionel was an experienced boater who was in talks with Logan to design something new for his growing family.

Logan was still in the process of rejigging his company to work out of Canada, but aside from a small going-away party with a handful of friends, he didn't seem to have any strong feelings about leaving Florida for good. Dario, the advisor who would help guide them through the canal, was aboard as well. He accepted a coffee with a happy nod.

"We got a one-day pass," Logan said, catching her up.

Sophie wasn't sure if she was happy or disappointed, since it was common to spend the night tied up outside the channel in Lake Gatun.

"We're going to raft up with that cruiser and—there. That cat." He pointed to the catamaran that was motoring toward them.

"What's my job, Logan?" Biyen asked.

"You have three important jobs. The first one is to stay on the bow. Things could get busy and I need to know you're in a safe spot."

"You got it." Biyen gave him an enthusiastic thumbs-up. "What else?"

"Take lots of pictures. We're all going to be working, so we can't be looking around at the scenery."

Sophie had initially planned to be a line handler, but Logan had persuaded her to be a spare in case there were injuries. Things could get hairy if anyone lost their focus and failed to maintain tension or relieve it. Boats could swivel and cause the raft to shift. Hands could get caught. He also wanted her eyes on Biyen and needed her to prepare meals and keep everyone hydrated. It was going to be a long day. "Should I use my iPad or the camera?" Biyen asked.

"Both."

"Consider it done."

Tyrone, a linebacker, sent Sophie a perplexed look.

I know, she conveyed with a shrug.

"And the third one?" Biyen asked.

"Keep being awesome," Logan told him.

"You, too, Logan. That goes for everyone. Let's have fun today." Biyen gave a big, straight-armed clap of his hands. "I'm going to put a few things in my backpack so I'm ready for a day in the bow."

"Sounds good, bud. Put on some sunscreen, too." Sophie skimmed his hair as he went by. "I've got a breakfast casserole thing that'll be ready in about ten minutes. There's a vegan one for you and Biyen, Emil."

"Thanks, Sophie. Am I going to be the first to say it?" Emil scratched his hair and looked around, then directed his thumb at Logan. "I didn't expect this guy would ever get married, let alone marry this well. You're great. Your kid is great. He is a very lucky man."

"He knows," Logan said dryly, sending her a look that warmed her through.

He didn't get a chance to say anything else. It was time to tie up to form their raft. Logan's boat was deemed the most powerful so they were designated as the middle boat. Dario took the helm.

Once the men were fed and the galley tidied, Sophie joined Biyen in the bow.

Initially, Logan had planned to get his boat to Canada by himself, but it had morphed into this family trip. They had planned for it to be a disaster. If Biyen had grown tired of being cooped up on a boat, or Sophie sucked at homeschooling, or Logan got antsy with extra people in his space, they would have booked the necessary flights. Nolan had been prepared to come get Biyen if Sophie wanted to stay with Logan, and Reid and Emma were champing at the bit to keep Biyen in Raven's Cove if he wanted to be back at school with his friends.

So far, those conversations hadn't come up once.

They had left right after Christmas and the trip was exceeding all of their expectations. Biyen's Spanish was already better than Sophie's. He soaked up new information like a sponge, and he was giving Trystan a run for his money when it came to vlogging about his days.

Trystan, of course, was boosting his profile with shares to his own multimillions of followers, which certainly didn't hurt.

They were missing everyone and Sophie looked forward to getting home, but it was really nice to have this chance to gel as a family. Logan was in his element, happier on the water than anywhere else. Every night, after they made dinner and cleaned up, he and Biyen plotted their next day's course while Sophie read a book. Read. A. Book. Sometimes with a glass of wine, if she had her period.

Today, she didn't have her period. It had been a few days, actually. This morning, when the curiosity had got the better of her, she had used a test she had bought on their last day in Florida.

On the inside, she was freaking out, but she made herself stand at the rail with Biyen as they inched toward the first lock, trying to decide if telling Logan would be a distraction he didn't need today.

Logan came to stand beside them. "All good?"

"Uh-huh." Biyen took Logan's hand and said, "But I

think you should know that I love you for bringing me on this trip."

A sound came out of Logan as though he'd been punched in the gut.

"Buddy," he breathed.

"Yeah?"

Beneath his smile, Logan was so moved, his eyes misted. He swallowed.

"I love you, too. You and your mom. I love you both the most." Logan looked up at her and his emotive look faded to alarm.

"Are you crying? What's wrong?" He reached out to hold her arm, Biyen still between them.

"I wasn't going to say because I want you to be able to concentrate today, but…" She could hardly speak through her trembling lips. She had to run the heal of her hand under her eye. "It's not just us. We're three and a bit. Soon to be four."

"Are you kidding me?" Logan's jaw dropped. He grabbed onto the rail as though he needed to steady himself.

"You're gonna have a *baby*?" Biyen grinned up at Logan, but he soon got squashed as Logan pressed forward to hug her, seeming to burst a ball of sunshine through her whole body.

"Wait. Ack! Let me out!" Biyen wiggled free and clasped onto the rail. "Okay, now you can hug and kiss."

They did.

The End

If you enjoyed *Forgiving Her First Love*, you'll love the other books in…

Raven's Cove series

Book 1: *Marrying the Nanny*

Book 2: *Forgiving Her First Love*

Book 3: *Wanting a Family Man*
Coming soon!

Available now at your favorite online retailer!

Acknowledgement

While this story is fiction, it takes place on the unceded, traditional territory of the Heiltsuk people.

Exclusive Excerpt: Wanting a Family Man

Book 3 in the Raven's Cove Romance
Keep reading below this is coming soon!

OF THE MANY mistakes Cloe Vance had made in her twenty-three years, showing up in Raven's Cove unannounced was arguably one of the worst.

She'd been scared, though. Scared someone would tell her she wasn't allowed to come. Scared no one would tell her where her niece was. Scared that her phone would be tapped and tracked. Heck, she was even scared that she was becoming paranoid, which said everything about the state of her life these days.

She was a mess, which was exactly what she'd been trying to avoid when she'd aged out of foster care and started adulting. She had been determined to make smart, practical choices. She hadn't wanted to end up like her mother, yet here she was—broke, homeless, and fleeing a dangerous relationship with a Very Bad Man. She wasn't doing drugs to numb the pain, but she could see how alluring that type of escape could become.

She saw clearly how *all* the rotten stuff happened. When you felt like you were utterly alone in this world, it took only a little misplaced trust and allowing hope to override your gut. The next thing you knew, you had no job, no home, no friends. She had even lost her sister, which wasn't directly connected to her actions, but it felt as though it was.

This new perspective humbled her. It made her hate herself for judging her mother all those years ago. Being frightened and lonely wasn't a crime.

Being an accessory to money laundering was, though.

Somehow, Cloe had avoided being charged with that. She had cooperated and was still in a daze that she had walked out of the courthouse with her freedom.

Within days, she had liquidated her few remaining possessions and bought a bus ticket north. It was strange to be so untethered. As she had sat on the ferry from Port Angeles, Washington, into Victoria, Canada, she had felt like a castaway bobbing on an open sea.

She still felt adrift, even though she'd since left that ferry for a second bus that had taken her to the top of Vancouver Island where she had climbed aboard a second ferry that took her even farther up the coast and into the night.

She didn't stop for a proper sleep anywhere, just dozed in her seat, waking disoriented from confusing dreams.

When she walked off that last ferry, she found herself two miles from town. At midnight. The landing crew must have thought she was waiting for someone because they got in their car and disappeared, leaving her alone on the slip.

If she'd had a phone, maybe she could have hired a

rideshare or found a room. Instead, she studied the brochure she'd picked up off the ferry, waiting until there was enough light to see the road since there were no streetlights, then walked into Bella Bella.

It was terrifying and exhausting, yet peaceful. It felt good to be moving instead of sitting, breathing fresh air instead of stale A/C. It was mid-summer, so the breeze wasn't too cold. She could hear the steady hiss of waves and concentrated on that, trying to ignore the creaks and snaps in the brush that stopped her heart every few steps.

The town was barely coming awake. It was only a couple of streets in each direction, increasing her sense of having arrived at the edge of the earth. She was the coffee shop's first customer. She took her paper cup to the wharf, where she sipped while waiting for the water taxi that would take her into Raven's Cove.

Her brain was numb, forming no thoughts beyond, *Get to Raven's Cove.* That had been the only imperative in her head for months. Even before April, when she'd been told her sister had passed unexpectedly in a small plane crash.

After that terrible news, Cloe's urgency had intensified, fueled by urgent questions. *What will happen to Tiffany's baby? Who will look after Storm?*

The baby is with family, had been the message relayed through her lawyers. What family? Tiffany's almost-husband, Wilf, had three grown sons. Had one of them taken guardianship? Which one?

The need for answers, and to see for herself that Storm was safe and well-cared for, had kept Cloe alive through the twists and delays in the court case. If she hadn't been driven to survive for Storm, she might have given up entirely by now.

The water taxi growled into place against the wharf, releasing a handful of children wearing backpacks and babbling with excitement for whatever their day promised.

Cloe boarded and might have fallen asleep as the taxi rocked its way to Raven's Cove, but the coffee and the rush of finally arriving had her sitting up with anticipation as she came into—

Was this it?

She wasn't sure what she had expected, but definitely something grander. All she could see was a marina with a T-shaped wharf holding a variety of boats in their slips. Some were fishing boats, others were leisure craft.

On shore, there were maybe a dozen houses peeking from the forest on the hills above the collection of commercial buildings. A pub on the left was dwarfed by a huge industrial building behind it that wore a sign declaring it *Raven's Cove Marina and Shipyard*. Between that and the two lodges on the right stood what looked like the shortest strip mall in history. It held maybe three shops and had what might be a couple of apartments above it.

As the taxi closed in on the wharf, the land rose too high to reveal anything except the pub's patio, which jutted out to overlook the cove.

"Is this…it?" she asked the water taxi captain as she disembarked. Perhaps she'd been dropped off on the outskirts again. *Please don't make me walk another two miles.*

"Sure is," he said with a nod, as though he heard that a lot.

As she stepped onto the wharf, she hung back, letting the handful of fellow passengers go ahead while she shrugged into her backpack and brushed back her hoodie, trying to get her bearings.

Her ears were immediately accosted by the chill of her new pixie haircut. Yes, she had even left behind the chemical blonde she had saturated into her dark brown curls all these years. She wore no make-up, jewelry, or even a bra.

Slowly, she started toward the ramp, passing a man who was casting off a speedboat of some kind. She didn't know boats. This one looked like a convertible sportscar with a low, angled, wrap-around windshield and white seats in the bow.

The man straightened as she came even with him and she halted, stepping out of his way so they wouldn't risk knocking each other into the water.

Oh shit. He was *Trystan Fraser*.

A year and a half ago, Tiffany had sent her a link to a trailer for Never Alone with the text, *I'm dating this guy's dad!*

The Never Alone series chronicled Trystan's adventures and outdoor survival tips as he trekked into remote locations around the globe. He took only what he could carry, then documented how he was never really alone. There was always wildlife and insects and a thriving ecosystem around him.

Cloe had watched way too many hours of him talking intimately into the camera while she'd been in protective custody. That's what really made her falter into speechlessness—awe at facing her celebrity crush.

He was taller than she had expected, familiar yet infinitely more handsome, with his neatly trimmed dark hair and straight brows and strong bone structure beneath a naturally tanned complexion. He also radiated a dynamic self-confidence that was even more powerful in person than on screen. He was *sexier*, which was saying something because she lived for the handful of episodes where he took his shirt off.

While she stood there agog, mute and practically drooling, his gaze swept over her in a way that felt like male interest—which gave her a lurching yes-no response that swung wildly between invitation and rejection. He had a girlfriend, didn't he?

He gave her a friendly nod and a self-deprecating smile that said, *Yeah, I'm that guy from that show.*

Oh God. She winced inwardly. He must get this sort of fangirl reaction a lot. How mortifying.

"Are we leaving today or what?" another man asked, making her realize there were two men already inside the boat.

Did they see how obviously starstruck she was?

"Yeah." Trystan stepped around her and stepped aboard, using his foot to push the boat away from the wharf as he did. The engine was already rumbling. The boat motored into an arc away from the wharf.

Wait. Was that *them*? All of Wilf Fraser's sons? Which one had custody of Storm?

Cloe had glanced at their socials many times, hoping to spot her niece in one of their photos. That allowed her to belatedly recognize the man who remained on his feet at the helm. He was the eldest, Reid. The one who'd spoken was settling into the shotgun seat. He was the middle-brother, Logan. Trystan settled behind the driver's seat, facing backward.

He held her gaze another moment, then they were too far away for her to even call out to stop them.

She wanted to kick herself. Had she really just let them get away like that? She could have wept. What an *idiot*.

No crying, she scolded herself. She'd done enough of that. It fixed nothing. She was tired and hungry. That was the problem.

She decided to treat herself to breakfast in the pub-restaurant while she figured out her next move and took a table on the patio so she could watch for the men to return.

Over eggs and toast, she learned that yes, those had been the Fraser men heading to Bella Bella, where she'd just come from. Which figured. They hadn't had a baby with them, though. Did that mean Storm was still here with someone? Her nanny, maybe?

"I was hoping to speak to one of them," Cloe told the server when she brought her bill. "I don't have a phone. Do you know where I could leave a message?"

"Go into the office. Take the stairs beside the hardware store or…" She pointed to a house on the bluff that overlooked the marina. "That's where Reid and his wife live. Emma's probably home with the baby. You could talk to her."

Emma. That was the name of Tiff's nanny, wasn't it? She scraped the recesses of her mind for what Tiffany had said about her. She was from Australia, wasn't she? No. New Zealand?

That didn't matter. Cloe's heart clutched with nervous excitement at how close she was to seeing Storm.

"Thank you." She tipped as well as her dwindling cash would allow and left. Shouldering her small backpack, she made her way across the grassy verge where a couple of picnic tables overlooked the marina.

She was getting a better look at this place now that she was on foot. It was cute, but for someone who'd grown up in L.A., it was mind-bogglingly small.

All the essentials seemed to be here, though. A licensed eatery, a hardware store, a grocery store that also served as post office and liquor store, a laundromat, and finally, an espresso bar that also sold gifts, housewares, and ice cream.

She paused outside the grocery store to read the flyers on the corkboard, hoping to see a cheap room to rent. There was only an offer of free kittens and someone selling used tires.

As she reached the far side of what might be called a town square, she arrived at the two hotel-lodges. One was utilitarian, but looked newly refurbished. The other was likely the one that Tiffany had regarded as the jewel that would draw a wealthier clientele to the cove. It was built of massive logs and tons of glass. Each room had a wide balcony that overlooked the water.

That building was the first thing that struck Cloe as pure Tiff. Her sister had longed to be someone who 'did something.' She had wanted to be a boss—not the metaphorical kind. The kind who owned a company and hired people and was taken seriously. She had always been drawn to home décor and house flipping and everything high-end so all of this seemed right up her alley.

Cloe stepped inside long enough to learn from reception that even the rooms in the 'old' lodge were priced sky-high. Also, they were booked out through October and, no, they didn't need help in housekeeping at this time.

She tried not to let despondency get its claws into her. Dusk was hours away. Right now, her priority was to see Storm.

Her palms were sweating. Nerves chased her as she carried on to where the graveled forefront of the village forked into a lane on the left and a driveway on her right. The lane meandered toward sparsely placed farmhouses along the shoreline. The driveway rose to the top of a bluff where a tall, split-level house overlooked the marina.

For a moment, she stood and took in how impossibly beautiful this place was.

She had lived in cities for so long, she had started to think that wilderness like this only existed on television. There were no honks and air brakes, no skyscrapers, no crowds. There was only the calls of birds and the distant drone of a boat engine and the steady wash of the tide pushing against the shore. The air smelled of salt and pine and earth and sunshine.

She removed her backpack so she could take off her hoodie and tied the sleeves around her waist. Then she warmed in the morning sun as she hooked her backpack on one shoulder and finished her climb up the drive.

Her feet began to feel as though they were encased in concrete, though, slowing her step. Reality was sinking in. Losing her sister was something she'd compartmentalized while she'd been living in the isolation of a shitty hotel room, but her lateness in getting here—four months after her sister had died—curdled the eggs she'd eaten.

Tiffany wasn't here.

But her daughter was.

Swallowing the jagged lump from her throat only to have it lodge like broken glass in her chest, Cloe fisted her clammy hand and knocked.

"It's open." A woman's voice carried through the screened window beside the door.

Hesitantly, Cloe turned the knob and poked her head in, keeping her feet on the stoop. "Hello?"

"Hello?" The speaker was drying her hands on a tea towel as she came to the wide archway between the living room and kitchen. She was a little older than Cloe, close to thirty maybe. Her brown hair was bundled into a clip atop her head. She wore a green T-shirt and cutoff jeans. Her feet were bare.

"Sorry. I thought you would be—" She shrugged that off and gave Cloe a confused smile. "G'day. Can I help you?"

"I hope so. I'm, um…" Cloe wished she had found a

way to shower and dress in fresh clothes, not that she possessed such a thing. Should she ask for Mrs. Fraser? "Are you the nanny? Emma?"

"Yes. Can I help you?" Wariness edged into her tone. She came to the door and took hold of it, subtly forcing Cloe to retreat on the stoop.

"Hi. I'm Tiffany's sister, Cloe." She tried to find a friendly smile, but too many emotions were accosting her, making her mouth feel numb and quivery. "Is Storm here? I was hoping to see her."

Emma's shock was unmistakable. Her jaw went slack. Her eyes bugged out. Her hand twitched as though she wanted to slam the door in Cloe's face.

"She's down for her nap right now." Emma's voice turned thin and high. "Why don't you come in and sit down. Would you like something to drink?"

"Water would be great." Her throat had become a desert. "Thank you."

Cloe toed off her cheap, rubber-soled flats and left her bag by the door, then gratefully followed Emma into a beautiful kitchen with a granite island, modern cupboards, and stainless-steel appliances. A breakfast table sat in a nook that overlooked the sun-dappled water. A pair of French doors stood open to the wide deck, allowing the fresh air to fill the house with the intoxicating smell of summer and beach.

"Wow." Cloe couldn't help stepping outside to appreciate the breathtaking view. "This is beautiful."

"It is." Emma came out and searched the water as she

set the glass on a small table beside a lounger. "I'll check on the baby. Have a seat."

"Thanks." Cloe didn't get a chance to ask where Mrs. Fraser was. She sank onto the lounger, relaxing because she hadn't known how she would be received, but Emma was being really nice to her.

Finally, for the first time in way too long, something was going her way.

Have you read the bonus epilogue for Book One,
Marrying the Nanny?
Get it here and Dani will notify you when
Wanting a Family Man releases:

danicollins.com/marrying-the-nanny-epilogue

More Books by Dani Collins

Blue Spruce Lodge series

Book 1: *On the Edge*

Book 2: *From the Top*

Book 3: *In Too Deep*

Love in Montana series

Book 1: *Hometown Hero*

Book 2: *Blame the Mistletoe*

Book 3: *The Bachelor's Baby*

Book 4: *His Blushing Bride*

Book 5: *His Christmas Miracle*

Firefighters of Montana series

Book 2: *Scorch*

Other titles

Wedding at Mistletoe Chalet

Taken by the Raider

Available now at your favorite online retailer!

About the Author

Award winning and USA Today Bestselling Author, Dani Collins, has written more than two dozen romances ranging from sexy contemporary for Harlequin Presents, to romantic comedy, epic medieval fantasy and even some erotic romance. Lately she has also been writing rancher romance for Tule's Montana Born. Since she's a small town girl at heart, this makes her feel at home.

Dani lives in Canada with her high school sweetheart and two mostly-grown children as a love-letter to her small town roots.

Thank you for reading

Forgiving Her First Love

If you enjoyed this book, you can find more from all our great authors at TulePublishing.com, or from your favorite online retailer.

Printed in the USA
CPSIA information can be obtained
at www.ICGtesting.com
LVHW042244290824
789700LV00029B/433